IN
Dreams
Forgotten

Books by Tracie Peterson

www.traciepeterson.com

GOLDEN GATE SECRETS
In Places Hidden • In Dreams Forgotten

HEART OF THE FRONTIER
Treasured Grace • Beloved Hope
Cherished Mercy

THE HEART OF ALASKA***
In the Shadow of Denali • Out of the Ashes

SAPPHIRE BRIDES
A Treasure Concealed
A Beauty Refined • A Love Transformed

BRIDES OF SEATTLE
Steadfast Heart
Refining Fire • Love Everlasting

LONE STAR BRIDES
A Sensible Arrangement
A Moment in Time • A Matter of Heart
Lone Star Brides (3 in 1)

LAND OF SHINING WATER
The Icecutter's Daughter
The Quarryman's Bride • The Miner's Lady

LAND OF THE LONE STAR
Chasing the Sun
Touching the Sky • Taming the Wind

BRIDAL VEIL ISLAND*
To Have and To Hold
To Love and Cherish • To Honor and Trust

STRIKING A MATCH
Embers of Love
Hearts Aglow • Hope Rekindled

SONG OF ALASKA
Dawn's Prelude
Morning's Refrain • Twilight's Serenade

ALASKAN QUEST
Summer of the Midnight Sun
Under the Northern Lights
Whispers of Winter
Alaskan Quest (3 in 1)

BRIDES OF GALLATIN COUNTY
A Promise to Believe In
A Love to Last Forever
A Dream to Call My Own

THE BROADMOOR LEGACY*
A Daughter's Inheritance
An Unexpected Love • A Surrendered Heart

BELLS OF LOWELL*
Daughter of the Loom
A Fragile Design • These Tangled Threads

LIGHTS OF LOWELL*
A Tapestry of Hope
A Love Woven True • The Pattern of Her Heart

DESERT ROSES
Shadows of the Canyon
Across the Years • Beneath a Harvest Sky

HEIRS OF MONTANA
Land of My Heart • The Coming Storm
To Dream Anew • The Hope Within

LADIES OF LIBERTY
A Lady of High Regard
A Lady of Hidden Intent
A Lady of Secret Devotion

RIBBONS OF STEEL**
Distant Dreams • A Hope Beyond
A Promise for Tomorrow

RIBBONS WEST**
Westward the Dream
Separate Roads • Ties That Bind

WESTWARD CHRONICLES
A Shelter of Hope
Hidden in a Whisper • A Veiled Reflection

YUKON QUEST
Treasures of the North
Ashes and Ice • Rivers of Gold

All Things Hidden***
Beyond the Silence***
House of Secrets
A Slender Thread
What She Left for Me
Where My Heart Belongs

*with Judith Miller **with Judith Pella ***with Kimberley Woodhouse

GOLDEN GATE SECRETS

2

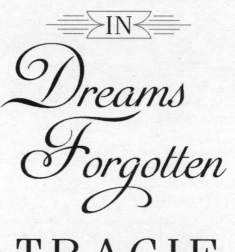

IN

Dreams Forgotten

TRACIE PETERSON

BETHANYHOUSE

a division of Baker Publishing Group
Minneapolis, Minnesota

Published by Bethany House Publishers
11400 Hampshire Avenue South
Bloomington, Minnesota 55438
www.bethanyhouse.com

Bethany House Publishers is a division of
Baker Publishing Group, Grand Rapids, Michigan

Printed in the United States of America

Library of Congress Cataloging-in-Publication Data
Names: Peterson, Tracie, author.
Title: In dreams forgotten / Tracie Peterson.
Description: Minneapolis, Minnesota : Bethany House, [2018] | Series: Golden gate secrets ; 2
Identifiers: LCCN 2018002431| ISBN 9780764219009 (trade paper) | ISBN 9781493413775 (e-book) | ISBN 9780764231216 (cloth) | ISBN 9780764231223 (large print)
Subjects: | GSAFD: Christian fiction.
Classification: LCC PS3566.E7717 I48 2018 | DDC 813/.54—dc23
LC record available at https://lccn.loc.gov/2018002431

Scripture quotations are from the King James Version of the Bible.

This is a work of historical reconstruction; the appearances of certain historical figures are therefore inevitable. All other characters, however, are products of the author's imagination, and any resemblance to actual persons, living or dead, is coincidental.

Cover design by LOOK Design Studio
Cover photography by Aimee Christenson

18 19 20 21 22 23 24   7 6 5 4 3 2 1

To Anna.

I am always amazed at how God puts people together,
but our friendship is definitely one of those things
that He carefully orchestrated for His glory.

You have taught me so much about the Hutterite
people and their love of Jesus and others. Your
kindness and love is something I will always
cherish. Thank you for being my friend.

—Tracie

CHAPTER

1

*J*udith Gladstone looked at the letter in her hands. It was creased and worn from folding and unfolding. The ink seemed to fade with each reading.

She smoothed the paper in a loving fashion. Her mother's delicate script and pleading words stirred her heart. "This is all I have to go on," Judith whispered to herself.

The letter was the only resource that might shed light on the past, as well as the future. She read it again, hoping it might give her an insight that up till now had eluded her.

Dear Edith,

I know you must be surprised to receive word from me after all these years, but I have learned that I am dying and feel I need to make an appeal for your forgiveness. I know that what I did was unforgiveable, but I hope you might find some way to manage a small bit of understanding and forgiveness for your sister.

My actions were born of desperation. You know the reasons why. I know that I deserve only your reproach and bitter avoidance, but I hope that the years might have eased matters between us.

Before I die, I long only to tell you that I am sorry, and yet those simple words are not enough to convey my deepest regret for what I did. For Judith's sake, I hope you will forgive me and perhaps try to help her. After all, she is blameless in this matter.

I had hoped to repay the money, but we never seemed capable of making enough to do so. I know the money wasn't all that important anyway, but I wanted to make the effort. Looking back now, knowing my death is imminent, I hope only to be at peace and knew I could not do so without at least writing this letter.

Knowing the pain I caused you and the situation itself, I never came home to rectify the matter. Leaving as I did was wrong, but returning seemed even worse. I don't know if you're still in San Francisco, but I pray you are and that this letter will reach you.

> *Begging your forgiveness,*
> *Lila*

Judith shook her head, still staring at the words. "Oh, Mother, what did you do that couldn't be forgiven? Why didn't you tell me about your sister? What does it all mean?"

She stretched her legs out on the cushioned window seat and gazed outside. Spring had come, and the sun pushed back the clouds to shine down on the world after days of rain.

"So why can't I put aside my gloom as easily?"

She didn't need to ask the question. Her desperation to understand her mother's secrets was like a cloud hanging over her. Lila and Homer Gladstone—her parents—had always insisted they had no living relatives, yet here was her mother's letter to prove otherwise.

Having been raised on an isolated ranch in southern Colorado, Judith had never really questioned her parents' honesty. There had been no suggestion of lies—no strange comments or objects to raise suspicions. Judith remembered asking about her grandparents and hearing brief explanations of their demise from illnesses or accidents. When asked about other relatives, her parents had always told her there were no other living relatives. When Judith had pressed to know if there ever had been, her mother had been quite clear on the matter.

"No, Judith. There is no one else."

"But there was," Judith said, looking again at the letter. "You had a sister named Edith."

Refolding the letter, Judith got to her feet. She tucked the missive back into its envelope and then slipped it into her pocket. She had spent weeks—months—poring over the well-worn letter, and to no avail. Coming to San Francisco had been her last hope, but so far she'd been unable to find out anything about Edith Whitley.

Of course, she'd only arrived the previous November, just four months ago. She had boarded a train in Denver without knowing what she might find in San Francisco. There had been precious little money after selling off her mother's remaining things and paying the family's debts, but Judith had taken some of it and bought the train ticket. She hoped it was the right thing to do and knew that once she reached her destination, she would have to immediately seek a job. That idea didn't seem so daunting, but navigating a big city had left her more than a little anxious.

But fate had been with her. On the train west, she'd made

the acquaintance of Camrianne Coulter and Kenzie Gifford. Both young women were traveling unaccompanied to the city on searches of their own, and it seemed only natural that the trio combine their resources to help one another.

Judith checked her appearance in the dresser mirror. She'd pinned her hair up in a bun as usual but had taken the time to use a hot iron to make ringlets on the sides and at the nape of her neck. She'd never had a lady's maid, and although there was a sweet young woman in the house named Liling who had recently started helping them with such matters, Judith was more comfortable doing for herself. She also reasoned that she wouldn't be staying here in the Coulter house forever, so it was best not to get too used to having servants.

"Are you ready?" Kenzie called from the hallway.

Judith opened the door of her room. "Yes, I'm afraid I got a little distracted."

Kenzie was a few inches taller than Judith, with striking red hair and shimmering blue eyes. Judith thought she was one of the most beautiful women she'd ever seen, but more than that, Kenzie had such a regal grace and elegance about her. She carried herself in a polished and confident manner that Judith wished she could emulate.

"If we don't hurry," Kenzie said, "Micah will arrive, and you'll have no time to talk to Caleb."

Judith swallowed the lump that had instantly formed in her throat. At the mere mention of Caleb's name, she felt all aflutter. Caleb was Camri Coulter's brother—the owner of the house Judith was living in and the man she had fallen in love with at first sight. Of course, he had no inkling of her feelings.

"I'm ready." She slipped on an emerald-colored jacket that complemented her plaid walking-out skirt. The outfit was something she'd purchased with her Christmas bonus.

"You aren't going to wear a hat? We'll be outside all day."
Kenzie had her own beautiful creation of gold woven straw,
white tulle, and flowers strategically pinned atop her auburn
hair.

"Oh, bother. I'm rather addlepated today." Judith went to
a peg behind the door and took down one of the two hats she
owned. It was a wide-brimmed green felt trimmed in rosettes
of blue and red. All three colors matched the shades in her skirt
and jacket. She hurried back to the mirror.

Kenzie gave a soft laugh. "At this rate, Caleb will have already
left on his date."

Judith frowned as she pinned the hat into place. "With Florence Brighton, I suppose."

"No, he's taking her to the opera tonight. Today he's attending
an engagement party of one of his friends, as I understand it."

"Well, she'll probably be there. It seems she's always around
when he is."

"Why don't you just tell Caleb how you feel about him?"

Judith shook her head. Kenzie was the only one she'd ever
confided in regarding her feelings for Caleb. "It wouldn't matter. He clearly doesn't feel that way about me."

"He might, if he knew how you felt." Kenzie shrugged. "But
have it your way. Far be it from me to make recommendations
about love. My life is proof that I'm not a good judge of such
matters." She had been stood up at the altar the year before
and had not recovered from the rejection.

They made their way downstairs as Judith did up the buttons on her jacket. They'd just reached the bottom step when
Camri came flying out of the dining room.

"I nearly forgot my gloves," she said, hurrying past them
up the stairs.

Kenzie shook her head. "It would seem I'm the only one in

control this morning, and I'm the one who didn't want to go on this picnic outing in the first place."

"But it'll be fun. You'll see." Judith gave Kenzie's arm a pat. She knew her friend didn't care to go on outings with Dr. Micah Fisher. He was rather sweet on Kenzie, but she had no interest in him.

"Caleb's probably in his study," Kenzie said, motioning down the hall. "Why don't you go speak with him, and I'll listen for Dr. Fisher."

Judith nodded and hurried away before Kenzie could change her mind. The study door was open, and she could see Caleb standing at his desk, reviewing some papers. He was dressed impeccably in a double-breasted beige tweed suit.

As she approached, he looked up with a wide smile. "I wondered if you'd make it before I had to leave."

"I'm sorry. I lost track of the time."

"Well, it seems to have been time well spent. You look lovely."

She looked away, feeling her cheeks grow warm. "Thank you. I might say the same of you. Well, perhaps lovely isn't the right word . . . ah, for a gentleman."

He laughed. "I'm happy with any compliment I can get. Now, what can I do for you?"

Judith thought of several answers she would like to give, but refrained. She drew a deep breath and met his gaze with a confidence she didn't feel. "I wondered if you'd had time to check on my matter."

Caleb looked momentarily blank, then seemed to understand. "I'm sorry, Judith. I'm afraid I've been so busy with this political corruption issue that looking for your aunt completely slipped my thoughts. But I'll make a note to myself."

She felt a stab of pain. He hadn't even thought of her or her desire to find her family. He was all she could ever seem to think

12

about, but he clearly didn't feel the same way. *And why should he? I'm just a poor, uneducated girl from nowhere. I haven't the money nor the beauty that Florence Brighton has, nor even the refinement and intelligence that Camri and Kenzie have.*

She tried not to let it bother her. "It's all right. Truly. I didn't want to bother you with it anyway, but Camri told me I should, and . . . well, I'm sorry."

She turned to go, but Caleb quickly crossed the distance and put out his hand to stop her.

"Wait—I'm the one who is sorry. Of course I want to help you. Don't apologize—this is my fault. I'm afraid all this city nonsense with Abraham Ruef and his corruption has taken my full attention."

Abraham Ruef was the power behind the mayor and the city's Board of Supervisors. It was well known that he ran San Francisco in a scheme of graft that rivaled New York City. Caleb and his former employer Henry Ambrewster had both fallen victim to his corruption. It had, in fact, cost Henry his life and seen Caleb shanghaied.

"It's quite all right, Caleb. The problems you're dealing with are much more important than my finding out if I still have a living relative. It will keep." At least she'd managed to get her letter back from him after he borrowed it, intending to investigate for her. She feared that, with all he had going on, he might misplace or lose it, and Judith couldn't bear to imagine that loss.

He smiled and patted her arm. "Thank you for understanding. I promise I'll get to it as soon as possible. Hopefully Monday I can give it more attention."

"Thank you, I—" The sound of the door knocker echoed down the hall. "I have to go. That will be Micah, and I don't want to keep him and the others waiting."

"Have a wonderful time. I wish I could join you. I think a picnic at the beach is just the thing for this beautiful day."

She nodded. "I'm sure it will be . . . very nice."

Judith set her mind on enjoying the day. Ten young people from church had come on the outing. They'd all squeezed into two cars, one owned by Micah and the other by a man named Thomas, who was particularly sweet on a woman in their group named Suzanna. He hadn't minded at all that she was snugly pressed between him and her girlfriend Maribelle. Their car was rounded out by another couple, Roman and Esther, who were newly engaged. Everyone but Thomas held a basket packed with goodies.

In Micah's car, Judith sat with Camri and Patrick in the back. Given Patrick's broad shoulders, it was a tight fit, but Camri didn't seem to mind cozying up to her fiancé. Kenzie was the unhappy one. With Judith wedged in the back, she was forced to take the front seat beside Micah.

Judith watched as Kenzie hugged a large picnic hamper to avoid any contact with the young doctor. It would have been nice if Kenzie could just allow for their friendship—if not something more. It was obvious her former fiancé had been a cad. Judith knew the wound ran deep, but Micah was highly regarded by one and all. All but Kenzie.

After a short drive, they arrived at a place on the beach. Blankets were spread, and the food was unpacked from the hampers. The men immediately began gathering dry driftwood for a fire while the women set up the meal.

"Oh, what delightful-looking pies," Maribelle declared.

"Judith made them," Camri announced. "She's quite gifted."

"What kind are they?" Maribelle turned one of the pies in her hand. "I can't tell, what with all the meringue."

"They're both chocolate cream," Camri replied. "You could hardly expect anything else from Judith. I've never met someone who enjoys chocolate more than she does."

Judith's cheeks warmed, but she focused on arranging the food. Once all the tasks were complete, grace was offered, and everyone began to eat as if they'd been without food for weeks. There was something about the sun and fresh salt air that stimulated their appetites.

For the most part, Judith found the day pleasant enough, although it was a little colder than she liked. They shared thoughts on current events and told stories of their youth. Judith even shared how she'd learned to rope a calf when she was only eight years old. The others thought this very impressive. While they continued to nibble on dessert, Thomas and Roman brought out their guitars. It wasn't long until they were caught up in a sing-along of hymns and folk songs. Judith enjoyed this the most. She loved music. She was accomplished on the piano, and at least while everyone was singing, no one was questioning her about her plans for the future.

As the sun slipped beyond the horizon, Micah lit the bonfire. The dry wood quickly caught, and soon they had a welcoming blaze. Judith was grateful for the warmth and scooted just a bit closer. The sea breeze was even chillier in the absence of the sun.

Kenzie leaned over to Camri. "We really should be getting back."

"Just another song or two," Camri encouraged, leaning against her fiancé. "This has been such a nice time."

"I wouldn't be mindin' if we sang through an entire hymnal," Patrick said, wrapping his arms around Camri.

Thomas began to strum the chords to a new song, and as everyone joined in to sing, Judith felt a sense of belonging that she'd never really known before.

"The day Thou gavest, Lord, is ended, the darkness falls at Thy behest; to Thee our morning hymns ascended, thy praise shall sanctify our rest," Thomas's rich baritone voice sang out above the rest.

The others sang on, but Judith sat back and thought about her parents. They had never spoken much about God. It wasn't until she'd met Camri that Judith had really heard someone other than a preacher talk about God and heaven. Once she'd started attending church with Camri and Kenzie, Judith had been surprised to realize that the emptiness in her life that she'd accredited to having no extended family had been filled by accepting that God loved her. It had been hard at first, because who could imagine that the God of the universe would care one whit about a lonely girl from Colorado?

"So be it, Lord! Thy throne shall never, like earth's proud empires, pass away; Thy kingdom stands and grows forever, till all Thy creatures own Thy sway."

When the last chords faded on the air, everyone seemed content to just sit in silence around the fire. It was the perfect ending to the day.

Later, when Micah dropped them off at the house, the sun had long since gone, and the skies had given over their swirls of orange and scarlet to the night. While Camri and Patrick disappeared up the lighted stairs into the house, Kenzie was waylaid by Micah, who apparently wanted to talk to her privately. Judith felt torn between going into the house and waiting so that Kenzie wouldn't be alone. She climbed the stairs to the first landing outside the small but beautiful house. She glanced at the windows lit in welcome. No doubt a fire was already crackling in the front room, and given the chill, Judith longed for its warmth. She glanced down at the car, where Kenzie was shaking her head and doing her best to sidestep

Micah. Judith didn't want Kenzie to be uncomfortable, but at the same time, she knew Kenzie could take care of herself. She also knew Micah was a gentleman. He wouldn't do anything untoward.

"You'll catch a chill out here," Caleb said, descending the stairs. "And it looks like rain."

The sight of him took Judith's breath away. In the light from the streetlamp, she could see he was dressed in his finest formal wear from head to toe. Black tails, white tie, and top hat. Florence Brighton had better appreciate him.

"I . . . uh, I was just waiting for Kenzie." Her mouth felt suddenly dry. Why couldn't he see the effect he had on her? "You look quite dashing." She cringed. She hadn't meant to say it out loud.

"Why, thank you." Caleb shrugged. "It's expected, where I'm going."

"The opera," Judith murmured.

"Yes, but first to a very formal dinner at the home of a very influential and very aloof family, who believe their presence to be a gift of the very finest order." He grinned.

Judith couldn't help but smile. "Sounds *very* delightful."

Caleb laughed heartily. "Just between you and me, I tend to side with Kipling. He said, 'San Francisco is a mad city—inhabited for the most part by perfectly insane people, whose women are of a remarkable beauty.'"

"Are you speaking of Rudyard Kipling?"

This question came from Kenzie, who had joined them on the steps.

Caleb nodded. "I am. He wrote it some years ago. I suspect he hoped Americans, or at least San Franciscans, would never read it, but a good friend of mine managed to write it down word for word and sent it to me as a welcome when I moved

17

to this fair city. And, I must say, it seems to prove itself true to me on a daily basis."

Kenzie shrugged. "So why do you stay?"

Caleb gave a slight bow. "A very good question, my dear lady, and one which would take far too long to answer and cause me to be late to my *very*"—he winked at Judith—"important social event." He then bowed quite formally. "I must bid you both, good evening." With that, he sprinted down the stairs.

"Well, I must say that was rather entertaining." Judith watched him start his Winton and climb into the driver's seat. "Sometimes he is a real puzzle to me."

"Why do you say that?"

"Well, right after he returned from being shanghaied, he talked about going into ministry work full-time."

"He does hold a Bible study for those sailors he helped," Kenzie offered.

"Yes, but he talked about leaving the law, since he inherited Mr. Ambrewster's money, and going into some sort of ministry. Instead he's just going to one party or meeting after another."

"Well, it hasn't been that long since his ordeal." Kenzie shrugged. "Maybe he needs some time to put it behind him."

Caleb had been shanghaied from the dance hall of Malcolm Daniels the previous August, after trying to rescue his Chinese housekeepers' daughter Liling. Until then, he had practiced law with Mr. Henry Ambrewster and earned the older man's undying respect and gratitude. In fact, Ambrewster had so favored Caleb that when Patrick Murdock had been accused of murder, Ambrewster had allowed Caleb to stray from their focus on corporate law to defend him.

"But he seemed so excited to go into ministry work," Judith said.

"Maybe God hasn't revealed to him what he should do,"

Kenzie countered as they climbed the steps to the house. "Or maybe He has revealed it, and cleaning up the corruption in this town is the direction He wants Caleb to go."

"Maybe, but he doesn't seem all that happy."

Kenzie paused at the door. "Maybe you're the unhappy one, so you believe he's just as miserable."

Judith nodded. "I suppose you might be right."

CHAPTER

2

"Well, now that Patrick's joined our church," Camri Coulter said at breakfast, "at least we know where the wedding will be."

"But when?" Judith asked, smearing her toast with jam. "Will you get married this year?"

"Oh goodness, yes." Camri sipped her tea, then put the cup down with an odd look on her face. "At least I hope so. Patrick doesn't want to get married until he has his business back up and running and he can furnish us a home of our own."

"But I thought that was part of the problem with the city corruption that Caleb is trying to defeat," Kenzie said, shaking her head when Mrs. Wong, the housekeeper, offered her the platter of ham. "I didn't think Patrick could get his construction business back until Abraham Ruef was defeated once and for all."

Ruef controlled every aspect of business in the city, and a more corrupt man there had never been. He was a lawyer who had formed the Union Labor Party only a few years earlier. He saw the potential of labor controlling the wealthy and set himself up to be the legal advisor to almost every businessman and

21

labor group in the city. He was well-known for taking bribes. In fact, he was known to insist on bribes, although he called them a retainer for any counsel that he might offer. He took in large amounts of money from those who wished to curry favor. Then, after taking out his portion—usually half or better—he shared the rest with the mayor, Board of Supervisors, and anyone else who could benefit him. He was into everyone's pocket, and everyone was operating out of his.

"Caleb has friends who are helping him," Camri murmured.

Choosing that moment to make a hurried appearance, Caleb popped into the dining room and snatched a piece of toast off his sister's plate. "Good morning, ladies. I wish I could stay, but Patrick and I have a meeting."

Camri nodded. "He told me all about it last night. I do hope you'll both be careful."

Caleb grinned, which always caused Judith's heart to skip a beat. He had an impish look on his face as he leaned down to kiss the top of Camri's head. "I'm always careful."

"Yes, so careful that you managed to get yourself shanghaied and might still be somewhere across the Pacific but for God's intercession," Camri replied.

"But that is the glory of it, sister dear. God is always interceding for me against the powers of darkness." Caleb straightened. He speared a piece of ham and put it on top of the toast. "I'll tell Patrick you send your love."

"Doesn't he have the decency to come inside so I can give it to him in person?" Camri asked.

"There isn't time. I already told you that. Our meeting is at seven thirty so that everyone still has time to get to their daily business."

"But why did you plan for a morning meeting?" Camri asked. "I would have thought the evening would be a better time."

Caleb shrugged. "I'm not running things. I'm just one of many who have a personal interest in the matter and am doing my part to see Ruef defeated, even if that means meeting at midnight on the docks." He headed for the door. "Try not to worry. I'll see you all this evening, as I plan to stay in. We can discuss it over supper, and I'll even insist Patrick join us." He paused and looked directly at Judith. "Maybe we can talk Judith into playing the piano for us, and you and Kenzie can sing."

Judith focused her attention on her plate, feeling more than a little flustered. Goodness, but Caleb could put her thoughts in a whirl. He was considerate and sweet to all of them—treating Kenzie and Judith just as he did his sister. But Judith didn't want him to treat her like a sister.

He hadn't even exited the house before Camri spoke up. "I do wish they'd get this business settled. I can't help but worry. Ruef has a lot of friends, and they won't sit idly by while Caleb and his associates seek to destroy his hold on the city."

"Yes, but most of Ruef's friends are bought and paid for," Kenzie pointed out. "If the men figure out a way to cut off his funding, perhaps those friends will come over to our side."

"I'd like to think so, but I'm hardly convinced."

Judith could hear the concern in Camri's voice and quickly changed the subject. "What kind of gown are you considering for the wedding?"

"I would have liked to wear my mother's wedding gown, but our sister wore it and will not be parted from it, especially now that she's with child again. She hopes this time to have a daughter to whom she can pass it down."

Kenzie helped herself to a poached egg. "That hardly seems fair. Your mother's gown should be available to you as well as your sister."

Camri shrugged. "I didn't feel like fighting over it. Catherine

23

can be so headstrong, and I could see this turning into one of those fights that shakes the very foundations of the family. So my plan is to have a new gown designed to my preferences, one I can pass along to my own daughter—should I have one."

"And what are your preferences?" Judith asked.

"I'm not entirely sure. I've been reading about it and looking at hundreds of dress styles. Satin and chiffon are popular for wedding gowns, but so are silk and tulle. I've found several styles I like but want to try them on to be sure. There's a new shop in town devoted completely to bridal gowns, so I thought I might take a look."

"Oh, we could go with you. Make an afternoon of it on Saturday." Judith saw the frown that lined Kenzie's lips. "Well, I could go with you. I know Kenzie is usually busy on Saturdays helping her cousin."

"It would be nice to have your opinions." Camri looked at Kenzie. "Although I wouldn't want to cause you distress."

Kenzie shrugged. "It's of no matter to me. I'm not a china doll, and I won't break. I can accompany you too, if that's what you'd like."

Judith had to admit that Kenzie was far more accommodating now than she had been when they'd first come to the city. Given her wounded spirit after being jilted, Kenzie hadn't been very good company those first few weeks, but of late she was far more outspoken. Especially when Dr. Fisher tried to draw her attention.

Camri nodded. "I think it would be great fun, and since Caleb has been so gracious as to reimburse us all for the money we spent to keep up the household while he was missing, I feel as if I'm rich."

"Me too," Judith said. "It's a wonder, to be sure. I've never had much money in my life. My parents neither, but now my bank account has two hundred dollars in it. Seems completely odd to me, but there it sits."

Camri laughed. "I think we should plan to go out early and make a day of it. I will want both of you in my wedding as my attendants, so we can also consider your gowns. I think all of us in white with perhaps your gowns trimmed in pink might be nice. I want to have pink roses in my bouquet, and perhaps you could both have them in your hair. Or maybe a hat trimmed with pink roses and white feathers."

"Oh, I would love to be in your wedding." Judith put down her half-eaten toast. "I've never been a wedding attendant, and I can just imagine a hat like that." She sighed. "It would be just like a fairy tale, but it sounds very expensive, and two hundred dollars won't go very far once I start buying things like fancy hats."

"Silly goose," Camri chided. "My family will be paying for the wedding, or at least Caleb will be. He's already told me to have whatever I like. Since he has come into an unexpected fortune, he intends to see that I have the wedding of my dreams. So fear not. You needn't purchase a single thing."

Judith felt her cheeks warm. "Well, I didn't expect that, but then, I've never been around someone planning a wedding. Is it done like this all the time?"

Camri nodded. "The bride's family pays for the wedding. In days of old, it came with a dowry as well. The father of the bride would pay a dowry to the husband."

"Imagine someone paying your husband to marry you." Judith shook her head. "That seems rather insulting."

"Men have also paid for brides," Camri countered. "It just depends on the situation. Marriage was once far more of a business arrangement than a romantic one. I'm certain we'll see less and less of that, however, as women receive the right to vote and make their own choices."

"It's true," Kenzie said in an absent-minded fashion. "I knew women who were made to marry men arranged for them by their father." She seemed to come back to herself. "Saturday would be fine with me. Maybe we can have a bite to eat while we're out. I've heard of several new restaurants from Cousin George."

"I'll talk to Caleb and see if he might drive us and drop us off," Camri said, looking delighted with their plans. "We can always take the trolley back."

"I think it sounds grand." Judith was a romantic at heart. She had always found fairy tales about princesses and handsome princes to be her favorites. She'd even taken to reading more after Camri shared a romantic book written by Jane Austen with her.

"I also have some things I need to pick up," Kenzie said, pushing her plate aside. "I came here with mostly winter clothing, and while my mother is shipping my remaining wardrobe, I still have some purchases to make."

Judith nodded. "I'd love to do a little shopping as well."

"Then we shall have a full day of it," Camri said, getting to her feet. "But for now, I've promised to go to Henry Ambrewster's office and start an inventory, and you two must go to work making chocolate."

"Hardly that," Kenzie countered. "Boxing it and running the office will be our lot."

Judith giggled. "I'd actually like to try my hand at making it. I've imagined all sorts of ideas for new fillings."

Kenzie shrugged. "You should tell Cousin George. He might be of a mind to use your ideas. I heard him saying the other day that he needed to come up with some new ones."

"What fun that would be." Judith could only imagine how wonderful it might be to sit around discussing and developing recipes for new candies.

Humming quietly to herself, she went upstairs to fetch her coat and hat.

———

"The fact of the matter is that Ruef and his cronies must be stopped," Rudolph Spreckels stated. As one of the city's wealthiest men, he had a vested interest in ridding the town of Ruef's stranglehold. "And I believe that by working together, we can accomplish this."

Caleb looked around the room at the men who had gathered for this meeting. His soon-to-be brother-in-law Patrick Murdock gave a single nod of encouragement, while the others looked skeptical.

"You know full well that we agree with you. However, others have tried and failed. What makes you think we can be more successful?" a local businessman asked.

Caleb understood the man's frustration. He was only stating what everyone here was thinking.

Spreckels didn't have a chance to reply as Fremont Older, managing editor of the *San Francisco Bulletin*, stood. "I think we can succeed now, because we have more physical evidence. Not only that, but there are more of us willing to take a stand. We have power in numbers. If we stand together, then Ruef will have no one to intimidate."

"But he has so many of the common men in his employ," another man said, shaking his head. "Police officers and the chief of police himself, as well as firemen and most of the dock workers."

"So we must convince those men that they can be better off without Ruef as dictator," Older replied. "They know that it's just as easy to be on Ruef's bad side as his good. They've seen men beaten, shanghaied, and even killed. We need to help them to realize they're living on borrowed time."

Judge Winters spoke up. "We know there will always be under-handed men willing to do Ruef's bidding. I believe we should do what we can to draw them to our side, but the most important element is cutting off the head of this snake."

"I agree," Older said, nodding. "We are working to do that, but it will take money. That's why we've come together today. We need to know that we have your financial backing for our purpose."

"Fremont and I have pledged our support in the amount of five thousand dollars," Rudolph Spreckels reminded everyone. "As you know, William Langdon, our district attorney, has com-mitted himself to cleaning up the seamier parts of the city. Ruef might have arranged for him to be elected, but Langdon has shown himself to have his own agenda. I've spoken with him at length, and he's already put a federal investigation into motion. Our citizens are appalled at the way vice is allowed to run rampant, and we all know that this is a huge source of income for Ruef. As we clean up the Barbary Coast and other areas, we will deprive him of his bankroll."

"Not only that," Older added, "but I have been in touch with Special Prosecutor Francis Heney. He told me of his interest in helping us. I'm going to Washington, DC, to meet with him and President Roosevelt."

Caleb had heard rumors of this and could see that the an-nouncement did much to perk up the men around him.

"Do you believe the president will help us?" one of the other men asked.

"It looks very promising," Older replied. As a longtime news-paperman, he had many connections and a great many friends. "However, we're going to need to raise additional money. Prob-ably at least a hundred thousand dollars."

"That's a large sum," someone said from the back of the room.

"True, but if we all dig deep and encourage our friends to do likewise, we can raise it. After all, we'll find ourselves either giving it willingly to rid ourselves of Ruef, or giving it unwillingly to benefit him."

Judge Winters stood. "This is good news to my old ears. However, I'm afraid I'm due in court and must leave your company."

"I'm afraid it's time to end our meeting anyway," Spreckels stated. "We must all be about our business and not give any of Ruef's associates a chance to realize what we're actually doing. I will expect you all on Saturday afternoon at my home. We are hosting a fund-raiser for one of my wife's charities at two. Once things are under way, we will meet in my library. Feel free to use the French doors off the veranda if you'd rather not deal with the other guests."

"Until Saturday, then," Judge Winters said, getting to his feet. "And remember, each of you, this is a dangerous business we are about. Keep your eyes open and take no chances."

Most of the men gathered their things and exited the room. Some stayed behind to speak to Older. Caleb's heart was encouraged by the support of these good men, but he knew there was still so much to be done.

"Would we be headin' to yer office now?" Patrick asked.

"Yes. I'd imagine Camri is there already, and I don't want her to feel that she has to do the inventorying all by herself."

"She wouldn't care," Patrick said with a smile. "She likes bein' in charge."

"Don't I know it." Caleb laughed and took up his hat. "You've got your hands full with trying to keep my sister in line."

"Aye, but I'm thinkin' it won't be too unpleasant a task."

Caleb couldn't help but like the lighthearted Irishman. For all his woes and losses, Patrick seemed to always manage a positive spirit. It hadn't been easy, however. The last couple years had been brutal. Patrick had lost his father and business, and then just before Christmas he'd lost his only sister Ophelia to tuberculosis—the same disease that had taken their mother.

They made their way to where Caleb had parked his car. "You know, you really should learn to drive."

"Aye, I suppose it would be of use to me."

"I could teach you. I know you'd manage it in moments. The real problem is managing everyone else on the street."

"Most days it looks like a donnybrook between cable cars and automobiles," Patrick mused.

"And then you throw in the horse-drawn wagons and carriages and pedestrians, and it becomes a three-ringed circus." Caleb shook his head. "The world seemed much less complicated when we were boys."

He drove them downtown to the offices he'd once shared with Henry Ambrewster. Caleb had been there a few times since Henry's death and his own return to the city, but there had always been too much going on to perform more than a cursory search for his missing ledger. The ledger was crucial because it listed names and information relating to Ruef's graft. It had been hidden in Caleb's office desk drawer prior to his being shanghaied, but Patrick had said that Henry had it in hand the day he was killed. Caleb could only pray Henry had time to hide it before his assailant came to the office. If not, then their search was in vain.

As if reading his thoughts, Patrick spoke up. "I'm thinkin' this might be all for naught. The man who killed Ambrewster broke into the safe and took the money and would surely have taken the ledger as well. I doubt there was time for Ambrewster to be hidin' it."

"Maybe not, but I have to hope. That ledger contains a great deal of information that would benefit the special prosecutor should he agree to help us." Caleb pulled to the curb in front of the large six-story brick building that housed the office. "It would have been nice to have the money as well, since Ruef handled it himself and fingerprints could have been obtained, but the ledger would be enough to give the prosecutor plenty to go on."

They made their way to the third-floor office and found Camri already hard at work. She was standing near the top of a ladder, pulling dusty books from the top shelf in Henry's office.

"You shouldn't be up there," Caleb chided. "You'll get your skirts twisted and fall."

"You certainly have a lot of faith in my abilities," Camri called down.

"I don't question your abilities," Caleb replied. "It's the yardage of your skirt."

Patrick was already reaching up to help her. "Come down like a good lass, and I'll take yer place."

She glared at them both, then started down with an armful of books. When she reached the bottom, she raised her chin defiantly. "As you see, I am quite unharmed."

"And I mean to see ye stay that way," Patrick said, taking her place on the ladder.

Caleb looked around the office. The man who had killed Henry had made a mess of things that had not yet been cleaned up. The offices had been closed to everyone but the police, who had given at least a pretense of gathering evidence. Caleb didn't believe for a minute they would have turned over any evidence even if they'd found it. Most of them worked for Ruef, after all. Patrick had told him of warning Ambrewster to hide the ledger, but had Henry had the time? Patrick had been there, speaking to Ambrewster, probably no more than a few minutes before the killer came. There may not have been time to do much of anything. Of course, one benefit they had going for them—Ruef didn't know how Caleb was keeping track of information. Ruef would have had his man mostly looking for the papers Patrick had taken from his home, and those had been safely hidden in Caleb's house.

"Tell me again what the ledger looks like," Camri demanded as she started pulling books from the lower shelves.

"Beige with red leather binding."

She laughed. "Most of these books are beige with red leather binding."

Caleb nodded. "Which is why I chose that particular ledger. It's not at all noticeable. With it sitting on my desk, folks would just assume it to be another law book."

"Well, it makes finding it like looking for a needle in a haystack," Camri said, straightening with several dusty volumes in her arms. "And given that it's just as likely the murderer took it with him, I'm wondering if we're wasting our time."

Caleb looked around the room and shook his head. "Anything we do to help put Ruef away won't be a waste of time as far as I'm concerned."

3

*C*aleb enjoyed listening to Judith play the piano. She had such a passion for music, and it came out in the way she managed the keys. Her playing eased his worries from the day. They hadn't been able to locate the ledger, but they'd made great progress in the office and would probably know soon enough if it was there.

Judith started in on a Schubert piece, and Caleb stretched his hands out before the fire. A light rain had brought a chill to the air, and the fire compensated nicely.

"Ye look mighty content standin' here," Patrick said, joining him.

"I am. Life is good, despite the complications of Ruef and the losses in our lives." He glanced to where Camri and Kenzie were busy looking through some magazines. "While the ladies are otherwise occupied, I want to say something."

"Go on with yerself, then." There was an edge to Patrick's tone that suggested he knew what Caleb intended to say.

"Look, I know we've discussed this before, but I want you

to let me gift you with enough money to restart your family construction company."

Patrick raised a brow. "Aye, we've discussed it before, and my answer is the same. I can't be takin' the money. It wouldn't be right."

"I had a feeling you'd say that, but hear me out. Ruef took away everything your family owned and nearly cost you your life. Then he arranged to take Henry's life, and in turn, I inherited all of Henry's money. So in a way, if you took some of Henry's money and created your business, it would be like Henry was getting a small bit of revenge."

Patrick seemed to consider this a moment. "Aye, but with Ruef still in power, 'twould do no good. He'd simply see to my failure and perhaps my death. Then ye'd have to be answerin' to yer sister." He grinned. "It'll come round in time. I'm not worried about it. Right now the important thing is to see Ruef put behind bars."

"Yes, but Camri is planning a wedding as we speak. She wants our parents to journey out here from Chicago. I know you intend to wait to marry until you have your business restored and a house of your own, but you may need to swallow your pride and let me help. At least let me *loan* you the money."

Patrick shook his head. "Caleb, ye've come to be a good friend, but I won't let this come between us. Money can cause even the best of friendships to sour. Ophelia helped me to see that there are so many more important things than money and possessions."

"I quite agree." Caleb thought of the petite Ophelia and how she'd died so young. She had been sweet on him when he'd come to Patrick's rescue. Even now, the thought made him smile. "Your sister was a wise old soul despite her youth."

"Aye. She was that. I miss her talks in the evening. From the time Da passed on, we'd have them every night. Sometimes we'd talk about old memories and things we loved about Ma and Da, and other times we discussed the problems around us. She always had brilliant insight."

"She loved you a great deal. There's no denying that."

Patrick smiled. "She loved ye too. I would have been proud to have ye as family."

"You are family, Patrick. Whether you marry my sister or not, I'd still be proud to call you brother. I won't forget how you devoted yourself to finding me."

"I didn't have a choice. Your sister would have been down at the dance halls and docks herself if I hadn't taken the job."

Caleb laughed, drawing the attention of Camri. She put aside her magazine and came to join them at the fire.

"Why do I get the feeling that you're laughing at me?" she asked.

"Not at you, sister dear, but it is related to you. You bring joy to us. What can I say?" Caleb gave her his best innocent expression but knew she wasn't buying it.

"Don't be corrupting my fiancé," she said, moving to loop her arm through Patrick's. "I won't have you driving him off before I can get him down the aisle."

"Like anyone could drive me away from ye."

Patrick gazed down at her with such a look of love that it made Caleb even more certain the couple were meant to be together. It was all he had ever wanted for her—someone to love her and care for her. Their parents were so happy together, and their older sister Catherine was content in her match, but Camri had always been so headstrong and independent that Caleb worried she'd never allow herself to fall in love. He was glad to be wrong.

"Are we going to continue looking for the ledger tomorrow?" Camri asked.

"I suppose we should. We need the information to help put Ruef away. Do you mind coming down to help another day?" Caleb asked.

"Not at all. Since I no longer work at the candy factory and haven't yet found a project here to keep me busy, I find it boring just sitting around the house, planning a wedding that may never happen."

Patrick put his arm around her. "For sure it will be happenin'. You aren't goin' to get out of it that easy."

"I know you're right. We haven't even known each other but a few months, so there's wisdom in taking it slow." She shook her head. "But it doesn't seem like it's only been a few months. I feel like I've known you all of my life."

"I feel the same," Patrick assured, giving her shoulder a squeeze.

Camri straightened. "Well, I should probably just focus on a different project."

"What kind of project are you considering, sister?" Caleb knew Camri wasn't one to sit idle for long.

"I had thought about teaching at a college again, but with everything we've gone through the last few months, I'm really of a mind to work with the poor. I've talked to Pastor Fisher about it, and he believes we could create a place of safety and education, particularly for women. Given that you and your associates are working to clean up the town, there are going to be quite a few women and young girls displaced."

"What did Pastor Fisher suggest?" Patrick asked.

"If we could raise the funds to buy a large piece of property, then we could put up a building where the women could be housed and educated in order to be able to move on and support themselves. I thought perhaps I could put together a series of lectures or some such thing. I would appeal to those with the means to donate to the cause, then use the money from the ticket sales for the purchase of property."

"That would take a lot of time." Caleb considered the matter for a moment. There was no reason he couldn't hurry the process along, thanks to Henry's gift. "Why don't I purchase a piece of property? Perhaps something with a building already in place, even one in disrepair. I could hire Patrick to oversee fixing it up and making it safe."

Camri's eyes lit up. "That would be marvelous! Do you really think we might find something?"

Caleb smiled. "I don't know why not. Patrick, I know you've got your heart set on putting your business back together, but while we're working on that, why not work for me? You can save up some money and make your lovely wife-to-be happy."

"I'd like to be pleasin' her, to be sure," Patrick replied.

"Please say you'll help us," Camri begged. "You and I have talked about this so many times. Imagine if the women in your neighborhood felt they could come and get an education in order to better themselves."

"I can imagine it, and I suppose it might well suit us all for me to agree to such an arrangement."

Caleb put his hand on Patrick's shoulder. "I'll expect only your best work." He grinned.

"And for sure ye'll be havin' it, boss."

Caleb laughed heartily. "No, I won't have you calling me boss. We're going to go on as we always have—as friends."

"This is so exciting. When can we start to look for properties?" Camri asked.

"Well, I need your help at the office, but Patrick can start tomorrow."

"Start what?" Judith asked from the piano. She had stopped playing and was looking at the trio with great interest.

"We're going to find a piece of property with a building on it to fix up. We'll use it for helping the poor," Camri replied. "Just like we discussed with Pastor Fisher."

"How exciting!" Judith got to her feet. "How can I help?"

"Well, for now I don't imagine there's much for you ladies to do," Caleb interjected. "If Patrick is willing, he can start looking tomorrow, and hopefully it won't take much time at all to locate a spot. Of course, it all depends on what you think would work best and where it should be."

"Well, it needs to be easy to get to. Transportation is already difficult for the poor," Camri replied.

Kenzie joined them. "Cousin George said there's a warehouse for sale just south of downtown. I could get the address for you, if you like. It might suit our needs, as it's near the bay. Cousin George had considered it for expanding his factory, but it required too much work to fix it up."

"That location sounds good," Camri said, nodding. "I like that idea. Why don't you call him right now?"

Kenzie nodded and headed off to the phone. Caleb knew from experience that his sister, once motivated about a project, would take off running without further thought to consulting anyone.

"It would probably be wise to speak with Pastor Fisher, as well," he reminded Camri. "We'll need the help of the church to make this work, and he should be consulted before we purchase any particular property. After all, this isn't going to be just our project. We'll need to form a board and solicit donations and funds for the everyday expenses. There's a great deal of paperwork that will need to be set up in order to make this all aboveboard. I can certainly see to that."

"I'll see if Pastor Fisher can go with me tomorrow," Patrick said.

Camri looked at him. "I do wish I could go."

Caleb hurried to put her mind at ease. "We won't purchase anything until you have a chance to see it, so don't fret."

"I'm not fretting. I just want to be a part of everything."

"And so you shall be." Caleb looked around the room. "What happened to Judith? I thought she would want to be in on this discussion."

"I don't know." Camri shook her head. "Perhaps she went with Kenzie."

But just then Kenzie returned with a piece of paper. "Here's the address for the warehouse." She handed it to Caleb.

"That does seem like a good location." Caleb handed the paper to Patrick. "I'll leave it up to you."

Judith slipped away unseen and made her way upstairs. She wanted to be excited about Camri's project to help the poor, but she couldn't help feeling frustrated that no one seemed at all interested in helping her. She'd been willing to delay her search until Caleb could be found, knowing that she'd gone all these years without having any other family members. But Caleb had been home for some time now, and he had promised to help her find her aunt. So far, he hadn't kept his promise.

She closed her bedroom door and went to the dressing table. She plopped down on the chair and propped her elbows on the tabletop. She sighed and rested her chin in her hands. Her reflection in the mirror told the story. She couldn't hide her disappointment. No one seemed to care about her feelings.

A sigh escaped her lips. Somewhere in the city she had an

aunt—perhaps cousins. At least she hoped that might be the case. She hoped there might be a great many relatives to whom she could lay claim. All of her life, she'd wanted to be part of a big family.

"But right now I'd settle for knowing about just one aunt."

She straightened and began to pull pins from her hair. She had a mild headache and figured she would just spend the rest of the evening in her room. If anyone missed her—not that she expected they would—she would simply explain that she'd needed to rest.

Long baby-fine blond hair fell about her shoulders. When her hair was down like this, Judith thought she looked much younger than her years. She would be twenty-five in September, and yet she could easily pass for sixteen. Maybe that was why Caleb saw her as nothing more than his sister's friend. Then again, maybe he saw her as nothing more than that because she had nothing to offer him. She wasn't stylish or well-bred. Her family name meant nothing to anyone, and she certainly couldn't offer him a dowry.

"Maybe I should have stayed in Colorado and gotten a job cooking at a ranch." At least there she would have known her place. Here, she had a hard time figuring out what it was she was meant to do. Camri would have her go to school and further her education, while Kenzie would have her swear off all romantic entanglements. Both women were trained to participate in a much higher society than Judith had ever managed.

She sighed again and shook her head. "I don't belong here. I'm not sure I belong anywhere."

She quickly undressed and settled into her nightclothes. Taking up her book, Judith went to her lovely bed. She'd never had anything like this growing up. Her small bed at the ranch had been supported by ropes. The mattress had been filled with straw and was comfortable enough, but it was nowhere near as luxurious as the bed she now enjoyed. This bed was large enough for two people, perhaps even three, and the mattress was twice as thick and filled with down.

Mrs. Wong, the housekeeper, kept the bedding fresh and newly pressed. Judith always found her room in perfect order when she came home, and even now the covers had been turned down and bedside lamp lit. It seemed so strange to have someone wait on her hand and foot.

All her life, work was just a part of daily living. Everyone on the small ranch had to pull their weight, even the dog. Judith's days had always been filled with cooking and sewing, gardening and caring for the animals, as well as cleaning and washing. Her day started at dawn and went well past dark. When she was much younger, her mother had taken several hours in the middle of the day to school Judith. She had taught her to read and write and do simple arithmetic. But music had been Judith's real love. The other studies seemed unimportant. Music had the power to transport her to places far away, places she'd only heard about but wanted very much to see. Now books were beginning to do that as well.

There had never been time for pleasure reading as a child. Once her studies were complete, she was always needed elsewhere. But Camri had shared a great many books with her and encouraged Judith to let the stories sweep her away into another time and place. The first novel Judith read was Jane Austen's *Pride and Prejudice*. What an amazing story that turned out to be! She could easily imagine herself playing the part of Elizabeth Bennett's sister Jane. Jane was soft-spoken, even shy and demure, while Lizzy was given to speaking her mind and standing up for herself. Lizzy made her think of Camri.

After that, Judith read *Little Women*, a story in two volumes detailing the lives of four sisters and their family's trials and difficulties. Both *Pride and Prejudice* and *Little Women* contained the vision of family life that Judith had always wanted for herself. It was so easy to imagine all the laughter and love shared amidst a large family.

Before she could get settled in bed, a knock sounded on her door. She got up to see who it was and found Camri on the other side.

"You left without a word. Are you all right?" Camri asked.

Judith nodded. "I have a bit of a headache and thought it best to retire. I was just getting into bed."

"Would you like something for your head? I'm sure Mrs. Wong could fix you up a tea that would help."

"No, thank you. I'm sure I'll be just fine in the morning."

Camri seemed less than convinced. "I hope you know that I care a great deal about you. You've become a very dear friend. I'm sure that in time we'll find your aunt."

"I would like to think so too, but I can't fool myself. San Francisco is so big, and there are so many people. I hardly believe it will be simple to find one out of the thousands."

"Caleb will know what needs to be done. I'm sure he's already been asking questions."

"He's been very busy with other things, no doubt. I can't blame him, even if I wished it were otherwise." Judith put her hand to her head. "Now, if you don't mind, I'm going to go to bed. Please give my excuses to the others. I didn't mean to be rude."

"Of course I'll tell them. They'll understand." Camri gave her a hug, something that Judith still found rather awkward. "Hopefully you'll feel better in the morning."

"I'm sure I will. Good night."

"Good night, dear friend."

Judith waited until Camri was several steps down the hallway before closing the door. Leaning against it, she fought back tears. In spite of Camri's confidence that they would find Edith Whitley, Judith found her spirits sinking. Maybe it had been a mistake to come here after all.

CHAPTER 4

"Brother of mine, I wish to speak to you." Camri entered Caleb's office without waiting for his invitation. Caleb looked up from his desk. "What is it?"

"Judith."

He frowned. "Judith?"

Camri nodded and took a seat opposite his desk. "Yes. Judith. You promised to help her find her aunt. If you haven't time to do it, then I want you to hire someone. She was good enough to put aside her search in order to help me find you, and I feel we owe it to her."

He gaped at her. "I completely forgot. *Again.* I meant to do more, but the Ruef situation and finding my ledger has me preoccupied. I promise I'll make inquiries today. Judge Winters is coming to see me this morning, so I'll start with him."

"Thank you. I have a feeling Judith's departure last night had to do with her discouragement. We were, after all, caught up in scheming over a piece of property. I fear she may have thought we were choosing to focus on another matter rather than her own."

"I don't doubt it. I feel terrible for putting it off." Caleb shook his head. "I promise I'll make it up to her."

Camri got to her feet. "Wonderful. Now, I must be off. I have several things to do before I meet you downtown at the office." She came around the desk and leaned down to kiss the top of his head. "It is so good to have you home again. Mother and Father are both improving just knowing you're safe. I'm sure they'll be completely well by summer, and then perhaps we can invite them to come stay here for a few months."

"Well, there's hardly space for everyone, what with Judith and Kenzie living here."

"They could share a room, or I could share with one of them for a short time so that Mother and Father could have my room. It's not that difficult a matter to resolve."

"They'll be coming in the fall for your wedding, remember."

Camri frowned. "If there is a wedding. I know I was just as insistent that we take our time and get to know each other, but sometimes I fear it will never work out."

"Don't go being all doom and gloom, Camrianne. You know as well as I do that God has a plan even in this. Patrick is a good man, albeit a proud one. And even though he is proud, I don't think it's such a pride as to lead him to sin. He wants to be a good husband and provider, and that is a godly virtue. Don't try to force him to be other than he is."

She nodded. "I won't. I promise."

Caleb finished sorting through the papers he'd brought home from Henry's office. Most of it was correspondence and invoices. It was important that he familiarize himself with every aspect of Henry's dealings. After all, now that he was responsible for them, he needed to see every obligation met.

"Judge Winters come now," Mrs. Wong announced from the open door.

Caleb smiled and stood to pull on his coat. "Please show him in, and then would you please bring us some coffee and maybe some of those cookies you baked yesterday?"

Mrs. Wong smiled and nodded. "I bring them plenty quick." She scurried off down the hall, and Caleb could hear her telling Judge Winters that he was welcome to make his way to Caleb's study.

Moments later, the older man entered the room.

"Judge Winters, thank you for coming today."

"My pleasure, Caleb." The two clasped hands more in friendship than formal greeting.

"Let's sit by the fire," Caleb said, leading the way. "Mrs. Wong is bringing us coffee and some of the most amazing cookies you'll ever taste."

"Indeed? Well, that sounds like a wonderful way to spend a morning."

"Is it still raining?"

The judge nodded. "Lightly, but steadily." He took a seat. "I trust things are moving ahead in your investigations of Ruef."

"To a point. I'm still trying to locate my ledger of notes. We've been going through the office with no luck. Henry had an extensive library, and we have to go book by book, just in case he managed to put the ledger in with the other volumes. I fear, however, that his murderer probably absconded with it. Patrick feels certain Henry would have had little time to hide it."

Judge Winters nodded. "Well, let's hope it turns out otherwise."

"Whether or not it does, I feel confident I can regather the information. At least I hope to do so." Caleb took his seat just as Mrs. Wong wheeled in the tea cart with their refreshments.

She put the cart near the fireplace, then quickly poured two cups of coffee. "You want cream and sugar?" she asked, looking to the judge.

"No, just black, please."

"Same for me, Mrs. Wong." Caleb smiled. "And would you close my door when you leave?"

"I will." Mrs. Wong handed them each a cup and saucer. "You want me to serve cookies?"

"No, we'll manage. Thank you." Caleb put his coffee aside and got up as the old Chinese woman exited the room. He picked up the plate of cookies and brought it to the small end table that sat between the two chairs. "It'll be simpler if I put them here, as we are sure to devour them even before we need another cup of coffee."

The judge chuckled. "And what, might I ask, is in these marvels of baking?"

"I'm not completely certain. I know they contain almond and coconut, some ginger too, if I recall, and lots of butter." He grinned and took his seat while the judge helped himself to the cookies.

The judge's eyes widened. "These *are* delicious. Just seem to melt in my mouth."

"Exactly. I can eat a half dozen without even realizing it."

They enjoyed the cookies and coffee for several minutes while chatting about nothing more important than the latest plays each had seen. Finally, Caleb got down to business.

"I've gone through Henry's papers. I contacted most of the businesses we represented and have recommended them to other associates. I believe I've managed to pay all the remaining bills and have notified everyone who ever did business with Henry."

"To tell them you are closing the firm?"

"Yes."

The judge nodded. "So your decision is final." It was more of a statement than a question.

"Yes. I know God is calling me to something else. Right now I feel certain it is to help full-time with Ruef's demise, but after that, I cannot say. Camrianne has her heart set on running a relief station for women down on their luck. I believe she hopes to educate and train them for various jobs that will give them a better life."

"A commendable task, to be sure."

"I'll continue with the law if that is what the Lord wants, but for the moment, His will for my life seems cloudy at best."

"Ruef's affairs will no doubt keep you plenty busy."

"Yes. I know Spreckels and Older have been glad for the extra help. Especially since I'm doing it at no cost to the association."

The judge finished his coffee, and Caleb rose to refill his cup. "I also have another matter to discuss with you."

The judge looked up at him in anticipation.

Caleb leaned back against the fireplace mantel. "One of Camri's friends, Judith Gladstone, is staying here with us. She came to San Francisco because of a letter her mother wrote. Judith was always told she had no living family with exception to her parents, but upon her mother's death, Judith discovered a newly written letter addressed to an Edith Whitley of San Francisco. According to the letter, she would be Judith's aunt."

"I see. Was there an address?"

"No. That's the problem. The letter stated that Judith's mother didn't even know if this Edith Whitley still lived in San Francisco. From what the letter offered, I believe Edith would possibly have had money. The letter implies money was taken by Judith's mother, but also that she knew it was of no consequence. To me it suggests wealth. I have promised to help Judith find her aunt—if possible. I was hoping you might have some suggestions."

"Well, it just so happens that I once knew an Edith Whitley who was quite wealthy."

Caleb could hardly believe their good fortune. "You know her?"

"Knew her. She's dead."

His heart sank. "Dead?"

"I'm afraid so. She and her husband, along with their daughter, died several years ago when they were abroad. I'm good friends with her mother-in-law, Ann Whitley."

"Clark Whitley's widow?" Caleb whistled. "That is a wealthy bunch, to be sure. I never even considered that family." He knew from living in San Francisco that Clark Whitley had made a fortune in shipping, railroads, and steel.

"I don't know if their Edith is the same woman you're looking for, but it sounds possible. I know there was some family intrigue years ago."

"Perhaps involving Edith's sister, Lila?"

The judge shrugged. "It is possible. The family says little or nothing about it, and it happened before I made their acquaintance. If I were you, I'd write Mrs. Whitley a letter. I'll write one of my own, introducing you to her and letting her know that you aren't some sort of madman trying to start up a scheme." He smiled. "It's at least worth a try."

Caleb nodded. "I appreciate that, Judge Winters. Judith has been more than patient, and I am determined to see this through."

Judith found herself surrounded on the church grounds by a dozen children. The church was holding its weekly free luncheon for the poor, and she had been put in charge of the children once again. She didn't mind. Not really. She loved being with the little ones and hearing their animated play. They didn't seem to mind or notice their poverty when busy at a game of tag or hide-and-seek.

"Miss Gladstone, can we climb those?" one boy asked, pointing to several flowering trees.

"Oh, goodness no. You wouldn't want to smell like a girl, would you?"

The boy frowned. "No. Why would I smell like a girl?"

"Because those trees are covered in flowers, and they use flowers like that to make perfume. And only girls wear flowery perfume."

The boy seemed to consider this for a moment, then ran off to join his friends. Judith saw him talking to them and pointing at the tree. No doubt he was explaining the matter. She smiled to herself. She'd overheard the boys discussing tree climbing earlier and had managed to think up an excuse for why they shouldn't, rather than just telling them no. She was quickly learning that saying no to a child only seemed to egg them on to a stronger determination to do something.

One of the little girls, who was named Agnes, took a tumble and began to cry. Judith quickly scooped her up and offered comfort. The child was only four or five years old and so tiny for her age.

"There, there. Let me see if you've hurt yourself." Judith raised the child's dress hem just enough to reveal scraped knees. "It doesn't look too bad. Why don't you just rest with me for a few minutes?"

The teary-eyed child nodded and wrapped her arms around

Judith's neck. Judith hadn't been raised around children, but she found she liked them very much. She seemed to have a natural knack for understanding them and talking to them. Where other adults seemed hardly able to spare the time, Judith enjoyed chatting with the little ones.

"Miss Gladstone, Fin stole my ribbon," a little girl declared, tugging on Judith's apron.

The boy she knew only as Fin stood to one side with a smug look on his face. He seemed to be daring Judith to make him give it back.

"Oh, Rebecca, surely not. What would a boy ever want with a ribbon? Goodness, you don't suppose he means to wear it?" Judith said, pretending to be aghast.

Several of Fin's friends had joined him, and Judith's comment made them snort in laughter.

"Go ahead, Fin, wear the ribbon. You'll make a pretty girl," one of the boys teased.

That was Fin's undoing. He tossed the dirty ribbon to the ground. "Let's go kick the ball around." He marched toward the side of the church where a large ball awaited.

Rebecca hurried to retrieve her ribbon. She dusted it off and folded it carefully, as if it were her prized possession. It probably was. The children had very little. Their clothes were threadbare and patched, mismatched, and generally too large or too small. A ribbon was probably the only special thing Rebecca owned.

A thought came to mind. Judith had enough money that she could easily buy ribbons for all the girls. Better still, she could make them dolls out of remnant material. She could make quite a few with little more than a few yards of cotton and some stuffing. Of course, she'd need to make clothes for each one, but that wouldn't be hard. She could do it in the evenings after work.

But I'd need to make something for the boys too. That would be more difficult. She had no idea what might suit their fancy. She'd have to think about it and perhaps ask Patrick or Caleb.

Dr. Fisher came out of the church. He saw Judith and waved, then in what seemed almost an afterthought, decided to join her on the lawn. "Isn't it a lovely day? I worried it would rain."

"So did I." She glanced toward the church. "Did you have any sick to contend with?" As both a doctor and the pastor's son, Micah visited the weekly luncheon to offer free medical services whenever he was able to do so.

"Nothing too dire. A couple of expectant mothers and one case of rheumatism." Micah smiled. "And how are things going out here?"

"Just fine. The children are always such a pleasure to be with."

"Did Kenzie not come with you today?" He glanced around. "I didn't see her inside."

"No, her cousin needed her help with some extra work over the lunch hour. He was none too happy about me leaving either, but I assured him I would race back to work as soon as possible."

"I'd be happy to drive you back. My father was just praying with the women, and I'm sure they'll be by shortly to collect their little ones."

As if by unspoken agreement, the women began to exit the church and call to their children. Judith received several hugs before the rambunctious gang raced off to join their mothers.

"I suppose that was much too timely to be anything but God's planning so that I wouldn't have to walk or run back downtown." Judith smiled at Micah. "Yes, I would be most grateful for a ride."

"Wonderful. Come along, and we can discuss what you'll be doing the rest of the day."

"Or we could talk about Kenzie." She nearly giggled at his look of surprise. "I know how you feel about her."

"I feel abused by her most of the time," Micah said, opening the car door with a smirk. "She is just as fiery as that red hair of hers."

Judith said nothing until they started down the road. "She has been hurt quite deeply, you know."

"Yes. Stood up at the altar."

"Exactly. She has sworn to never love another."

"That's foolish. She's young and beautiful and has so much to offer."

Judith could hear the longing in his voice. "Yes, but you're a doctor, and you know that deep wounds take time to heal. Give her time, Micah."

He glanced at her and smiled. "I don't have any other choice—do I?"

She smiled. "No, not if you want to win her over."

He dropped Judith off at the factory door minutes later. "I appreciate the advice and will do my best to remain patient. However, as is often said, doctors make bad patients."

Judith had no chance to reply, as he maneuvered the car back into traffic and was gone. He was such a nice man, and Kenzie could do much worse than to accept his attention.

The scent of chocolate welcomed Judith as she entered the factory. She put aside her hat and outer coat, then donned her work apron and set to filling boxes with candy. It wasn't at all a difficult job. The most strenuous thing was sometimes having to fetch the crates of boxes or trays of chocolates when the delivery boys were too busy. Judith found sitting at the table arranging candies gave her plenty of time to think. Maybe too much.

Usually she dwelled on dreams of the past—her dreams and

those of her parents. When she was young, they had always talked about the large place they'd have one day. Her father wanted to run five thousand head of Angus beef, as well as raise a few fine riding horses. Judith's mother talked from time to time about how wonderful it would be to have servants who could cook and clean so that she could enjoy riding those fine horses. Sadly, none of their dreams ever came to pass.

Judith's dreams had always been of having brothers and sisters, aunts and uncles, cousins and grandparents. She often day-dreamed about large family gatherings—especially at Christmastime.

"Miss Gladstone, I need you to fill a rush order for one of our best customers," George Lake said, startling her out of her thoughts.

"Of course. Which arrangement?"

"The assorted creams—no nuts." He looked at the paper in his hand. "I need twenty made up immediately. I'll send Kenzie to attach the ribbons."

"I'll have them done before you know it." Judith gave the short man her best smile. George Lake was always so serious and anxious. She wished he could find some peace, but he always feared saboteurs were lurking around every corner. It seemed the chocolate industry in San Francisco was full of espionage and rivalry.

By five o'clock, the boxes were filled, trimmed, and waiting for delivery. Kenzie had said very little. She had been rather distant, in fact, and Judith couldn't help but wonder what was bothering her. Even Judith's attempts at small talk on the cable car home went unanswered. Kenzie excused it as nothing more than being tired, but Judith wondered if she were pining for her lost love. She sank into these moods at times, and there was nothing to do but wait for her to come out of them again.

Once they returned home for the evening, Judith was determined to mention Micah and his kindness in driving her back to work. If she spoke well of the young doctor, maybe Kenzie would start to think of him in a different light.

But then she saw Caleb dressed for an evening out, and all other thoughts left her head. She hated that he'd no doubt spend his time in the company of some beautiful woman. Probably that Florence Brighton. Her beauty was renowned. Even Camri had talked about how her black hair and green eyes gave her an exotic look that drew attention from men and women alike.

No one would ever speak of Judith in such a manner. Blond hair and blue eyes could hardly be considered exotic.

"Patrick and I will be gone for a while this evening," Camri told Judith as they crossed paths in the upstairs hall. "Don't worry about us if we're late. He's promised to take me to see the warehouse property Kenzie's cousin told us about."

"I hope it's suitable."

"Patrick and Pastor Fisher tell me it looks very promising. I'm excited to see it. Caleb is going with Patrick and the pastor tomorrow, and if we all agree on it, then Caleb will purchase it. It's all so exciting." Camri hurried toward the stairs. "I'll see you later."

Judith nodded. It would be a quiet evening with just herself and Kenzie to fill the hours.

She no sooner thought this than Kenzie came rushing out of her bedroom, coat and hat in hand.

"Where are you headed in such a rush?" Judith asked.

Kenzie didn't even pause to answer. "I promised Cousin George I'd accompany him to an organ recital. I told you on the way home from work, remember? We're going to get some supper out first." She flew down the stairs, not even waiting for Judith's response.

Frowning, Judith shook her head. Kenzie had said nothing of a recital. She'd not said much of anything.

She sighed. Once again, she was to face the evening alone. It seemed to happen more and more often. And there would be no chance to talk to Caleb and see if he had learned anything about her aunt.

Judith felt a wave of self-pity settle over her. "Well, there's nothing to be done about it. I'll just change my clothes and settle in to have a nice quiet time to myself. It's not like I don't know how to do that."

She quickly slipped into a worn gingham blouse and brown wool skirt. Both were articles she'd brought with her from Colorado, and both had been her best clothes prior to purchasing new ones for herself in San Francisco. She had to admit she loved her newer things. She had two plain navy blue skirts and two equally simple white blouses for work. Added to this was a bevy of undergarments and two fashionable dresses. One, the plaid she'd purchased with her Christmas bonus, and the second was a more formal gown handed down to her from Camri. The latter was something she'd only worn a few times but cherished just the same. She'd never had anything so lovely. The blue of the silk material complemented her eyes, and the lace trim made her feel delicate and pretty. Completely different than her life on the ranch.

In truth, everything about living here made her feel different than she had as a child. Growing up, there had never been quite enough of anything, and the lack of necessities wore down her parents' spirits like a bad tooth.

Judith made her way downstairs, noting the beauty of the house. Her mother had lived with so little, and yet if their presumptions were correct, her family had money. At least enough that her mother knew it hadn't been very important that she'd taken some of it.

"You like to eat supper now?" Mrs. Wong asked, appearing at the bottom of the stairs.

Judith nodded. "I suppose so. It's just going to be me, so you needn't make a fuss."

Mrs. Wong offered her a sympathetic smile. "You like to have supper in front room with fire?"

She thought about it a moment. "Yes, that sounds very nice."

The housekeeper smiled and bobbed her head. Judith gave it no more thought. She wasn't all that hungry anyway.

She made her way to the piano and sat down to play out her misery. Without benefit of written music, she pulled from memory a repertoire of songs. The rich tones of the well-made piano filled the air and took away some of her sadness. By the time Mrs. Wong returned with a tray, Judith was feeling marginally better. Perhaps it wasn't so bad to have the evening to herself. There was the piano and books to be read and no one to bother her.

She squared her shoulders and made her way to where Mrs. Wong had set up her meal on a small table. "I am just fine by myself, and if I never find any family . . . I'll be fine then too."

She sat down and bowed her head. At least she now understood who God was and that He loved her. Coming to know God had filled most of the emptiness inside her.

"Thank you, Lord, for this food and for Your love. I don't mean to think lightly of all You've done to bring me to this place, nor of the friends You've given me. I am thankful. But . . . if You wouldn't mind . . . I would very much like to find my aunt."

She paused for a moment, thinking of Caleb and how much she cared for him. Might she pray that he could return her feelings? No, it was probably best to leave it unsaid. She'd already asked for help with her aunt. She didn't know if there was a limit to what one could pray for, but she didn't want to risk things by asking for more. At least if she could find her aunt, then she could leave this house and perhaps forget about Caleb Coulter, as he so easily seemed to forget about her.

5

*J*udith startled at the sound of the front door slamming shut. She'd been reading in the front room and had dozed off. A quick glance at the clock revealed it was only eight-thirty. Sitting up straight, she couldn't help but wonder who had come home and why they were in such a rage. She started to get up but heard Mrs. Wong in the hall.

"Mr. Caleb, you back early."

"Yes, well, there seemed to be no reason not to come home."

"I take your hat and coat."

"Thank you. I won't need anything else. Please take the rest of the night for yourself and your family." His tone was curt—clipped. Completely unlike him.

Judith saw him storm off down the hall. Something had definitely put him in a foul mood. She'd never seen him like this before. What could have happened?

For several long moments, she did nothing but ponder the matter. She knew he was going out with friends—including

Miss Brighton. Perhaps Miss Brighton had been rude or even insulting. One could hope.

Judith chided herself. "That isn't kind. I must have a better spirit about such matters." Still, if Florence was the cause of Caleb's anger, then perhaps he would no longer have any interest in her, and that could be an answer to prayer. Was it all right to hope Miss Brighton had been ill-behaved?

She walked to the piano, still thinking. Prayer and looking to God for answers was so new to her. So too was dealing with a man she loved. How could she offer him help? She knew Caleb enjoyed music. Perhaps if she played that nocturne he loved so much, he would calm down and be at peace again.

Sitting down to the keys, Judith drew in a deep breath and began to play. She let the music speak her feelings, hoping—wishing—Caleb might understand her heart.

It wasn't long till he appeared in the doorway. He leaned against the wall for a moment, a hint of a smile on his lips. Judith pretended not to notice him. Instead she focused on the music and prayed God would heal whatever hurt he had experienced that night.

Make him happy, Lord, but don't let him love Florence Brighton.

When the final notes of the Chopin nocturne faded, Judith looked up and smiled. She didn't say anything, knowing that words would probably do nothing to help.

"Your music is like a salve to my wounded spirit. Thank you." Caleb came to stand by the piano.

"You're welcome." She began to play again, this time choosing Handel.

"I know that melody, but I can't place it."

"It's Handel's 'Largo' from the opera *Serse*."

"Ah, yes. I remember now."

"Mother told me it was an abysmal failure when Handel first played it for the public. Can you imagine? Such sweet, somber music, a failure? I've always felt there was something of the very heart and soul of Handel in this song."

"Perhaps whoever called it a failure lacked any real depth of soul," Caleb countered. "And maybe knew nothing of the heart."

She smiled. "My thoughts exactly."

He drew a deep breath and let it go. "It would seem there are a great many such people in San Francisco."

She continued to play. "Why do you say that?"

"Because I was with a group of them tonight." He crossed the room to his favorite chair and sat.

Judith finished the piece and then quietly closed the lid of the piano to cover the keys. She got to her feet and, without waiting for an invitation, joined Caleb near the fire. "I'm a good listener if you'd like to talk."

He looked at her with such depth of emotion that Judith wondered if she'd made a mistake. How could she possibly maintain a façade of calm and ease if he continued to look at her like that?

"So many of the people I once considered friends have no interest in spiritual matters," he said. "One of them asked me tonight to share about when I was shanghaied. I did so, telling them how God encouraged me to share the Bible with my fellow prisoners. They scoffed at this, telling me I would have been better off planning an attack. They spoke of how they would have mutinied and taken over the ship.

"I continued, trying my best to explain the depth of feeling I had for God and how I wanted to share that with others. I told them that I intended to go into some sort of ministry work, and they laughed."

Judith could well imagine. "They don't understand. They've probably never had cause to believe they need God."

"Well, I know from experience that such a time will come into the life of each man . . . and woman." He fell silent.

Perhaps Florence Brighton was one of the people who had scoffed. The way Caleb had said the word *woman*, it seemed this might be at the crux of his misery.

"Did Miss Brighton feel the same as the others?" Judith asked quietly.

"Florence?" he said, sarcasm dripping in his tone. "She started the entire conversation about the foolishness of believing in an unseen force—a divine deity. She said she'd received better advice from a fortune-teller than any minister who'd ever droned on from the Bible. It saddened me to the heart."

"I'm sorry. I know you must care very much about her." Judith tried not to let her feelings show. "Perhaps she was simply out of sorts."

He looked at her and shook his head. "No. Florence has made clear her lack of spiritual interest. She has declared herself to be an atheist—a person who doesn't believe in the existence of God."

"But why?"

Caleb shrugged. "Who can say? I truly thought I could change her mind."

"I admit that I don't know much about God. I've only just come to understand His love for me. No, that's not quite right. I still don't understand that, but I have come to believe it is there." She smiled. "But I do remember Pastor Fisher saying that only God could change a heart."

Caleb considered her words for a moment and then nodded. "Of course, you're right. I suppose I thought that I had some great abiding wisdom that could reach her in her unbelief. It was truly humbling to be laughed at for my faith."

"I would imagine so." Judith didn't know what else to say. She felt sorry for Caleb. He was such a kind man with a loving nature unlike any she'd ever known.

"They see no value in my helping others to know God. They find it boring and completely lacking in purpose for their lives. They can't understand that in helping their fellow man, they help themselves."

"Perhaps they truly have never been shown the way."

"What do you mean?"

"Just that I know how that is. When I was young, I never knew people like you or Pastor Fisher. My parents were not religious people. They were kind and good to most everyone they met, but they didn't attend church or even read the Bible.

"I was taught right from wrong, but I never knew what that right and wrong was based on. I presumed that good was when a person felt best and benefitted others most, while wrong left a person troubled and guilt-ridden. For instance, I knew it was wrong to steal, not because the Bible said so, but because it hurt other people."

His expression showed genuine interest. "And nothing was ever said about God being displeased or that we needed Him in order to overcome sin?"

She shook her head. "Nothing was ever said about sin. I'm not sure I ever even heard the word before my father died. The closest thing to a sermon I'd ever heard preached before coming here was the funeral services for my father and mother. Even so, my first real understanding of sin came from Camri."

"Well, I'll be. I had no idea a person could be without knowledge of sin. Even my friends understand the meaning of sin."

"But understanding what a word means is hardly the same as understanding the effects of it on one's life."

He looked at her oddly, his eyes narrowing ever so slightly. "You are quite wise, Judith. For all your isolated upbringing, you understand things that elude me."

"Pastor Fisher said that we all have our crosses to bear, but we shouldn't think we bear them alone. He promised to speak more about it as we drew nearer to Easter. I'm looking forward to hearing what he has to say. It all seems so amazing." She realized her tone had become excited. She forced herself to calm down by gazing at the fire. "I'm sorry. I didn't mean to gush. I just got a little carried away." She paused again and shook her head. "That probably sounds funny to you, since you grew up with such teachings and know all about these things."

"Not at all. I'm humbled by your enthusiasm. You make me consider the world and the hearts of men through other eyes."

"Until I came here, I felt something missing in my life." Judith kept her gaze on the flames. "I always thought it was the lack of siblings or grandparents. Even though I knew very little about such relationships, I had heard stories. One of my father's hired men came from a family with twelve brothers and sisters. He used to tell me all about things they did and how they never felt lonely because they were never alone." She smiled and shrugged. "While I, on the other hand, always felt lonely, because I was always alone. But when Camri told me about God and then took me to church, I felt like I was suddenly let in on a secret. The more I learned, the less I felt alone, and when Pastor Fisher asked if anyone wanted to know Jesus as their own Savior, I nearly jumped over the pew."

Caleb chuckled, and it eased her nervousness. "I would have likcd to see that."

"I thought it was so amazing that God sent Jesus to die for me. Why should God even care about some poor girl from Colorado? Why should He have even noticed my being here? But Pastor Fisher said God had even numbered the hairs on my head—that He had put me together in my mother—that He knew each intimate detail of my being. Isn't that marvelous?" She didn't try to hide the wonder in her voice.

"It is marvelous. I think, in fact, that in my disappointment, I have forgotten just how marvelous."

"Well, maybe not forgotten, but perhaps it's just become common to you. After all, you've known about it a lot longer than I have. I just hope that I can learn more and more."

"I suppose it's hard for me to understand a heart that rejects God." Caleb said nothing for a moment, then continued. "Maybe I wouldn't make a good preacher after all. I attended theological training along with learning the law. I know the Bible, but perhaps that isn't enough. You see, I grew up with people of faith, and to me it seems the most natural thing in the world to turn to God. Especially in times of need." His expression seemed almost pained.

"But not everyone grows up that way, Caleb. Some people learn to rely on themselves when needs arise."

"I can't imagine that. Was that how it was for you?" He still seemed genuinely interested, and it touched Judith in a way nothing else could.

"I was taught I only had myself to depend on. I remember when I was just six years old, I encountered a rattlesnake. I screamed in terror. My mother, on the other hand, picked up a hoe and chopped off the snake's head. She then reprimanded me for screaming and told me it served no purpose and that I needed to learn that the only person I could count on saving me . . . was me. After all, she might not be there next time."

"That's terrible."

"At the time I thought her the bravest person in the world, and I vowed to be just like her and fear nothing. Although, later she told me she had her own fears . . . she just never gave in to them."

"So she died still not believing in God?"

"I honestly don't know what she believed. I mean, we said grace over the meal." Judith shrugged. "So my parents must have believed that God existed, but nothing much was ever said about Him. I grew up without any real understanding or knowledge of God."

"I'm sorry, Judith. I didn't know, but now that I do, I promise I will endeavor to do whatever I can to help you in your study of Him."

She felt her chest tighten. He was so near . . . so wonderfully near. She looked down at the beautiful rug, trying to calm her nerves. "Thank—thank you."

"You're welcome, although I hardly deserve any thanks. I should have paid more attention. But there is one matter on which I've improved. I spoke to Judge Winters today about finding your aunt."

Judith's head snapped up. "You did?"

"Yes. I'm sorry it took me so long to do so."

She forgot all about her weeks of frustration. "Did you learn anything?"

"I'm not sure. I have a lead, but I don't want to say anything until I know something more certain. Will you trust me to see it through this time?"

She nodded. "I would trust you with anything, Caleb."

He beamed at her. "Then I will learn what I can and tell you as soon as I know something certain. You can count on me. I won't put the matter aside until we find out the truth."

Judith felt overcome with love for him. He had no idea of her thoughts or how he made her feel, but it didn't matter. Caleb Coulter was the man her heart had chosen, and whether anything ever came of it, nothing would alter her feelings for him.

CHAPTER

6

*K*enzie Gifford sat at the table, helping Mrs. Wong and Liling with the kerosene lamps. Despite having electricity, the lamps were still used often, and as such, needed cleaning. Mrs. Wong hadn't been comfortable when Kenzie offered her help. She was the housekeeper, and to have one of the ladies she cared for helping clean lamps didn't make sense. However, with Liling's help, Kenzie finally managed to help her understand the situation.

Earlier that morning, Caleb had dropped the girls off to shop for wedding gowns on his way to view the new property everyone agreed should be purchased to house displaced women and children.

Kenzie had tried to get caught up in Camri's excitement about her wedding, but found it impossible. After just a few shops, Kenzie thought she might burst into tears and suffer a complete collapse. Arthur's betrayal and abandonment on their wedding day was a wound that never seemed to heal. She finally told her friends that she wasn't feeling up to the ordeal and took the cable car home.

Upon arriving at the house, however, Kenzie learned that Dr. Micah Fisher was coming to play chess with Caleb later that morning. If she remained at home and Micah knew she was there, he would insist on speaking with her unless she was otherwise occupied. So she immediately set out to be exactly that.

Mrs. Wong had refused to order Kenzie to any particular task. She told Kenzie to do whatever she felt like. Having had her share of experience cleaning lamp chimneys, Kenzie grabbed an apron and set to work.

After a while, the doorbell rang, and Mrs. Wong went upstairs to answer it. Kenzie found herself straining to hear if it was Micah, but being downstairs in the Wong's section of the house made it difficult.

Finally, Mrs. Wong returned and sat back down at the table. "Mr. Micah here now."

Kenzie nodded. "And you said nothing to him about my being here?"

"I tell him nothing. You safe." The housekeeper smiled in a conspiratorial manner.

Liling sat across the table, trimming lamp wicks. The petite woman's trials in the past kept her somber, but there was a contentment about her even in doing this menial task. Freedom had ways of putting even the most damaged soul at rest. Just a few months ago, Malcolm Daniels, the same man who had arranged for Caleb to be shanghaied, had held Liling prisoner in his dance hall brothel. He had won her in a game or bought her, Kenzie couldn't recall which. Not that it mattered. She had been a prisoner nevertheless and forced to live the life of a prostitute. Her parents had despaired of ever seeing her again, but thanks to Caleb and Patrick Murdock, she had been rescued and was here now.

Kenzie took up a piece of newspaper and crushed it into a ball just as Mrs. Wong had shown her. The paper did an amazing job of removing soot from the glass. Back home, Kenzie would have soaked the chimneys in soapy water and then scrubbed them. Her parents hadn't been eager to get their home electrified. Neither the risk nor the cost enticed them to modernize. She would have to write to her mother about the newspaper trick.

"You take clean lamps to bedrooms," Mrs. Wong instructed Liling. "They ready."

Liling was only two years younger than Kenzie, but it looked like they were separated by a half dozen or more. She was slim and petite with huge dark eyes and jet black hair. Kenzie thought at first that Liling would be fragile—even sickly from all that she'd endured—but surprisingly she was strong, even fierce in nature. Perhaps her years of torment had grown in her a strength that could only come through adversity.

"Be sure put them in correct room," Mrs. Wong admonished.

"Mama, I know where to take the lamps. You don't have to worry." Liling gathered up three lamps and cradled them to her breast. "I'll be very fast."

"Fast not as important as doing it right," her mother countered.

Kenzie couldn't help but smile. She'd heard similar things all of her life from her own mother. In fact, at times like this, she really missed her mother.

"You don't have to keep working," Mrs. Wong said.

"I know." Kenzie pushed the newspaper wad into the chimney from the bottom. Thankfully her hands were small enough to fit through the opening of the glass. "But I want to. It keeps me occupied."

"You want tea?"

"Tea would be very nice." Kenzie was starting to get hungry, and Mrs. Wong always served cakes or cookies with her tea.

She turned her attention back to the lamp. She was pressing the paper against the glass to clear away the smudgy soot when without warning it shattered. She let out a yelp of pain as a piece of glass sliced through her fingers.

"You hurt!" Mrs. Wong said, coming to her side. "You bleeding."

Kenzie felt her head swim at the sight of her own blood pooling on the table. "Oh, dear."

Mrs. Wong helped Kenzie get the ring of remaining glass off her wrist. Next she grabbed a clean towel and handed it to Kenzie. "For your hand. I get water to clean."

Kenzie took the towel, but for some reason she couldn't figure out what she was supposed to do. She looked at her fingers and saw the blood continuing to flow. She felt her head grow hot. What was wrong with her? Why was there so much blood?

———

"That was an amateur choice, Micah," Caleb teased. "I'll have your queen in two more moves." He slid his bishop into place.

"I guess my mind isn't on the game." Micah leaned back and shrugged. "What can I say?"

"I don't suppose our resident redhead has anything to do with it?"

"She vexes me, I won't lie." Micah studied the chess board. "There's just something about her that intrigues me."

Caleb chuckled. "Maybe because she says no to your advances. That's got to be a first."

Micah looked up and shrugged. "What can I say? I'm a dashingly handsome man." He grinned. "Maybe Kenzie needs an eye examination."

"Well, you are a doctor."

Micah started to move one of his pawns, then shook his head. "You're right. I've made a mess of this game, and no matter what I do now, it's yours to win." He leaned back in his chair. "Want to start another?"

"Not if you're not going to pay any more attention than you did to this one." Caleb too eased back. "You should just surprise her. Bring her flowers or take her on a picnic."

"Ha! She'd throw the flowers in my face and refuse to even speak to me. I'd have to tie her up to get her to go anywhere with me. Maybe if you were to invite Judith for an outing and then suggest Kenzie come along for the sake of propriety, I could just happen to join you somewhere and make it a foursome."

Caleb looked at him thoughtfully. "Judith is a very nice young woman. Terribly young, I suppose."

"She's twenty-four. I heard her tell Camri that much."

"Twenty-four, eh?" Caleb nodded. "Not as bad as I figured."

"Sounds like you've given this some thought." Micah could see he'd hit upon the truth. "So why do you feel she's a 'very nice young woman'?" He held up his hands at Caleb's frown. "Not that I don't think the same, but this is something more personal. I can tell."

"I can't really say what I feel. I know I feel sorry for her. She wants so much to know who her family is and why her mother lied." He shrugged. "Honestly, my mind has been going in so many different directions. I'm still trying to work through this mess related to Ruef. Oh, and we finally found my ledger."

"Oh, really? Where?"

"It was in Henry's office. I was certain it had been taken by his murderer, but bless Henry, he had the foresight to act quickly after Patrick warned him. He tucked the ledger in between some law books. The covers were very similar, so we didn't realize what it was until we opened it."

"I'm sure that will be helpful to your case."

Caleb nodded. "It will be. There all sorts of names and dates—amounts of money given and so forth. That combined with the papers Patrick managed to take from Ruef's house will be solid evidence against the graft going on. Then this morning I finalized an agreement to purchase an old warehouse on the bay. We're going to turn it into a place of temporary lodging and education for women and children. Given all that's happening with Langdon cleaning up vice in this town, there will no doubt be a great many women in need of help."

"No doubt." Micah smiled. "Let me know what I can do."

"Your skills as a physician will definitely be needed."

"I pledge to do what I can. However, in turn, maybe you can help me figure out how to get Kenzie to see me as something other than her enemy."

"I hardly think she sees you as an—"

"Dr. Micah! Dr. Micah!" Liling cried out at the top of her lungs. She burst into Caleb's study, white-faced. "You have to come to the kitchen. Miss Kenzie's cut her hand, and she's bleeding!"

Micah shot up from his seat. "Liling, go to my car and fetch my bag. Hurry."

He raced down the back stairs and into the kitchen. Mrs. Wong was frantically cleaning blood from the table, and Kenzie sat pale-faced and silent. Her right hand was wrapped in a towel and clutched to her breast, but even so, Micah could see blood coming through the layers.

"She cut her fingers when glass break." Mrs. Wong pointed to the pieces of broken glass she'd put on the counter. "I clean it up so you can help her."

He reached for Kenzie's hand. "Kenzie, let me see how bad it is."

"It's fine," she barely whispered.

Micah had seen patients in shock and knew Kenzie was not faring well. "Mrs. Wong, I need the table." He didn't wait another moment but swept Kenzie into his arms and laid her on the table. He thought she might fight him, and when she didn't, he knew it wasn't a good sign.

Liling burst into the room and held up his black medical bag.

"Bring it here," he instructed, pulling off his coat. "Mrs. Wong, bring me some hot water."

"I have some brandy upstairs," Caleb called from the doorway.

Micah hadn't even realized Caleb had followed him downstairs. "Good. Bring it. I can use it to sterilize. And she might need some before this is over." He had all sorts of fears about what he'd find when he uncovered the wrapping on her hands.

Mrs. Wong produced a basin of hot water, then fetched towels and soap. By the time she brought those to the table, Micah had already rolled up his sleeves, taken several things from his bag, and was ready to wash his hands.

Kenzie lay on her back, pale and silent. She stared up at the ceiling, but Micah wasn't sure she was actually seeing anything.

"Liling, get some pillows and put them under her feet to raise her legs," he ordered.

The petite woman disappeared from the room and was back in a flash. Her mother helped her position the plump pillows under Kenzie's limbs. Once this was done, they stood back, awaiting instruction.

Micah washed up quickly, then motioned Mrs. Wong to hand him a towel. She quickly complied just as Caleb returned with the brandy. After drying, Micah reached for Kenzie's hand. She refused to let him pull the towel away.

"Kenzie, you mustn't fight me on this. I need to stitch you up."

77

She frowned, as if trying to make sense of his words, then relaxed her hold. Micah unwrapped the towel and found that she had deep slices in two fingers. Her ring finger was the worst. It was cut to the bone.

Kenzie looked at him and caught sight of her hand. "Oh, dear," she whispered and turned away.

Micah ignored the urge to offer her comfort. He could do that later. "Liling, quickly wash your hands, and then I want you to sit here, close beside me, and hold pressure on the little finger to stop the bleeding while I work on her ring finger. It's going to be an awkward fit, but I think we can manage because you're so small."

The young woman gave a nod and went to the basin. She lathered up her hands, then rinsed as her mother poured fresh water over them. Once this was done, Liling didn't even bother to dry her hands, but slid into place by Micah.

"Good, now take a clean towel and drape it across her hand and first three fingers, then under the ring finger and over the little one." He waited as Liling maneuvered the towel into place, then gave a nod. "Good. Now clasp her finger with the towel and pinch the cut together."

Again he waited while Liling complied. Once she was situated, he let go of his hold on Kenzie's ring finger and went to work.

The cut, though deep, was clean and smooth. He washed out the wound, which had slowed in its flow. The action stirred up the bleeding again, but it couldn't be helped.

"Caleb, pour some brandy over her finger." He waited while Caleb did exactly that. Kenzie winced, but didn't move. "Now, Liling, I need you to keep holding the little finger, but also to pinch closed the ring finger while I thread my needle."

Liling easily accomplished this.

Micah dug into his bag and produced a small envelope. "Liling,

I want you to release pressure on the finger when I say so. I'm going to pour this powder into the wound. It'll help numb it. Ready?"

She nodded.

"Now." Liling released her hold, and Micah quickly sprinkled the white powder into the oozing cut. "All right, hold it tight again just in case." He set the envelope aside and motioned to Caleb to pour some brandy over his hands as well as the needle and thread.

"Kenzie, I need you to hold very still. Hopefully the medicine will help with the pain, but it may still hurt. Caleb, you hold her shoulders down, just in case."

Caleb moved into place.

"I won't move," Kenzie said in a whisper.

Micah glanced for a moment into her blue eyes. That was a mistake. He looked away quickly and focused on the wound. "All right. Here we go."

He refused to think about the woman on the table as anything more than a patient. It wouldn't serve him well to concern himself with feelings and emotions at this point in the battle. However, even though he'd stitched body parts hundreds of times, Micah found himself feeling a little nervous as he stuck Kenzie's finger with the needle.

She was as good as her word and never moved. Micah quickly stitched the finger, then wrapped it for protection. Once that was done, he repeated the entire procedure for her little finger. She never uttered a single word or protest during the entire operation, but her ashen color and clenched jaw made it clear that she was in pain.

Micah looked at Caleb. "Give her a drink. A big one. She's earned it, and it will help with the pain." He could see the perspiration edging her hairline.

"Mrs. Wong, I need a glass," Caleb said as he opened the bottle.

A small snifter was produced, and Caleb poured a liberal amount of brandy into the glass. That done, he went to the opposite side of the table and put one arm under Kenzie's head.

"Kenzie, you heard the doctor—drink," Caleb said, holding the rim of the glass to her mouth.

She did as instructed but gasped and sputtered as the liquid passed her lips. "I don't . . . I don't drink alcohol," she said, trying to push the glass away.

"You do today—doctor's orders," Micah declared. "Be a good girl."

She didn't offer further protest, which told Micah that the injury and repair had exhausted her ability to fight.

"Thank you, everyone, for your help," he said. "This could have been much more difficult if you hadn't been here."

"What now?" Caleb asked, handing the brandy bottle and empty glass to Mrs. Wong.

"I think she needs to rest."

"I'll carry her upstairs," Caleb said. Then he shook his head. "Why don't you carry her? I don't want to accidentally hurt her. I'll lead the way and open doors—turn down covers, that sort of thing."

Micah knew what his friend was doing, but he didn't mind at all. He liked the idea of carrying Kenzie—even if he had to climb two flights of stairs. "Just let me put things away."

"I am perfectly . . . perfectly . . . able to walk." Kenzie said, trying to sit up. She only got halfway, however, before she stopped, blinked several times, and fell back. "Give me a minute."

Micah laughed and shoved the last of his things into his bag. "It's going to take more than a minute before you feel better. You've had a good shock to your system." He handed his bag to Liling. "Would you please put this on the table by the front door?"

"Of course." She took the bag and disappeared.

"Now, for you." Micah picked up Kenzie with little effort. She couldn't have weighed all that much. "All right, Caleb, lead the way."

Micah glanced down to find Kenzie watching him. To his surprise, she smiled in a drunken, lopsided way. "You're very bossy," she said, her eyebrows rising in surprise. No doubt she was starting to feel the effects of the liquor.

Micah couldn't help laughing. "I am. Just remember that, and we'll get along fine." He began climbing the narrow stairs.

"I can be . . . bossy . . . too," she said, closing her eyes.

Micah smiled. "A fact I know quite well."

Caleb began to despair when he didn't hear anything from Ann Whitley. He'd written to her days earlier, asking for a chance to meet with her privately. Poor Judith was nearly beside herself, and Caleb could offer her nothing.

After Kenzie's accident on Saturday, he had just about decided to break with social etiquette and call Mrs. Whitley directly when a card came from the Whitley mansion, instructing Caleb to come on Monday afternoon at three. The timing was perfect. Judith would be at work, which was just as well. Caleb knew she would only have wanted to accompany him, and for this first visit, he was determined to go alone. That way, if Ann's daughter-in-law didn't prove to be the Edith Whitley they were searching for, Judith wouldn't have to deal with it in public.

The Whitley mansion stood atop Nob Hill, surrounded by other well-appointed estates. This was the better part of town—the part where the likes of Spreckels, Crocker, Hopkins, and Stanford lived—men with prominent roles in California's success. Men whose names were whispered in awe by many and cursed by others.

Caleb parked his car and took a moment to marvel at the gleaming limestone masonry. The Beaux-Arts home sported eight white marble columns with Corinthian capitals on the main part of the two-story, hip-roofed house. The grand entryway was arched with an intricately detailed canopy molding. The two sets of floor-to-ceiling windows that graced either side of the entry were also trimmed in elaborately carved shields and swags. To each side of those, the east and west wings of the house jutted out. If one were to look down on the house from above, it would no doubt look like an I-shaped monstrosity amidst carefully groomed lawns and gardens.

Pulling off his driving gloves, Caleb speculated at the value of such a place. Even the rather ostentatious Queen Anne brownstone Henry had left him could hardly command a sum such as this house might. Although the real estate agent who was in the process of selling Henry's brownstone assured Caleb he would realize a hefty profit. Of course, so too would the agent.

Not wishing to be late, Caleb left his gloves in the car and made his way to the front door. He rang the bell and waited. A few moments later, a stern-faced butler appeared.

"May I help you?"

Caleb presented his calling card. "I was asked to come for a three o'clock meeting with Mrs. Whitley."

The butler took the card and gave a nod. "Come in, please."

The foyer was as grand as Caleb had expected. The highly-polished marble floors were nearly as reflective as the huge gilded mirror that hung left of the front door. An ornate receiving table sat in the middle of the floor, topped with a grand bouquet of roses and lilies, while matching mahogany staircases graced either side of the room. Glancing upward, Caleb could see that the stairs swept in a curve to an open second-floor balcony.

"May I take your hat, sir?" the butler asked. Caleb nodded and handed him his felt homburg.

After seeing to his things, the butler asked Caleb to follow him. He led Caleb from the foyer down a long and impressive salon filled with expensive mahogany and walnut tables, stylish sofas and chairs, and a massive stone fireplace that Caleb was confident he could stand up inside. The walls of the room were trimmed out in elaborate moldings and artwork, and the floors were decorated with expensive Aubusson rugs. At the very end of the salon, the butler turned right and paused in front of two massive oak doors. He gave a light knock, then opened the ten-foot-high door on the right.

"Madam, Mr. Coulter." He stepped back to allow Caleb to enter the room.

Caleb smiled and stepped into the large drawing room. Mrs. Whitley sat like a queen upon her throne, a long-haired, buff-colored cat asleep on her lap. The white-haired matriarch glanced up at him with an expression suggesting something between boredom and disdain.

"Thank you, Ramsay, that will be all." She waited until the butler had closed the drawing room door before speaking again. "Please be seated, Mr. Coulter."

He did as instructed, taking a leather wingback chair opposite her. "Thank you for having me, Mrs. Whitley. Judge Winters sends his regards."

She softened her expression just a bit. "You do realize that without his recommendation, I would not have agreed to see you."

"I presumed as much. I'm grateful for your willingness to give me a chance to explain my interest."

"Please do." She didn't move so much as a muscle, merely continued to stare at him like he was some sort of curiosity.

"As my letter explained, I am an attorney and have a client seeking to find Edith Whitley."

"And who is this client?"

"I'm not at liberty to say just yet. I thought it would be best to meet you and explain first."

"Then I suggest you get to it, young man." Her brow arched slightly. "And do so quickly. I will brook no nonsense."

CHAPTER 7

Ann Whitley had dealt with all manner of people, and Mr. Coulter did not intimidate or impress. From the time she was young, living a life of ease under the roof of her politically active father, to marrying a wealthy man, Ann had commanded all those around her. Caleb Coulter would certainly offer no challenge.

She considered the astute young man as he explained his circumstances. He was dressed fashionably and carefully groomed, two things that Ann Whitley valued above all. Breeding showed not only in the way one dressed, however, and as she listened to Mr. Coulter's choice of words and the way he in which he held himself, she could see he had grown up among the privileged.

"Judge Winters told me of the accident that claimed the life of your son, daughter-in-law, and granddaughter, so you might believe this a pointless search. I also realize the chances of your daughter-in-law being the same woman we seek are slim, but I felt I must start somewhere." He smiled.

"So this client of yours wishes to know if Edith had a sister."

"Yes."

His gaze never left her face, and Ann admired his strength. Usually people were unable to look her in the eye for long, but this young man seemed completely at ease.

"Very well," she said. "You may tell your client that Edith did have a sister, but I refuse to elaborate until your client agrees to meet me face-to-face."

"She'll be happy to do that," Mr. Coulter replied with a nod. "When might we come?"

Ann knew her calendar was clear but pretended to consider the matter. "I suppose I could manage a few moments on Saturday afternoon. Let's say at four. I'll have tea served."

"Thank you, Mrs. Whitley." Caleb Coulter got to his feet. "I won't take any more of your time."

Startled, her cat raised his head. Ann stroked the animal's soft fur. "I'll expect you on Saturday at four. Good day."

Caleb Coulter had no sooner left the room than Ann's son and grandson entered to learn what they could. They were insatiable snoops.

"Well, Mother. What was that all about?"

She looked at her son. "I'm not entirely sure, William. He has a client who has asked after Edith and whether or not she had a sister. I've invited him back on Saturday for tea. He's bringing his client then."

"Grandmother, do you suppose that was wise?"

She turned to her grandson. "Bill, what I would suppose is that at your age—what is it now, twenty-three?" He nodded. "At twenty-three, I believe you would know better than to question me."

The blond-haired young man gave a huff and sat down with his arms folded. "Wasn't it you who told me that a person who kept only himself for counsel was a fool?"

Unlike her docile and easily managed son, William Whitley

ll was far more difficult. On one hand, Ann was pleased to see strength in the boy that his father clearly lacked. On the other, she knew he wasn't completely under her control.

She gave him a hard look. "Just because I find no value in your counsel doesn't mean I refuse to seek it elsewhere."

Bill gave her a look that suggested he knew he wouldn't win the argument. He finally relaxed his arms. "So who is coming to see you on Saturday?"

"Mr. Coulter wouldn't say. Apparently he's been checking into Edith and her past. His client has some interest in learning the truth."

William sank into the chair beside his son. "What did you tell him?"

Ann shrugged and continued to pet the cat. "That Edith had a sister. And before you ask what else was offered, don't bother. I said nothing more, and the young man kept everything else to himself. He felt it important to wait until his client could be with me face-to-face."

"Do you suppose it's Edith's sister?" William asked. He sounded troubled—almost frightened.

"How in the world would I know?" Ann got to her feet, cradling the cat.

"What if it is? What if it's . . . Lila?"

"I suppose we shall cross that bridge when we come to it, but I will offer this: Lila knew very well where her sister lived. Furthermore, I hardly imagine she would send a lawyer to ask if Edith had a sister."

"But if not Lila, then . . ." He looked away, shaking his head.

"People are always trying to claim association by blood with the wealthy," Bill interjected. "This is probably nothing more than a scheme to bilk you out of your money, Grandmother."

She looked at the spoiled young man and smiled. "Well, you should know just how unsuccessful that can be."

———

Kenzie waited patiently as Micah examined her fingers. She hated that he was attentive, coming every day to see her progress. It was Friday, nearly a week after her accident, and she'd had about all of the attention she could manage.

"Don't you have anything better to do than come here every day to check on me?" she asked.

He glanced up. His new growth of beard did little to conceal his grin. "Nothing at all. Nothing anywhere nearly as important as this. Nor as much fun."

She felt his finger trace along the side of her palm and then up the center of her little finger. "Stop that at once."

"Now, now, Miss Gifford, I am a physician, and I'm only checking to see that you have feeling in your extremities."

"I can feel everything just fine. When are you going to take out the stitches?"

He continued holding her hand. "I believe I can remove the ones on the little finger today. The others need to stay in place another day or two."

She sighed. "I suppose you'll stop by to check on my finger each day until you're satisfied."

"Of course. I'm your doctor, and as such, I will be faithful to my responsibilities."

She rolled her eyes. "No doubt."

He drew out a pair of tweezers and a small pair of scissors. "Hold still." Without giving her any further instruction, he went to work removing the three stitches. "There. See how simple that was?" He smiled and finally let go of her hand. "I'll re-bandage your ring finger, and then you can go back to your affairs."

"Hardly that. You won't let me work at the factory, and that's where I should be."

"Tsk, tsk." He wagged his index finger in disapproval. "Factories are full of dirt and grime. You might get an infection. Besides, haven't you enjoyed your leisure time?"

Kenzie *had* enjoyed being able to rise late and do very little, but she wasn't about to admit that to Micah. Instead, she sat gritting her teeth while he reapplied a bandage to her finger.

"There. All done. However, I have something of a favor to ask you."

"A favor?" She shook her head. "I don't like the sound of that."

"Well, I figure you owe me, since I saved your life and all." He grinned, and she couldn't help but notice how his whole face lit up.

Keep your head, Kenzie.

"You hardly saved my life."

He put his hand on his chest and gave her a wounded look. "I'm hurt. You lost a great deal of blood, and had I not been able to stop the bleeding, you could easily have died."

She fought the urge to roll her eyes. "Very well. You saved my life. Thank you."

"But I'm not looking for thanks." He put away the rest of his things and closed his black bag. "I'm looking for someone to accompany me to a charity ball."

Kenzie stood up, shaking her head vehemently. "No. I will not go to any dance with you."

"Can't you dance?" he asked with a look of innocence.

"Yes." Her voice betrayed her exasperation. "I can dance. I just choose not to, and especially not with you."

He cocked his head to one side. "Why 'especially'? Are you afraid of me? Do I hold some magical power over you so that you can't help falling in love with me?"

She gave a most unladylike snort. "Hardly. I have no desire to discuss this with you, Dr. Fisher. Suffice it to say, I have put balls and soirees behind me."

It was hard not to remember the last ball she'd attended shortly before her wedding. Arthur had been so attentive—so wonderful. He had shown her every consideration, bringing her flowers and sweeping her off in his finest carriage. They had clearly been the most envied couple at the ball, and Kenzie had never felt more beautiful.

"You aren't listening to me," Micah said.

She looked at Micah and shrugged. "I seldom do."

He sobered. "Do you hate me so much that you won't even extend a simple kindness? Or are you afraid? Won't you at least tell me why?" His words were gentle and coaxing. "After all, you're leaving me to face the evening alone."

"I'm not afraid, and I'm sure with your handsome face, you'll have no difficulty getting any number of women to accompany you."

He leaned back with a smug expression. "So you think I'm handsome."

"Oh, good grief, you do exasperate a person. You know very well you're handsome and don't need me to tell you so."

"I'm glad you think so. It helps to be mutually attracted."

"We are not mutually anything. Now, why don't you run along and find yourself a date for the ball? I have things to tend to."

"I know you're afraid to trust me. Afraid to give your heart again, but I need your help. Most of the other young women I might ask are busy or would see it as something akin to a marriage proposal." Again, his tone took on a tenderness that Kenzie was defenseless against. "Please help me out."

She could see this was getting her nowhere. She had absolutely no desire to attend the ball, but neither did she want him thinking her afraid or ungrateful. Perhaps if she did attend, he would see for himself that they didn't belong together. Then he would leave her alone once and for all.

"Please say yes," he urged.

She made the mistake of looking into his eyes. The sarcastic glint was gone. "Very well. I'll go." She shook her head. "Although, I shouldn't, and perhaps—"

"No, you can't take it back now that you've given me your word." Micah got to his feet. "I'll be here tomorrow evening at six." He headed for the door, then paused to throw her a smile over his shoulder. "Try to look happy."

Kenzie would have thrown something at him had anything been nearby. He was incorrigible. She sighed and headed upstairs, but just as she reached the top step, she realized what he had said.

"Six tomorrow evening!" She felt a momentary sense of horror. Where was she to get a ball gown by then?

———

Caleb had purposefully held off telling Judith about the appointment on Saturday. He didn't want her to spend the week fretting, and besides, he wanted to further research the Whitleys. But now that it was Friday, he would have to let her know about their meeting and what he had learned.

He heard when she returned from work. Camri was in the front room and called to Judith. Caleb had asked his sister earlier in the day to let Judith know he needed to speak with her that evening, just in case he wasn't home.

Getting up to go to her, Caleb was surprised when Judith quickly rushed into his study. "Camri said you needed to talk to me."

He smiled. She looked so pretty, despite being dressed in her simple work clothes. Just seeing her brightened his day. "I do. Please come in and sit a moment." He caught a whiff of chocolate. "You smell like candy."

She was much too preoccupied to even hear what he'd said. Already she was making her way to the chairs by the fireplace. When she'd taken a seat, she looked up at him with an expression between fear and dread.

"Don't look so worried. It's not all that bad." He smiled. "I have some news for you. Some perhaps not exactly what you want to hear, but some good."

She looked up at him. "I'm listening."

He decided to remain standing and positioned himself in front of the fireplace. "I had a brief meeting this week with Ann Whitley. She is the mother-in-law of a woman named Edith Whitley."

"You found my aunt?"

"No, I didn't say that. I'm not sure if this Edith Whitley is your aunt or not. Mrs. Ann Whitley, however, has agreed to meet you tomorrow. We'll go for tea in the afternoon at four, and hopefully we can ask our questions and learn if her daughter-in-law was your aunt."

"Was?"

Caleb drew a deep breath. "That's the bad part. Mrs. Whitley's daughter-in-law died some years ago when she was abroad. The ship she was on with her husband and daughter sank off the coast of Italy, and they were drowned."

Judith looked momentarily stunned, but then tears formed in her eyes. "So even if she is my aunt, I won't ever have a chance to know her."

Her sadness touched him in an unexpected way. Caleb knelt down beside her chair and took her hand. "I'm sorry, Judith. I should have figured out an easier way to tell you. Still, it's very possible that this Edith Whitley isn't your aunt at all."

"I don't know which would be worse—having to start all over, or having it be true. I had really hoped to have family still living."

"And perhaps you do. Don't let yourself be defeated by this. We'll go and speak with Mrs. Whitley, and if Edith was your aunt, then perhaps she had other family—children who didn't accompany her to Europe. You might have cousins. Mrs. Whitley should be able to tell us, if that is the case."

Judith wiped away a tear with her free hand. "If she's my aunt, it'll be like losing Mama all over again. I'll be alone."

"Never." Caleb stroked her hand. "You'll never be alone. You have me and Camri and Kenzie. We might not be related by blood, but you are family just the same."

She gave him a weak smile. "I appreciate that. Truly I do. I don't mean to sound ungrateful."

"And you don't." He smiled. "This is a trying situation, and I intend to be there for you every step of the way."

Something stirred in his heart that he didn't quite understand. He wanted nothing more than to offer Judith comfort and protection just as he would give to Camri. But he felt something else for Judith that had nothing whatsoever to do with being a brother. Right now, more than anything, he wanted to hold her in his arms. Kiss away her tears.

Shocked by his own feelings, Caleb dropped her hand and jumped to his feet. "We will go to Mrs. Whitley tomorrow. We're to be there by four, so you should be ready to go by three thirty." He began to pace. "Don't worry about a thing. I'll drive us there, and should things become uncomfortable, we'll leave."

She looked at him oddly. Caleb wanted to ask her what she was thinking but figured it was better to let the matter drop.

"What should I wear?" she asked.

He stopped in midstep. "Ah . . . that's entirely up to you. The Whitleys are very wealthy and no doubt expect everything prim and proper." He didn't know what else to tell her. She was hardly in a position to impress the old woman, no matter what she wore. "It promises to be warm, and I know your wardrobe is limited. You might check with the others and see if they can lend you something. I wouldn't want you to faint."

Judith smiled at this and got to her feet. "I may be emotional about losing family, Caleb, but I'm not a weakling. I've never fainted and don't plan to start."

He felt his sense of ease return. "I know you're a very strong woman."

"I'm learning it's not my strength, but God's." She looked away. "I'll do my best not to embarrass you tomorrow."

Caleb frowned. "Why would you ever think I'd be embarrassed by you?"

She shrugged. "I'm just a poor girl from Colorado. I don't have the polish and style that Kenzie and Camri have." He started to protest, but she shook her head. "It's the truth, but it doesn't trouble me. I'm learning all that I can. However, I wouldn't want you to be uncomfortable or thought less of because you were with me."

Against his will, Caleb moved toward her. "I think you are an amazing woman—beautiful and sensible, with more than enough polish and style. You could never embarrass me. I'm honored to escort you." He gazed deep into her eyes, and for a moment lost all reason. "I . . . you . . . are perfect just as you are."

He stepped back, knowing that if he didn't, he might well try to kiss her after all.

Turning his back on her, he walked to his desk. "I need to

get back to work." He glanced up and found her watching him with a look on her face that suggested she might have been receptive to his kiss. He sat down to keep from going back to her. "Tomorrow, then?"

She nodded. "I'll be ready at three thirty."

*J*udith fussed with her hair for another minute before giving up. She had brushed and twirled every piece into submission, and although it looked good, she wasn't sure it would be good enough.

Standing, she checked her reflection one more time. She'd borrowed a beautiful salmon-colored tea dress from Camri, and it felt heavenly. The cotton eyelet material was lightweight, and the charmeuse lining was silky on her skin. Judith ran her fingers along the darker pink braided trim that outlined the bodice, waist, and hem. She looked every bit as stylish as the women in the magazines.

She drew in a deep breath and let it out slowly. It was nearly three thirty, and she couldn't delay any longer. Her nerves were stretched taut just at the thought of spending the afternoon with Caleb, much less meeting a woman who might or might not have information about her family.

Taking up her gloves and purse, Judith whispered a prayer. "I don't know what will happen today, Lord, but I pray You'll be by my side." She checked the purse to make sure her mother's letter was inside. It was. She had no idea if she would need it, but it might be important to take.

She tucked the purse under her arm and pulled on her gloves as she made her way downstairs. Camri was waiting for her with a large-brimmed hat.

"I nearly forgot about this. Sit here, and I'll pin it on for you," Camri said.

"I'm so nervous that I hadn't even thought about a hat."

Camri fussed with it for a moment, then stood back. "There. You look perfect."

Judith jumped up and went to the hallway mirror. The hat was straw, painted ivory and trimmed in feathers and ribbon rosettes dyed the same color as the dress. "Oh, this is so pretty. What if I damage it?" She turned to look at Camri. "Maybe this is a mistake."

"Calm yourself. It's only a dress and hat. If something happens to it—well, that's life. You mustn't let it concern you for a moment." Camri gave her a hug. "Now, come on. Caleb is already at the car, waiting."

The thought of seeing Caleb made her stomach flutter. She wondered if he would think her outfit pretty. She hoped so. She could never rival the looks of Florence Brighton, but she was determined not to embarrass Caleb at the Whitley mansion.

Camri walked with her down the steps to the car. Caleb stood watching until the last couple of steps, when he moved forward to take Judith's hand. "You look beautiful."

"Camri lent me the dress, and I think it's wonderful."

"It isn't just the dress," Caleb said, patting her arm. "*You* are beautiful, Judith."

She felt her cheeks grow warm. "Thank you."

He helped her into the car, then waved to Camri. "Don't worry about us if we're not back right away."

Judith had no idea what he meant by that but decided against asking him. Perhaps he knew more about Mrs. Whitley than he was letting on. Perhaps there were other plans afoot. A part of her wanted to run for the safety of her room.

Silly, this is the very reason you came to San Francisco.

She watched as Caleb flipped a switch in the car, then went to crank life into the motor. What had started for her as love at first sight was growing deeper. She loved to watch the way he moved—the way he seemed completely oblivious to his effect on women. She loved his spirit, as well. He was gentle and kind to everyone he met, and even when people treated him with less than respect, he was always congenial.

"There," Caleb said, getting into the driver's seat. "We're set to go. Are you excited?" He glanced at her with a smile.

Judith drew a deep breath. "I am, but I'm also terribly nervous."

He reached over and squeezed her gloved hand. "Don't be. I'll be with you every step of the way."

She lost herself for a moment in his dark brown eyes. They reminded her of the chocolate Mr. Lake made at his candy factory. "Thank you," she barely managed to whisper. Why couldn't he see the way he made her feel—the way she'd come to care for him?

"All right then, hold on to your hat."

Judith did so, saying very little on the ride to the Whitley estate. The day was lovely and warm, just as Caleb had warned. It would have been a perfect day for a picnic or a walk along the beach. For a moment, Judith wished she might be doing either of those things rather than the task at hand. She knew it was silly to be so nervous. After all, this Mrs. Whitley might not be able to give her any information at all.

Lord, I don't know how to even pray about this, but please help me get through this meeting without making a fool of myself. If it's not too selfish of me to ask, then please let me find my Aunt Edith.

"You're awfully quiet," Caleb said.

"I've just been praying."

He gave her a nod. "Prayer's always the answer. I can't tell you the number of times it has helped me face adversity and trials. Not that this meeting should be either, but I know you understand my meaning."

He couldn't know just how much this felt like a trial. A testing, to be exact, for Judith felt certain she'd never faced anything quite so overwhelming. Even the trip to San Francisco hadn't left her feeling so intimidated.

As they made their way closer to the Whitley neighborhood, the wealth of the owners became apparent. Judith had seen these beautiful homes from a distance, but she hadn't realized just how massive the houses were. Not only that, but the lawns and gardens were extensive and beautifully kept. Even the trees were carefully groomed.

Before she knew it, Caleb was turning into one of the well-manicured drives and pulling to a stop in front of a large stone house. Judith tried to remain calm.

"Are you all right?" Caleb asked before getting out of the car.

"I think so. I hope so." She tried to swallow the lump in her throat. "Oh, Caleb, what if I do something wrong? What if I make a fool of myself?"

He smiled reassuringly. "Just be yourself and don't worry about the rest. Mrs. Whitley makes a game out of trying to intimidate people. Just remember that, and then maybe it won't seem so bad."

"All right."

She waited as he came around to help her from the car. In many ways, she dreaded what she would learn once they were inside, but at the same time, she felt like a moth drawn to the flame. It would have been impossible to turn back.

Caleb rang the bell, and almost immediately the front door opened to reveal a very formal-looking butler. He nodded at Caleb, then looked at Judith. She gave him a nervous smile that faded quickly at his frown.

"Please come in," he finally said.

Judith tried to think of what she might have already done wrong. Why would he frown in such a manner?

After taking Caleb's hat, the butler led them into a large open room. Judith tried not to react in amazement at the opulence. She wanted to look everywhere at once but knew that would be the wrong thing to do. Somehow, she found the strength to keep her gaze straight ahead. Maybe later, on the way out, she would have a chance to take it all in.

The butler moved to the far end of the room, turned right, and then knocked on a very large door. He opened it without waiting for a response and stepped into the room. Caleb patted Judith's arm again. She fought back tears of fear and the urge to throw herself into his arms.

"Mrs. Whitley, Mr. Coulter and . . ." The butler looked back at them.

"Miss Gladstone," Caleb filled in.

"Mr. Coulter and Miss Gladstone."

He stepped aside, and Caleb led Judith forward. Mrs. Whitley had been sitting with her back to them, but at the announcement she rose and turned with a rather stern look. Her expression changed almost immediately, however, to one of astonishment as she looked at Judith.

"Cora," she whispered.

Judith looked around, thinking perhaps someone had joined them, but there was no one else in the room.

Mrs. Whitley quickly recovered. "Please be seated. Ramsay, bring the tea." She sank back into her chair while Caleb guided Judith to a seat just across from the old woman.

"Mrs. Whitley, I'd like to introduce Judith Gladstone. She is my client."

Judith waited for the older woman to say something. Anything. When Mrs. Whitley only stared at her, Judith wondered if she should speak. She fumbled with her purse and pulled out the letter.

"What have you there, child?" Mrs. Whitley demanded.

"A . . . letter. From my . . . mother." Judith extended the envelope to the old woman.

"Is this why you're looking for Edith Whitley?"

Judith nodded, continuing to hold out the letter. "My mother wrote it to a woman named Edith Whitley . . . her sister."

Mrs. Whitley finally took the letter from Judith. Without pause, she pulled it from the envelope then unfolded it to read. The silence in the room felt suffocating. Judith looked at Caleb. He gave her a hint of a nod and smile. Neither did anything to comfort her. Perhaps this had all been a big mistake.

Finally, Mrs. Whitley lowered the letter. Her hands were shaking, but whether from age or something else, Judith couldn't say. Again, all the old woman would do was stare at her. Judith was beginning to think they should just excuse themselves and go.

"Miss . . . may I call you Judith?" Mrs. Whitley asked.

"Of course."

"Judith, I am quite glad you came today."

Without giving it much thought, Judith found herself blurting out the question on her heart. "Have we come to the right place? Do you know if my mother and your daughter-in-law were related?"

"Yes." Mrs. Whitley's tone was matter-of-fact as she gave a nod.

Judith felt as if her throat might close. She could hardly draw breath. "Did you . . . did you know my mother?"

Again Mrs. Whitley nodded. This time, however, she got to her feet. "I'd like to show you something."

Caleb rose and extended his hand to Judith. She stood, feeling her knees wobble. The old woman crossed to a set of pocket doors on the far side of the room. She pushed back the doors to reveal a smaller sitting room and entered without another word.

Caleb gave Judith's arm a tug. She walked with him to where Mrs. Whitley stood in the next room. When Caleb stopped, she glanced up. They stood in front of the fireplace. A large oil painting graced the wall above the mantel.

"This is my son Nelson and his wife, Edith, and their daughter . . . Cora."

Judith looked at the faces of each person. She lingered on the face of Edith who looked very much like Judith's mother. In fact, they looked so much alike that for a moment Judith felt that she was looking at a painting of her mother. But it was when she saw the face of the younger woman in the painting that Judith felt her mouth drop open. It was like looking at a painting of herself.

Cora was the very image of Judith. No wonder the older woman had murmured that name.

Judith's knees began to shake, and she clung to Caleb for support. What did this mean?

Caleb put his arm around her. He seemed to understand that she was close to collapse.

"I know this must come as a shock to you, dear Judith, but there is simply no other way to explain," Mrs. Whitley said.

Judith shook her head. "I . . . don't understand."

The old woman's expression softened in a way it hadn't since they'd arrived. She stepped forward and reached out to touch Judith's cheek. "Edith wasn't your aunt, my dear. She was your mother."

*T*hank you for letting me borrow this ball gown." Kenzie fingered the dark blue beaded silk with tulle overlay. "It's stunning."

Camri smiled. "It is pretty, and you're lucky it arrived last week. It's one of only two such gowns I own. Mother promised to send all of my things, but apparently the other ball gown will arrive in a later shipment."

"I have several gowns back home. My life with Arthur seemed to demand such finery. I never thought to need them again. Mother is sending my summer clothes, but I doubt she'll think to send the gowns as well. Frankly, if she did, I'd probably sell them."

"I wouldn't. You might need them. After all, Micah is quite social."

Kenzie looked at her sharply. "I'm only doing this once. I don't plan to ever go to another event with him."

"But why not? Micah's very nice, and it's obvious he's taken an interest in you."

"I don't want him to take an interest." Kenzie walked over to Camri's window and looked out on the sunny day.

"I don't understand why not." Camri knew her friend was still nursing a broken heart, but perhaps it was time to let the good doctor help her heal. "Micah is a good man, Kenzie."

"So was Arthur. Or at least I thought him to be."

"But just because one man is less than admirable doesn't mean all men are a waste of your affections. Patrick and Caleb are good examples. They have their flaws, but they are good and trustworthy."

Kenzie turned and fixed Camri with a frown. "You hardly know what kind of man Patrick is. You've only known him a few months."

"With some people you can just tell what kind of person they are. Like you. When I first met you, I knew I would like you, that you would be the kind of woman I could trust to be my friend. I've always been a good judge of character."

"Well, apparently I'm not."

"Then maybe you should trust the impressions of those who are."

Kenzie shook her head. "Honestly, Camri, I'd rather not discuss this. If I could get out of going to the dance, I would."

"Then why did you agree to go?"

"I don't know. I suppose because of pride or a sense of obligation. I wasn't thinking clearly."

"Isn't it possible that part of you really wants to go with Micah to the dance? It has been a long time since you allowed yourself to enjoy an evening out. Why don't you look at this as a new start?"

The look on her friend's face was enough to reveal her heart. Kenzie was still unable to move past the heartbreak she'd suffered. Camri tried to choose her words carefully.

"I don't wish to offend, but I know you value honesty."

"I do," Kenzie replied. "So just say what you will." She came back to the bed, where Camri had laid out the gown.

"It seems to me that you never really had a chance to say good-bye to Arthur. That makes it difficult to put him behind you. Maybe you could write him a letter and tell him how much he hurt you—how his deception and betrayal crushed your spirit. Perhaps that would even cause him to reconsider his actions."

"To what point?"

Camri shrugged. "Maybe he'd realize that you still care and make things right."

Kenzie shook her head. "I don't know that I want that, Camri. I knew when Arthur first started trying to win me over that it was a mistake. I don't fit in his world, and his family was only too glad to point that out to me. I wish I'd listened to my heart and kept up my guard."

"But love can overcome all. If you two are really meant for each other, then maybe you should give him another chance."

"Camri, he made it very clear that he wasn't interested in a life with me. Why in the world would I put myself in that position again?"

"Well, if you still love him—"

"I think I'll always care for him."

"But that isn't the same as being in love with him."

Camri could see by Kenzie's expression that the comment had taken her by surprise. Camri waited, wondering if her friend would realize the impact of her statement.

"But I must still be in love," Kenzie said, shaking her head. She sat down on the corner of the bed. "I pledged that I would love him forever."

"His betrayal was crushing. Perhaps it killed the love you felt for him, but your pain won't allow you to see it. I don't claim to be an authority on the matter, as you well know, but perhaps you aren't in love with Arthur and just haven't yet figured out what to feel toward him."

Kenzie stared past Camri—no doubt seeing nothing. "But how could I not love him?"

"Things happen to change how we feel about people. Love is not a guaranteed emotion. The love shared between a man and woman requires constant work—nurturing. If not, it dies."

"Love can die? I suppose I never thought of that being possible."

"Well, like I said, I'm no expert, so perhaps I'm all wrong, but it seems to me that just as hate can die, love too can cease to exist. Sometimes we cling to what we know rather than accept the changes that frighten us. Perhaps if you can find a way to accept what happened, then you could learn to love again. Maybe give your heart to Micah. Or if not him, someone else."

"But Arthur still has my heart. Maybe it's not the love I thought we shared, but he ripped my heart from me when he betrayed me."

"Then maybe it's time you reclaimed your heart so it can heal. Write to him, Kenzie. Tell him the truth. Tell him every painful thought and feeling that he caused. Tell him you're taking back your heart—your life. Don't let Arthur Morgan continue to dictate your feelings. He may have ruined that day, but don't let him have the rest of your life."

Kenzie squared her shoulders and looked up. "You may be right, Camri. I would never have considered it before, but there is something satisfying in imagining him reading such a letter." She got to her feet. "I'll go tend to it right now."

"There's plenty of stationery in the small sitting room desk."

"Yes, I remember." Kenzie headed to the door. "Thank you."

"I'll have Liling and Mrs. Wong steam out the wrinkles in

this dress and bring it to your room." Camri smiled despite the seriousness of the previous moments. "I think you're going to be surprised at how much you'll enjoy yourself this evening—once you have this letter behind you."

———

Ann Whitley could see that her granddaughter was about to faint. "Young man, you should probably help Judith to a chair."

Mr. Coulter had no sooner nodded than Judith's knees gave way. "I've got you. Don't worry." He lifted her easily and carried her to a chair. He whispered something in her ear, then unpinned her hat and used it to fan her face.

After ringing for Ramsay, Ann came to Judith's side. "I am sorry, child. There was no easy way to tell you."

Judith looked up at her, shaking her head. "How can any of this be true?"

"Mr. Coulter, would you bring that chair closer?" Ann motioned to an overstuffed chintz chair by the fireplace.

"Of course." He put aside Judith's hat, then quickly did Ann's bidding and positioned the chair beside Judith's.

Ann took a seat and reached out to pat her granddaughter's hand. Ramsay appeared with tea. "Quickly, Ramsay, bring Judith a cup of tea. She's unwell."

Ramsay had been with Ann for over forty years, having come to the house as a footman. He was younger than Ann by a decade but had proven himself worthy of her trust. He brought Judith's tea. "Would you care for sugar or lemon?"

Judith shook her head and took the saucer and cup with shaky hands. Without a word, she sipped the contents. Ann waited until a little color returned to her face. Meanwhile, Ramsay served her and Mr. Coulter their tea, then offered them a variety of tea cakes, sandwiches, and cookies. Ann chose several for herself, and Mr. Coulter did likewise. He offered some of his own to Judith, but she shook her head.

"Ramsay, prepare a plate with an assortment for Judith," Ann said.

The butler did as instructed and deposited a selection of refreshments on the side table by Judith. Once they were served, Ramsay looked to Ann. She gave a nod, and he quickly exited the room, pulling the pocket doors closed behind him.

"Are you feeling better, my dear?" she asked.

Judith seemed to rally. "Yes, I'm fine. I'm sorry for behaving as I did. I've never fainted before."

Ann smiled. "You were quite entitled. Do have something to eat, however. It will make you feel better."

Judith looked at the plate of tea cakes and then back to Ann. "Maybe in a minute."

"Of course. Take your time. Meanwhile, I'll try to explain your past to you."

"Please do. I . . ." Judith fell silent, shaking her head.

Ann took a deep breath and began. "I have—or rather *had*—two sons. Nelson and William. Nelson was my firstborn and fell in love with a beautiful young woman named Edith Morley. Edith had a twin sister named Lila. They were identical in every way but personality. Where Edith was docile and well-behaved, Lila was headstrong and wild."

She paused to drink her tea and let Judith absorb the story so far. Then she continued. "Nelson and Edith announced their engagement, and Lila was unhappy about it. She always seemed to need to outdo Edith. Perhaps it was because Edith was the firstborn, who can say. After the engagement was announced, however, Lila became even more difficult for her parents to handle. As Edith's wedding approached, Lila announced she had fallen in love with a cowboy named Homer Gladstone. She wanted to have a double wedding with her sister. Of course, to a well-to-do family like the Morleys, Homer was an unacceptable choice for their daughter. They forbid further involvement, but Lila refused to listen. She ran away with the young man and married him. Two weeks later, Edith and Nelson were married in an elaborate wedding. Lila's absence was explained as illness, and no one in society knew what she'd done until much later."

Judith remained silent, nibbling a cookie. Ann knew there would be time in the days to come to go into more detail, but for now it seemed important to give her granddaughter a brief understanding of all that had happened, and why.

"Nelson and Edith went to Europe on their wedding trip. They were gone for three months, and during that time, Lila and Homer were found and brought to the Morley estate. Lila's father—your grandfather—declared he would have the marriage annulled. However, Lila announced that she was with child, and so the marriage would stand. It was decided to make the best of the situation, so Lila's father bought them a small ranch east of Oakland, and there they set up housekeeping.

"When Nelson and Edith returned from abroad, they were established here, as my husband and I desired. They were given the second story of the west wing and were happily settled. Edith learned that she too would have a child, and we were all delighted. Everything seemed to be going fine until the time came for Lila to have her baby."

Judith put the cookie aside. "My mother . . . my . . . she had a baby?"

"Yes, but the baby died, and Lila nearly lost her life. When she finally did recover, the doctor said she would never be able to have children of her own. She was devastated."

"How awful," Judith murmured.

"It was indeed. She was two months recovering from the

111

ordeal—at least physically. By the time she was up and around, Edith had given birth to twin daughters, Cora and Judith."

"Me?" Judith asked. Her expression full of disbelief. "Cora wasn't just my sister? We were twins?"

"Yes. It was such a joyous occasion. Nelson was prouder than any papa could ever be. Edith apologized for not giving him sons, but he told her that he was thrilled with his daughters and that sons could come later. Sadly, two boys were later born, but neither survived."

"I can hardly believe that I had a sister and brothers." Judith looked at Mr. Coulter. "I never imagined all of this."

"Mrs. Whitley," Mr. Coulter interjected, "which twin was born first, Cora or Judith?"

"Judith. However, the girls appeared to be identical, and as you can see from the painting—that proved to be true."

"So what happened?" Judith asked, shaking her head. "Why did my mother . . ." She again seemed unable to speak the question and lowered her gaze to the floor.

"Why did Lila take you?"

Judith's face lifted. "Yes."

"Her grief drove her, of that we all agreed. A week after you were born, she and Homer came to the house on the pretense of congratulating Edith and Nelson. We invited them to stay with us while they were in San Francisco, since Lila and Edith's parents were out of town.

"They were given a guest room in the west wing, at Edith's insistence. She loved her sister dearly. They had always been very close, at least from Edith's perspective. Edith was instrumental in your grandparents accepting and helping Lila after she had shamed and disobeyed them with her marriage. We had no way of knowing that Lila and Homer had come planning to take you."

"But maybe that wasn't their plan originally," Judith said. "Maybe it just happened, and once it did, they knew there was no going back."

"No, I'm afraid they knew very well what they were doing. You see, unknown to any of us, Homer had sold the ranch. They had money enough to live on for some time. Not only that, but Lila took some money from the house. Nelson kept a large sum in his desk. Homer had seen it and told Lila about it, and before they slipped away with you, she took the money, as well."

"That's what she was talking about in the letter." Judith turned to Mr. Coulter. "She said she'd hoped to repay the money." He nodded and she looked back at Ann. Understanding was beginning to finally dawn. "This explains everything in the letter."

"I'm afraid it does. Lila and Homer had planned well in advance to take you. We believe it was Lila's plan, however. Homer was devoted to her and would have done anything for her—and did. The very next morning—Sunday—Lila went to speak to Edith and tell her good-bye. The rest of us were attending church. Even Nelson had come with us. Edith was still confined to bed, but with the servants there, and knowing her sister would be with her, we thought nothing of leaving. Apparently Lila had counted on this. She went to Edith and explained that they were leaving and had already said their good-byes to the rest of us. Edith protested the short visit, but Lila promised they would return again soon. She said nothing out of the ordinary—gave no hint of having sold the ranch or anything else. She visited for a few minutes and then said farewell and was gone."

"But how did she take me?"

Ann remembered that afternoon as if it were yesterday. "We

came home from church around one. By then, the household was being turned upside down. Apparently just before Lila went to say good-bye to Edith, she slipped into the nursery to say good-bye to the babies and bring the nurse a cup of tea. We figure the tea had been drugged, because the nurse said she fell asleep almost immediately. Meanwhile, from what we can figure out, Homer slipped in and took you while Lila visited with Edith. He left a bundle in your place so your absence wasn't noticed until some hours later when the nurse woke up."

"But surely other servants would have noticed Gladstone with the baby," Mr. Coulter commented.

Ann shrugged. "Ramsay said he noticed only that Gladstone was carrying a small valise. We presumed he put Judith inside."

"But didn't Edith . . . my mother . . . think it strange that the nurse wasn't coming to check on her or bring her the babies?" Judith asked.

"Edith was taking medication given to her by the doctor. It made her sleep quite a bit. Once Lila left, she fell asleep. It wasn't until close to the time we returned that the nurse came to check on her and ask if someone had brought you to her. When Edith told her no, a thorough search was immediately started. It wasn't long before everyone presumed the worst—that Lila had taken you. The police were summoned against Edith's desires. She didn't want her sister getting in trouble with the law and had hoped we could just find the Gladstones and deal with them privately. However, my husband and I refused to do it that way. We spared no expense and hired private detectives as well, but there was no sign of them. They had planned it out so well that we never got so much as a hint as to where they had gone. They simply vanished. And with them, you."

Judith began to cry softly, and Mr. Coulter stood. "Perhaps

it would be best if we were to go and let Judith consider all that you've told her."

Ann shook her head. "Nonsense. This is her home now. She's my granddaughter, and she'll stay with me."

Judith jumped up, and her teacup and saucer clattered to the floor. "No, I can't stay here. I don't belong here."

"You're distraught, child. I'll have Ramsay call for the doctor. He can give you something to help you rest."

"No!"

Judith surprised Ann by running from the room. "Wait!"

"Maybe you should give her some time."

Ann turned to Caleb Coulter. "She's my granddaughter. I think I know best."

"You might have known what was best for Cora, but Judith is a different person. She has her own personality and needs. Please try to understand that." Caleb picked up Judith's forgotten hat.

Without another word, he exited the room, leaving Ann aghast. She wasn't used to people refusing her, especially in matters of family, and she wasn't about to start now.

She got up and crossed the room to ring for Ramsay. Now that she knew Judith was her granddaughter, she intended to see her established in her proper place, and no one was going to stop her.

CHAPTER

10

*C*aleb easily caught up to Judith as she stormed off down the drive. He pulled the car alongside her and stopped. "Why don't you get in, and I'll drive to the park?"

She looked at him for a moment as if he'd lost his mind. Then her expression changed, and she nodded. She got into the car without giving Caleb time to help her. She almost sat on Camri's hat, but he retrieved it in time and handed it to her. Caleb drove to Golden Gate Park and stopped the car near a large stand of trees. For several minutes, he said nothing. He leaned back and pulled off his driving gloves and prayed that God would give him the wisdom to help Judith. He cared about her and knew that she was hurting from the shock of all she'd learned.

"I don't understand any of this," Judith finally murmured. "How could my mother and father have lied to me all my life? How could they seem to be such good people and yet have done such a hideous, heartless thing?"

"Pain makes people do things they might not otherwise do.

From what your grandmother said, your mother was grieving—desperate after the loss of her baby."

Judith looked at him. Her blue eyes were wet with tears. "Caleb, I thought I knew my parents. I loved them. I thought they loved me. How could they steal me away from my real parents, my sister?"

The tears slipped down her cheeks, and her voice broke. "How can I ever believe anyone ever again?" She let go of her purse and buried her face in her gloved hands.

Caleb put his arm around her. "I'm so sorry, Judith. I know this is hurting you, and I wish there was something I could do to lessen your pain. It was a terrible thing that was done to you and to your family."

She leaned into him and began to sob in earnest. Caleb had never felt more moved. He wanted only to comfort her—to make her pain and fears go away. He wanted to promise her that she never had to return to the Whitley mansion unless she wanted to. He wanted to say a lot of things, but for the moment, silence seemed the right choice.

He wasn't sure how long they sat there. He was grateful that he'd found a somewhat secluded spot to park, since there were people everywhere. When the sun was shining in San Francisco, you could be sure that its people would be outdoors, enjoying the day.

Judith finally seemed to calm, but she didn't pull away from him. Caleb found he didn't want her to move. He liked the feel of her in his arms and the smell of her rose-scented hair.

"You know," he said softly, "you don't have to go back. I won't let Mrs. Whitley force you to live there, even if she is your grandmother."

"I always wanted a grandmother," Judith replied, hardly louder than a whisper.

"I can understand that. I always enjoyed my grandparents, but they weren't trying to control my life and make me into something I wasn't. I have a feeling that Mrs. Whitley knows no other way. She is used to having things done as she orders them."

Judith straightened. "Oh, Caleb, this is all so hard. I thought coming here I would find an aunt—maybe cousins. I thought I would have a connection to family again."

"And so you do, even if it isn't what you thought it would be."

"But I'm so confused. I'm not even the person I thought I was. I'm not Judith Gladstone. I'm Judith Whitley, and I don't even know who she is."

Caleb turned her face to his. "You're still Judith. The rest will sort itself out in time, but the things that make you who you are, those things are still a part of you. Nothing can change that."

"But my life was a lie. My memories, my joys and sorrows—all lies. Everything was built on deception. Everything except for the name Judith. I'm surprised they didn't change that as well."

"Frankly, so am I, but I'm glad they didn't. I rather like the name." He smiled at her. "And I rather like the young woman who bears it."

———

Judith didn't know what to think of Caleb's comment about liking her. Now probably wasn't the time to declare her feelings for him, but she knew they were stronger than ever. Just having his arms around her as she cried, being able to put her head on his shoulder . . . her feelings for him were only too apparent. She only hoped she hadn't made a fool of herself, and that she wouldn't with the things she was about to say.

"Caleb, I appreciate what you've done for me. I couldn't have made it through this without you. Besides Camri and Kenzie, you are the only one I trust." She took a moment to pin her hat back in place.

"And I don't take that trust lightly. I'll help you through this in any way I can. I promise you that."

She gave a little nod. "So advise me what to do now."

He considered this for a moment, not at all appearing eager to move his arm from around her shoulders. Judith remained close, hoping his nearness might give her strength.

"Mrs. Whitley will be in contact. She knows where I live, but not that you live there, so for a short time you can remain hidden, if you like. However, we both know she isn't going to go away."

"No, I don't suppose so."

"She also has plenty of money, so she'll no doubt hire someone to locate you. It would be best to forego working at the candy factory. Unless, of course, you don't mind her finding you right away."

"I can't see abandoning Mr. Lake. He's looking to expand his business. He even wants to hire some additional people." She paused to smile. "Of course, he has to find someone he can trust. Someone who isn't a spy for Ghirardelli."

Caleb smiled. "Of course. However, know that you will be vulnerable coming and going from the factory—perhaps even at the factory. If Mrs. Whitley so desires it, she might even have someone try to force you back to her house."

Judith thought of the older woman and had no doubt Caleb was right. "I'll do whatever you think is right."

"We'll pray about it, Judith. Together. God obviously has a plan even in this. He's known about your circumstances since before it happened, and I know He will have answers for you. For us."

She liked the sound of that. She would like very much for there to be an "us" where Caleb Coulter was concerned.

"Have I told you how beautiful you are tonight?" Micah asked Kenzie.

"At least a dozen times." She allowed him to take her arm as he led her into the hotel ballroom.

There must have been at least two hundred people in the room. Some were dancing, some talked in groups, and still others were enjoying refreshments from a large spread of culinary delights off to the far side of the room.

From what Kenzie had seen and heard, the tickets to the event had cost more than she made in a month working for Cousin George at the candy factory. She didn't know if Micah had been given the tickets or had purchased them to support the charity event, but either way, it made her feel even more obligated to stay the entire evening.

"You've been awfully quiet. I doubt you said more than two words on the drive here," Micah said.

Kenzie glanced his way. He was far more handsome than she wanted him to be, resplendent in his formal wear. She found it hard to stop looking at him. "I suppose I don't have anything to say."

His lips curled up ever so slightly at the corners, and Kenzie found herself wondering what it might be like to kiss him.

This is ridiculous and I need to stop. I can't let myself fall in love again. It's too painful and unproductive.

"Well, if you don't wish to talk, then how about a dance?" Micah asked.

"No. I don't want to dance either."

He cocked his head to one side. "Then what do you want to do? I noticed they have a lovely garden courtyard. We might take a moonlight stroll."

"Absolutely not!" She quickly looked back at the dancers.

Chuckling, Micah leaned closer. "You were awfully brave to come tonight."

Kenzie shook her head. "Bravery had nothing to do with this. It's merely obligation."

He was undeterred. "Then in light of obligation, given all I've done for you, you at least owe me one dance. A waltz, I think."

She considered protesting but knew he'd only keep nagging her until she gave in. Still, she wasn't going to make this easy on him. He'd tormented her all week by insisting he had to check on her fingers. She'd been made to endure his poking and prodding, not to mention his conversation.

"I agreed to come with you, but never said I would dance." She kept her gaze fixed on the waltzing couples on the dance floor. The orchestra was playing a beautiful piece of music that Kenzie thought she'd once heard on an outing with Arthur. It made her a little sad.

"I believe agreeing to accompany me to a ball is in effect agreeing to dance. In fact, the more I think about it, the more I'm convinced you owe me several dances."

Kenzie knew she'd overplayed her hand. "One dance."

"A waltz."

She drew a deep breath and turned to face him. "Very well. A waltz. They're playing one now. Let's go."

He chuckled. "Oh, no. I am going to have a complete dance with you. Not a few steps in a final refrain."

"Very well." She wanted to tell him how unreasonable he was for pressing her for so much more than she wanted to give, but she was afraid she would only encourage him.

Thankfully, the next dance was a reel, and the one after that was a lively two-step performed to the new ragtime music. Kenzie liked the beat of the modern songs. They were cheery and made her momentarily forget her past. When the music ended, a brief intermission was announced to give the musicians a break. Kenzie breathed a sigh. It was a reprieve and would postpone the inevitable a few minutes longer.

Micah smiled at her as if reading her mind. "They'll get around to another waltz, don't you worry."

"I wasn't worried." She glanced around. "I'm rather hungry."

Without waiting for him to respond, she made her way to the refreshment table. A man in a crisp white coat picked up a small china plate while she contemplated the cornucopia of choices. She had no idea if Micah had followed her, nor did she want to know. She pointed to one of the pastry creations topped with cheese and a dollop of something she didn't recognize. The server quickly placed one on the plate. She pointed to one of the tiny watercress sandwiches, and he nodded and added it to the plate.

"I don't believe we've been introduced," an older man said from beside her.

Kenzie looked up and shook her head. "No. We haven't." She turned back to the table and pointed to one of the chocolate-covered strawberries.

"I'm Daniel Crosby."

She looked at him with what she hoped was an expression of indifference. He didn't seem to care and beamed a smile at her from behind his waxed mustache.

"And you are?"

"Here with me," Micah said before she could speak.

Kenzie turned to see the two men exchange a look. Micah's seemed to dare the other man to challenge his claim, while Mr. Crosby's expression was smug and self-assured.

Kenzie turned back to the server who held her plate. "That's all I care for, thank you."

He nodded, put a napkin under the plate, and handed it to her. She moved away from the table to where other people were sampling their food and discussing the topics of the day. She tried not to concern herself with what exchange might be taking place between Micah and Mr. Crosby, but she had to admit she was curious.

She glanced down at her plate and contemplated whether eating the food there was worth removing her gloves. Before she could decide, Micah was at her side.

"If I'd known you were hungry, I would have taken you out to dinner first."

"No, you wouldn't have, because I wouldn't have allowed it." She gave a little shrug. "Besides, I'm not as hungry as I thought."

The musicians began tuning up again. Micah smiled. "They're leading off with a waltz."

Kenzie glanced down at the plate in her hands. "I only just got my food."

He took the plate from her. "And you also just told me that you weren't hungry." He handed the plate to a serving girl, then turned back to Kenzie and extended his hand. "I believe this is our dance."

She let him lead her out onto the dance floor as the orchestra began to play. Without any warning at all, he took a possessive hold of her and swept her into the swirl of other dancers. Kenzie easily fell into the steps. It hadn't been that long ago that she'd danced with Arthur.

"You're very light on your feet," Micah said.

"As are you."

She didn't know what else to say for fear she might comment on how his movements were much smoother than those of her former fiancé. She closed her eyes and tried to will herself back in time.

For just a moment, she imagined that she was in Arthur's arms. She'd left her letter for him with Mrs. Wong. It wouldn't be posted until Monday, but now that it was written, Kenzie found herself second-guessing the idea. She had told him everything she'd thought and felt when word came that he wouldn't be marrying her. She told him of her humiliation and sorrow, as well as the anger and heartbreak.

"You aren't dancing with me," Micah scolded. "That means you owe me another waltz."

She opened her eyes. "I most assuredly am dancing with you, and I do not owe you anything more."

"Kenzie," his voice was almost accusing.

A wave of intense emotion washed over her, but Kenzie did her best to smother it. She didn't want to break down in front of all these people, but especially not in front of Micah.

"I'm done dancing." She tried to pull away, but he held her fast.

"What have I done to make you so afraid?"

She began to tremble. It was like he could see into her soul. "I'm not afraid." She tried to make each word a sentence unto itself.

"You're shaking like a leaf. Either you're afraid, or you're ill."

"Why can't you leave me alone? I've made it clear I'm not interested in anything you have in mind."

He continued to gaze into her eyes. "I'll leave you alone if you answer my question."

"What question?" The music built to a crescendo, and for a moment, Kenzie wasn't sure he'd heard her. She was about to ask again when he spoke.

"Why are you so afraid to love again?"

She misstepped, but Micah easily corrected. "I'm not afraid of anything. Furthermore, I can't—I *won't* love again because . . ."

She tried to think of some excuse, but nothing came to mind. At one time she might have told him she was still in love with Arthur, but after her talk with Camri, she wasn't at all sure what she felt.

"Just leave me be!" She yanked her hand from his and walked from the ballroom as the music came to an end.

She hurried to reclaim her wrap, then headed out of the hotel and into the night. The sound of footsteps following left her no doubt that Micah was right behind her.

"Kenzie, please wait."

Against her will, she did as he asked. Turning, she could see the concern in his expression. He stepped forward. "I'm sorry. I didn't mean to upset you. Let me drive you home."

She acquiesced and waited while the valet brought the car around. All the way home, she sat tense and guarded. She knew he would speak again and demand she answer more questions. She felt so miserable that she wasn't sure she wouldn't answer anything he asked, just to be rid of him.

To her surprise however, Micah said nothing until he'd pulled up in front of Caleb's house and stopped the car. She started to get out, but he caught her hand.

"I never meant to hurt you, Kenzie. You know that. You must know how I feel about you. However, I'm also worried. I don't think you've allowed yourself to understand the situation for what it is."

"What are you talking about?" She couldn't keep the exasperation from her voice. It was better to react in anger than admit he stirred up feelings in her she'd just as soon forget.

"When I was just starting out as a doctor, I made rounds with an older physician who worked here in the city. We went to the home of a woman who'd given birth just a few days earlier, in order to check on her and the baby. When we got there, we found that the infant had died. The mother, however, refused to acknowledge it. She sat rocking the dead baby and wouldn't let us take him from her."

"What has that to do with me?" Kenzie forced herself to meet his gaze.

Micah hadn't seemed to hear her question. "We tried to explain to her that the child was dead, but she assured us he wasn't. While my associate tried to reason with her, I found the husband and asked him to call the funeral home, which he did. He was beside himself and had been trying to get her to give him the child for the last eight or more hours. As best he could reckon, the baby had died in the night, and when they got up and found him lifeless, his wife refused to see the truth of the matter.

"No matter what anyone did, the mother couldn't give up the idea that the baby was still alive."

It began to dawn on Kenzie what Micah was trying to tell her. "Dr. Fisher, you needn't continue. You think I'm like that mother, but you're wrong. That mother held on to her child, believing he might still be alive and everyone else wrong. She refused to let him go on the hope that he still lived. As for me, I am neither holding on to my failed love affair, nor do I desire to do so. I do not hope that it still lives, nor am I expecting to resurrect my dead heart. I have neither the hope nor the desire to ever love again. It's simply too painful."

She quickly exited the car before he could stop her and raced up the stairs for the safety of home. Once she was inside with the door between them, Kenzie vowed she would never again allow Micah Fisher to persuade her to accompany him anywhere.

CHAPTER 11

*S*unday proved to be as lovely as Saturday. Caleb announced at breakfast that he had something to tend to before church, but that he would come back to drive everyone just prior to the services. Camri had assured him that given the pretty day, she and Patrick wouldn't mind the walk. Kenzie, who had been in a black mood all morning, said nothing, but Judith conveyed her approval of walking and left it at that. She reasoned that perhaps in trying to soothe Kenzie's distress, she might be able to forget her own misery for a time.

On the way to church, she stuck by Kenzie's side and tried to make small talk, but the redhead would have nothing to do with it. Judith had no idea why Kenzie was so quiet. She knew from Camri asking her about the dance that Kenzie had come home rather early. However, besides that, no one was saying much on the subject, so Judith thought perhaps it was best to avoid the topic.

Throughout the services, Judith tried to focus on the sermon but found her thoughts going back to Mrs. Whitley—her grandmother. She had shattered Judith's world completely.

She had stripped Judith of her past and all that she knew to be true. It left Judith feeling vulnerable and confused. It also left her with so many questions. Questions that no one could answer. The entire matter had kept her awake for a good part of the night.

Why had her mother—no, she wasn't Judith's mother. Why had Lila taken her? Lied to her? Why had her parents—no, they weren't her parents. How in the world could she sort it all out? From her earliest memories, she'd known Lila and Homer to be Mother and Father, but now she knew they were her aunt and uncle—not her parents. She pressed her gloved finger to her throbbing temple.

Lord, I don't know how to make sense of this.

The congregation stood to sing the benediction, and Judith rose with them, but her heart had no interest in the song. Caleb had assured her that she didn't have to make any decisions right away, but he had also been certain her grandmother would start an immediate search for her in order to make her move to the Whitley mansion. Judith didn't like the idea of being hunted down.

As the congregation began to leave the little church, Judith was still lost in thought. As much as she wanted to be with Caleb, she knew that walking home would do her more good.

"I'm going to walk. Would you like to accompany me?" she asked Kenzie.

"Of course." Kenzie headed for the door. She gave a curt nod to the pastor and Mrs. Fisher but turned away as Micah approached. Mrs. Fisher frowned and murmured something to her husband.

Judith didn't know what had happened, but Kenzie clearly wanted nothing to do with Micah. She smiled at the Fishers, trying to smooth over the discomfort of the moment.

"I very much appreciated your sermon today, Pastor Fisher. Thank you."

He smiled and shook her hand. "You are quite welcome. I find the story of Ruth compelling."

Judith nodded. Kenzie looked impatient. "Well then, good day." She turned and hurried down the church steps with Kenzie at her side.

"I know you're unhappy, Kenzie," Judith said as they made their way home. "I'm not trying to pry, but I want you to know that I care about your feelings. If Micah was out of line last night, I think you should say something to Caleb. After all, they are friends, and since you are under Caleb's protection, so to speak, he could take the matter in hand."

Kenzie shook her head. "He wasn't out of line. Not really. I'm afraid I'm just out of sorts. I had no desire to go on a social outing, much less a dance. I should have stuck to my initial decision and refused, but I allowed Micah to goad me into it. Now it's behind me, however, so I just want to forget about it."

Judith could understand wanting to put matters behind her. "I won't say another word about it."

"What of your own circumstances?" Kenzie asked. "I heard the discussion at breakfast regarding your family. That must have been a shock."

"Yes. It was that and so much more. The entire foundation of my life as I knew it was built on nothing but lies. I can't begin to figure out how to move forward with this knowledge. My grandmother wants me to live with her now, but I don't know her. I don't know anything about my real family."

Kenzie slowed her pace a bit and sighed. "It's going to be difficult to sort it all out. Just remember, however, that you have friends who care about you. Caleb won't make you leave, of that you can be certain. I think he cares for you."

Judith shook her head. "I don't know what he feels. I'd like to believe he cares. Well, I know he cares, but I mean romantically."

They reached the house and made their way inside. Judith's confusion only increased when Mrs. Wong presented an invitation that had been left for her in care of Caleb. It proved to be an invitation to tea at the Whitley mansion that afternoon.

"Oh, dear." She looked at Kenzie and shook her head. "She's already pursuing me, just as Caleb said she would."

Kenzie looked at the card and handed it back to Judith as Camri made her way into the house. She was still smiling after her time spent with Patrick. She took one look at Judith, however, and sobered. "Are you all right?"

"Mrs. Whitley has requested Judith come for tea at four," Kenzie replied.

"I won't go," Judith said. "I don't want to be alone with her . . . not yet. And I know Caleb said he'd be gone a good part of the afternoon."

"Yes, he has some previous obligation to Miss Brighton," Camri said, pulling off her gloves. "I don't think he wanted to go, but he felt he couldn't get out of it. After all, he tried to do just that this morning before church, but she wouldn't receive him."

Judith had wondered what Caleb had to do that morning that was so important. She sighed, feeling a sense of both annoyance and jealousy. "I don't know what to do."

Camri put her gloves on the table, then started to unpin her hat. "What if Kenzie and I go with you? Patrick is busy until evening, so I'm free. We could meet Mrs. Whitley and help ease the tension. You two could talk, and then when you felt you'd had enough, we could leave. You wouldn't have to worry about being alone."

Judith looked at Kenzie. "Would you be willing to do that?"

"Of course," Kenzie replied. "But don't feel that you have to go. Mrs. Whitley will just have to live with her disappointment if you choose otherwise."

Judith nodded. "If I have the two of you with me, I shan't be afraid."

"I'll have Mrs. Wong send a note to tell Mrs. Whitley that you'll be there and that we'll be accompanying you. If she doesn't approve and sends word to protest, then you can simply tell her no and be done with it. However, I doubt she will do that."

"I don't think she'd do anything to jeopardize getting to know you better," Kenzie added.

"Nor do I." Judith forced a smile. "Thank you both. I couldn't do it without you."

After a light lunch, Judith went to lie down for a little while. She couldn't stop thinking about Mrs. Whitley and how imposing she had been. Caleb had told Judith to pay her no mind, but that was easier said than done.

When it came time to leave, Judith was a nervous wreck. She dressed simply in her plaid suit and made her way downstairs, where the girls awaited her. She bit her lower lip as she pulled on her gloves.

"Don't fret so," Camri chided. "Nothing will happen to you. We won't allow it. Kenzie and I can be very vocal when we need to be."

Judith nodded. "Thank you again for going with me. I wouldn't have gone otherwise."

They walked the many blocks to Nob Hill, conversing about how there were more and more flowers in bloom and how lovely the day was. Judith felt herself growing wary as they approached the gates to the Whitley estate. Maybe she was making a mistake. Maybe she should just forget about it.

Looking up at the two-story mansion with all its fancy trim

and beautiful design, Judith had a thought. This was the home where she was born. This was where she would have grown up—where her sister Cora did grow up.

"It's quite the house," Camri said, glancing around at the grounds. "And the lawn is pretty. I'd love to explore the gardens."

"I was just thinking about how I was supposed to have grown up here. I can't even imagine what that would have been like. Wait until you see the inside. There are all sorts of paintings and sculptures. Oh, and the furniture is some of the most beautiful pieces you could imagine." Judith tried to swallow the lump in her throat. Her mouth was much too dry, however. She would actually be grateful for Mrs. Whitley's tea.

Ramsay, the butler, opened the door almost before Camri could ring. He nodded to Kenzie and Camri, then actually smiled at Judith.

"Please come in. Madam is waiting for you in the garden. I'll show you the way."

He led them through the same long, high-ceilinged room that Judith had passed through before, but this time she noticed large double doors on the left side. These opened onto a room that bore the same polished floors and several beautiful carpets done in pale blue, rose, and ivory. She couldn't imagine how hard it must be to keep something like that clean. Having had to beat more than her share of rag rugs, Judith could only marvel at the spotless beauty of the carpets.

On the far wall stood open French doors. Ramsay exited here, and the girls followed, passing into an outdoor haven of trees and shrubbery. Potted flowers were strategically placed amidst chairs and benches, and in the middle of the courtyard, a marble table stood festooned with plates of delectable goodies. Behind it, a uniformed young woman stood ready to serve.

"Enjoy the gardens. Mrs. Whitley will join you soon."

Once he was gone, Camri shook her head. "I knew Caleb said the Whitleys were rich, but I had no idea they had this kind of wealth. Did you see the painting at the end of the gallery? I'm sure it was a Degas."

"It is impressive," Kenzie admitted.

Judith was far too nervous to sit, so she pretended to be interested in the potted flowers. "These are so pretty." She gently touched one of the delicate blooms.

Mrs. Whitley stepped into the courtyard. She was dressed regally in a flowing navy gown trimmed with a lacy high neck and long sleeves. Judith pushed down the urge to flee and prayed for the strength to face what was yet to come.

"Thank you for agreeing to join me." Ann Whitley walked up to the table, where the trio of young women stood. "I know this has been very hard on you, Judith dear. Now, introduce me to your friends."

Judith nodded. "This is Caleb Coulter's sister, Miss Camrianne Coulter. And this is Miss Kenzie Gifford."

Ann could see that her granddaughter was more than a little uncomfortable. "Such unusual names. You shall have to tell me where you came by them. Miss Coulter, Miss Gifford, I am Ann Whitley, Judith's grandmother."

"I'm pleased to meet you, Mrs. Whitley," Miss Coulter responded. "You have a lovely home."

"Thank you."

Miss Gifford nodded. "It is indeed lovely, and I too am pleased to make your acquaintance."

They were lovely, well-groomed, and properly clad young women. It was evident they had been brought up with some modicum of social awareness.

"I've arranged for tea under the trellis. I believe we will be quite happy there." Ann glanced at the maid. "You may serve us now."

The young woman nodded and immediately went to work while Ann led them to the place she'd had prepared.

"This is so pretty," Judith said as they reached the lace-covered table. She admired the large, low arrangement of flowers. "And these are beautiful." She touched the edges of a pink rose.

Hothouse flowers had been delivered only that morning—not an easy feat on a Sunday, but quite possible when one was willing to pay for the privilege. Ann took a seat on a cloth-covered chair. "I love roses."

They took their places, and within a few minutes, Margery served the tea. She placed two multitiered serving dishes on the table. One held a bevy of small sandwiches and tiny tarts that looked filled with meat. The other was filled with fruits and cheese. After they had each chosen what they wanted, Margery returned and replaced the serving dishes with two identical pieces, these filled with all manner of desserts.

"I was afraid you might refuse to come," Ann said to begin the conversation. "I know you were quite upset yesterday."

"It's hard to learn that your entire life has been a lie." Judith sipped her tea.

Ann stirred cream into her tea. "It was impossible to find happiness in this house for years after you were taken. I can honestly say that your mother never recovered from losing you, nor did your parents ever give up hope of one day finding you again. You were always meant to be here."

"Please tell me about . . . my mother, if you would."

It was clear her granddaughter still had no desire to talk about moving into the house. Ann would do whatever she could to convince Judith that it was the right thing to do. However, the matter could wait.

"She was a charming, warmhearted woman. When I first met her, I wasn't at all sure that I wanted her for a daughter-in-law, however. She was so quiet and reserved, and I feared she'd be swallowed up in our boisterous and active life. But she adapted well. She particularly loved the gardens and music."

"I love music as well," Judith said.

"Judith is quite adept at playing piano," Miss Coulter offered.

Ann smiled. "Her mother was as well."

"I learned from my—Lila."

Ann nodded. At least that abominable woman had done one thing right. "Edith played throughout the time she carried you and your sister. No doubt that love of music was passed on to you both. Cora too loved music, but she preferred to sing."

Judith looked wistfully into her tea. "It's so hard to imagine having a sister. I wish I could have known her."

"I still have many of her things. Your mother's as well. They're yours now."

"Oh, no. I couldn't take them." Judith shifted in her chair, her cheeks coloring.

"But of course, you will. When you move in, I will put you in the rooms your parents had. I know you'll come to love being here—where you were always meant to be. We'll have a great deal of time to go through all of their things and talk about the past."

After a brief moment, Judith said, "You mentioned at our first meeting that my mother had other babies?"

Again, she avoided the matter of moving in. Ann remained composed, however. Had this been one of her other grandchildren, she wouldn't have allowed for it, but given this was a delicate matter and Judith was clearly afraid, Ann was determined to be accepting.

"She did. She gave birth to a boy in 1885, and they called him

Clark after my husband. Unfortunately, he contracted measles when he was four and died. There was also another boy called James who was born in 1888. He was eight years old when he fell from his horse and broke his neck. Your mother and father were devastated, as were we all. Poor Cora mourned perhaps more than any of us. She was completely devoted to the boys."

Judith bowed her head. "That is so sad."

"Has your family always been in San Francisco, Mrs. Whitley?" Miss Coulter asked.

Ann smiled. Camri Coulter was clearly the least intimidated of the trio. "No. I was born in New York. I met Mr. Whitley there, and we were married there as well. We didn't come west until his good friend Leland Stanford encouraged him to make the move. I was unhappy to leave New York and all my friends, but once we were established, I found contentment. San Francisco and its society has blossomed over the years."

"It is a lovely city. At first I wasn't at all sure I'd like it here," Miss Coulter replied, "but now that I've become engaged, I find I like it very much."

Ann nodded and turned back to Judith. "Why don't you tell me where you've been all these years? Tell me about your life with Lila and Homer."

CHAPTER
12

*J*udith immediately felt a sense of relief when her grandmother dropped the subject of having her move in. She wasn't sure why this woman was so insistent, but it made her uncomfortable.

"We, uh, had a small ranch in Colorado. Out in the middle of nowhere." Judith remembered the isolation of her home. "We rarely went to town, which was some distance from the ranch. I didn't have playmates or attend a school. My mother—Lila taught me at home. She taught me the piano, as well, but I guess I mentioned that." She looked at her hands.

"Did you always live there?"

Judith looked up to meet her grandmother's gaze. "For as long as I have memory. We never had much money, and I didn't learn until my mother . . . died that the place was mortgaged. Papa . . ." Judith shook her head in exasperation. "I don't know what to call anyone anymore."

Camri was first to comment. "They did raise you, so it's only natural that you would refer to them as your parents."

Mrs. Whitley put more cream in her tea. "I'm certain in

time you will feel less ill at ease, but I hope you will call me Grandmother." She smiled, but there was still a fierceness to her expression. "Your cousins and sister did, and it seems only right that you should too."

Judith nodded. "I think I can manage that . . . Grandmother."

The older woman nodded. "Thank you. Now, please continue. You grew up on a ranch."

"Yes. My father was a cattleman, as you already know. He loved working outside and had a small herd of cattle. It provided the money we lived on. Each fall, he sold off what he could, and we bought what we needed for the next year and paid the hired men. Some years were worse than others, and the hired men had to accept room and board and very little pay.

"My . . . mother and I gardened and cared for the other livestock. We had chickens galore, a couple of goats, and a milk cow. There was also a dog named Mack. He was a good guard dog and a bit of a mutt." Judith smiled. "I've always liked animals."

"I have a cat," Mrs. Whitley said. "He's nearly the same color as the stone on this house, so I named him Mr. Stone." She smiled. "I'm sure you'll see him around."

"We didn't have cats because they would pester the chickens. Mack had a run-in with the rooster, and after that, he pretty much left the chickens alone."

"It sounds as if you had a very hard life."

Judith shook her head. "It didn't seem that way at the time. There was always plenty of work to be done, and I did long for more family. I always wanted siblings and grandparents. My mother—" Again she hesitated. Judith sighed. "My mother always said there was no one else."

"Did she ever talk of the past?"

"No. Not really. A few times she started to mention some

memory, but usually she'd stop and say it wasn't important. When Papa died, she told me that she didn't know what she would do. She'd never loved anyone but him. I asked her how they met, and she said she'd met him during a riding lesson. That was the first time I'd ever heard her speak of such things."

Mrs. Whitley nodded. "They did meet that way. Homer was one of the grooms on your grandparents' estate. Your mother's parents."

"Where did they live?"

"Just outside the city and to the south. They owned a large horse farm. They raised the most beautiful Arabians, and people came from far and wide to purchase those horses."

"What happened to them?"

"Your grandmother passed away first. Her health failed her after Lila stole you away. She was beside herself, having lost not only a granddaughter but also a daughter. She tried to offer consolation to Edith, but of course none could be had. Not for either one. Your grandmother lost hope and took to her bed. The strain was too much, and she died. After that, your grandfather focused on the horses, but when little James was killed, he was devastated."

"You mean James died at their farm?"

"Yes," her grandmother replied, her tone becoming somber. "Your grandfather was teaching James to ride. Your mother and Lila had learned early to master horses, and she knew her father was an excellent teacher. However, something happened, and the horse spooked. Before your grandfather could reach them, the horse bolted, and James fell and broke his neck. He died immediately. Your grandfather was so grief-stricken that he shot the horse and vowed to have nothing more to do with the animals. He sold the ranch and moved to a small town to the north. He died in early 1899, which was the reason your mother and father took Cora and went abroad. Nelson had hoped it might restore your mother's spirits. She had so much loss in her life. When I learned that their ship had gone down and they were drowned, I was beside myself. My son was dead, and his family . . . The loss was acute. So you see, it's important to me that you come here and take your rightful place."

"But I don't know you." Judith tried to speak gently. She didn't want the old woman to think that she was without sympathy, but she wanted to make her feelings clear. "I want to know you better first."

"Living here would allow for that, don't you think?"

"It would, but it would also be very uncomfortable for me. I would rather get to know you a little bit at a time."

"You are a Whitley, Judith. You belong here, and in many aspects, don't you think you owe it to me . . . to yourself?"

"Judith owes you nothing," Camri said in a protective manner. "She's been just as much a victim in all of this as you and the others. You must allow that her entire world has been set on its ear, while the foundation of yours remains solid. Judith needs to handle this in whatever manner makes sense to her. You must give her time."

The look on Mrs. Whitley's face showed that she wasn't used to anyone standing up to her in such a manner. Judith wanted to say something to calm the tension, but was frankly glad that Camri had interceded.

A man walked out into the garden. "Mother, I was told you were entertaining Judith today." He looked at Judith, and his mouth dropped open. "Good grief, I can see why you had no doubt of her being Nelson's daughter. There can be no question of that."

Judith considered the man. He was rather stocky with tawny

hair that bore a fair share of gray. She tried to force some recognition or sense of familiarity, but there was none. Meanwhile, he assessed her as though he might be buying a horse.

"This is your Uncle William, Judith. He is your father's younger brother."

"I'm . . . pleased to meet you." She wondered at his previous comment. "Why would you doubt I was your brother's daughter?" The question came out before she'd really had a chance to consider it.

William shrugged. "A rich man has many relatives."

"I beg your pardon?"

"Simply put," he said, "there is always someone who wishes to gain a share of the family money. You could have simply learned of the kidnapping and decided it was a way to get some of our money for yourself."

"What an awful thing to say," Kenzie interjected. "Rude too."

"I meant no rudeness," he replied, although he didn't sound overly sincere. "I presume these are your friends?"

"Yes." Judith introduced them. She felt strangely wary of this man, however. Why should he be concerned about her seeking their money? She didn't even want to move into their home.

"How did you all meet?" he asked.

She barely heard the question but managed to answer. "We met on the train coming to San Francisco. Camri invited us to live with her in her brother's house. He was away at the time, but has since returned."

"So you live at the Coulter house," her grandmother stated.

Too late, Judith realized her mistake. "Yes. I do." She got to her feet. "I believe we should be returning home. Thank you for asking us here today, but Kenzie and I have work tomorrow and need to prepare for that."

"Work? Nonsense, child. You have no need to work. You

have access to a vast fortune now." Her grandmother shook her head. "I won't have you working."

"That's really her choice," Kenzie said, standing beside Judith.

"Yes," Camri reiterated. "Women today have choices that they've lacked before. I, myself, am college educated and hope to teach at one of the area colleges. Women needn't remain idle if they'd rather do something more." She rose and smiled at the older woman. "We have come a long way toward our independence."

"Be that as it may," Mrs. Whitley began, "no granddaughter of mine need ever toil for a living."

"But I like my job," Judith said. She looked at her uncle. "And I have no desire to take your money. I didn't seek you out for that reason."

"William meant nothing by his comment, so don't give it another thought," Mrs. Whitley quickly stated, giving him a scathing look. She began to rise, and William quickly helped her with her chair. "I am sorry you feel you must leave, Judith. Please know that you are always welcome here. You needn't send a request to come—simply arrive. I do hope that soon you will be willing to call this place your home." She rang for the butler.

"Thank you, Mrs. Whitley . . . Grandmother." Judith could see that Camri and Kenzie had already moved to the door.

Ramsay reappeared, and Mrs. Whitley nodded toward him. "Ramsay will show you out. The house is quite large, and I wouldn't have you lose your way. Hopefully in time you'll come to know it better."

The butler led them back through the massive house and to the front door. Judith was glad to be outside once again. Even on that short walk, she had begun to feel like the house was a prison.

144

"That was an ordeal," she murmured.

"That old woman is definitely all that Caleb said she was," Camri replied and set off down the drive. "It's clear she rules this house. You'll have to be on your guard with her."

Kenzie followed Camri, leaving Judith to bring up the rear. Judith hesitated for a moment, glancing back at the house. A part of her longed to know more about these people, while an equal part wanted to run away and never return. It was as if a battle raged inside for possession of her heart.

"Grandmother can be rather formidable."

Judith turned to find the owner of the voice. He was tall, with a head of thick, golden hair. His blue eyes seemed to twinkle in delight. She cocked her head to one side. "Do I know you?"

"Let me introduce myself," he said with a chuckle. "I'm William Whitley the Second. But you can call me Bill, since we are cousins."

His jovial spirit immediately put Judith at ease. "I'm Judith."

"Yes, I know. You look exactly like your sister, although I doubt I ever saw her wearing plaid."

Judith glanced down at her gown. Was plaid not acceptable? She looked back up to meet Bill's amused expression.

"It's beautiful," he said. "It would have done Cora a world of good. She always wore such pasty colors. You look stunning."

Judith smiled. "Thank you, Bill."

He nodded toward the house. "Don't let the old dragon scare you away for long. I'd really like to get to know you better. Cora and I always got along well. She confided in me, and I in her. I can't imagine that you and I wouldn't do the same someday."

Not knowing what to say, Judith simply gave a nod. Camri and Kenzie were waiting for her near the front gates. "I must go."

"Please come back soon." He gave her a dazzling smile. "This house could use some cheer."

"I . . . I'm sure I'll see you again." She hurried to the gates, not quite knowing what to make of the handsome young man.

"Who was that?" Camri asked.

Judith glanced over her shoulder and smiled. "William Whitley the Second. My cousin."

CHAPTER
13

*C*amri recorded the comments of every man who spoke at the meeting. They were all here to see Abraham Ruef put in jail, and none were shy about saying as much. In fact, more than once the conversations had gotten quite heated. Had lynch mobs still been in fashion, Camri felt certain Ruef would already be dead.

"The federal government is willing to assist us to a degree," Fremont Older declared. "That will give us the additional boost we've needed."

Camri scribbled down his comments. She had learned shorthand out of boredom originally, but over the years had found it useful. When Caleb brought the request to take notes to her, Camri had been happy to help. After all, it got her out of the house and into the company of Patrick. Other women might have preferred a night out on the town, enjoying dinner and perhaps the opera, but Camri was devoted to the war against Ruef. This was exciting and history making. And seeing Ruef behind bars would mean she and Patrick could finally set a wedding date.

She couldn't suppress a smile as she glanced toward her husband-to-be. He didn't seem to notice her gaze, and Camri was glad. She liked to study him when he didn't realize she was watching. She wanted to memorize every aspect of his face, from his beautiful blue eyes to his full lips and handsome nose. Well, at least she thought his nose was handsome, despite it having been broken on more than one occasion in his younger years.

She put aside her consideration of the man she'd come to love more than life and focused on the meeting. She'd been taught from an early age that women could do most anything they set their minds to, but it was still hard to convince the rest of the world. Because of this, women had to work twice as hard to convince men that they could manage some of the same jobs. Most of the men present had looked askance at her attendance. Several of the men who regularly attended these meetings had brought male secretaries to assist in keeping notes and told Caleb that they would have the notes typed up for his use. He needn't have his sister present. Caleb, however, wanted his own record. He had confided in Camri that he wasn't convinced all of the men were on the same side. He wanted her to detail not only what was said, but if she saw things going on behind the scenes, he wanted notes on that as well.

"I believe, given all that we've been able to do in the last week," William Langdon announced, "that it won't be long before we can bring formal charges against Ruef. Until then, I urge you to do what you can to protect yourselves. Say nothing to anyone else about our dealings."

Once the meeting broke up, Camri stood and began to put her things away. Patrick came to stand behind her, and when she straightened, he whispered in her ear.

"Ye're a fine-lookin' lass, you know. I've half a mind to marry ye."

She smiled and turned to face him. "I'm sorry, but I'm already engaged, and my fiancé would not approve of your talking love to me."

Patrick grinned. "No, for sure he would not want anyone else talking love to ye."

Caleb joined them. "I think the meeting went well. We're making progress. The ledger and papers I turned over to Langdon have proven very helpful. He's been able to get signed affidavits from some of Ruef's victims."

"Do you think they'll be able to bring indictments against Ruef very soon?" Camri asked.

He shrugged. "These things take time. If we rush it, we might make mistakes and have to start all over again. Of course, then Ruef would be aware of our dealings and would have the time and money to thwart our efforts. At least Langdon's actions against vice have shown folks that Ruef's stronghold can be broken. That's brought some folks out of hiding, and they're willing to join the cause."

"I was surprised to hear what Spreckels had to say about the city's growth," Patrick said as Camri tucked her notes into a satchel.

"I was too, frankly. I had no idea it had nearly doubled in the last five years." Caleb took up his hat. "It's no wonder Ruef has been pushing extra hard to control every aspect of growth. With all the outside interest in investing in San Francisco, he can no doubt already taste the profits coming his way."

Patrick led the way from the room. Camri returned the conversation to her concerns about time. "I know these things take time, but surely we can count on Ruef's grip being loosened enough that Patrick can reclaim his construction business."

"I'm working on it," Caleb said. "I've drawn up papers, and Judge Winters is going to help me push for the return of his property, since Patrick was cleared of all charges. Ruef won't like having to give anything back, however, so we must be certain to do everything in meticulous order. Besides, now that we have purchased the warehouse, Patrick has his hands full with making repairs."

"Coulter, I wonder if you'd spare me a minute," Fremont Older said as they tried to leave the building.

Caleb glanced at Patrick. "Do you mind waiting?"

"We'll just start walkin'. Ye can pick us up along the way." Patrick put his arm around Camri. "That way we can do some spoonin'."

Caleb chuckled. "I'll be with you shortly."

Patrick drew Camri along with him. She knew he would sense her frustration and want to know what was wrong. The trouble was, he knew what was wrong. She wanted to set their wedding date and couldn't until he could settle his business matters.

Clouds had moved in during the day, and a hint of fog was threatening to settle on top of the city. The dampness chilled her to the bone. She handed her satchel to Patrick in order to pull on her gloves.

"Now I have ye all to myself," he said, taking a possessive hold on her elbow.

"You could have me all to yourself all the time if you would just marry me."

He laughed, which wasn't at all the response Camri wanted. She looked up at him and pulled her arm away at the same time.

"I was serious. You just keep me guessing and waiting."

"Just as they keep me guessin' and waitin'. Ye heard yer brother. It takes time, and he's doin' everythin' he can."

"Well, I'm beginning to think you don't mind the wait as much as I do." She tried not to sound like a pouty child, but knew that despite her efforts that was exactly her tone.

"Maybe ye shouldn't think so much, given the fact that ye're makin' no sense. For sure ye need to pray for a bit more patience."

"It isn't patience I need. It's a wedding date. My mother keeps asking me so they can make plans to be here. Then there are all the other things that need to be arranged. The church and minister, my dress and those of my attendants, not to mention the reception."

"Then don't."

She frowned and stopped midstep. "Don't what?"

"Mention the reception." He crossed his arms and looked at her. "I want to marry ye as much as ye want to marry me, but I cannot until I can support ye."

"But you're working for Caleb now and making a wage."

"Aye, but that's not the same as havin' my business returned to me. Besides, we agreed the first of the pay would be goin' to furnish my sister with a headstone." He shook his head. "Camri, we've been all around this bush and beat it several times. There's nothin' hidin' within that hasn't come to light. We just need to bide our time."

She let go an exasperated breath and started off down the road. She knew he was right, but it didn't change matters. She needed to be able to set a date. She wanted to be able to dream about that day—to arrange for flowers and cakes and all manner of things that would make the day perfect. It surprised her to feel so passionate about the planning, but she couldn't help herself. She knew it didn't matter to Patrick as much as it did to her, but she wanted that day to be perfect. Patrick would be happy just to show up before a judge after giving her five minutes' warning.

"Ye aren't goin' to be changin' my mind with yer anger." His Irish brogue always thickened when he was irritated.

She slowed her steps. "I didn't think I could. Nobody cares what I want in this matter. You don't understand what it means to me. What it would mean to any bride."

"Camrianne, that's hardly fair. I do care, and for sure ye know that."

"Then why can't you swallow your pride and accept my brother's help?" She stopped again and fixed him with her most serious gaze. "I was perfectly willing to wait until fall so that we could better know each other. If you were to take Caleb's offer, then we could set the date and be done with it."

"Don't be goin' down that path again. I've told ye my reasons. Why can't ye care about what this means to me?"

It was Camri's turn to cross her arms. "I care as much about what you want as you care about what I want."

"Then we're in agreement." He had the audacity to grin.

"Oh!" She waved her arms in exasperation. "You are impossible."

Again she started stalking off down the road, and just as she'd known he would, Patrick easily caught up to walk beside her.

"If we're goin' to fight about this every time we're alone, then I'm not goin' to be alone with ye."

"Fine. Then we won't be alone." Now she was starting to get really mad.

A car approached from behind, and Camri turned to see if it was Caleb. It was. Thank goodness. When he drew alongside them, Camri hardly waited for him to stop before she had the door open and was climbing into the back. She started to pull the door closed behind her, but Patrick took hold of it before she could and slid into the seat beside her.

"Is something wrong?" Caleb asked.

"Patrick is too pig-headed to see God's blessing being offered to him."

"And Camri is used to bossin' everyone around and can't stand it when someone dares to defy her."

"Oh!" She shuddered. "You're impossible. Maybe it's a good thing you don't want to set a wedding date."

"Maybe it is."

Caleb said nothing for a minute, and Camri felt a wave of guilt wash over her. She hadn't meant for any of this to happen. She had agreed to support Patrick in his task of reclaiming his business. She had promised to be patient and endure whatever time it took. So why was she being so out of sorts now?

"I think it's a good thing you're coming to this conclusion now," Caleb finally said, glancing over his shoulder. "I've been thinking that perhaps the two of you aren't suited for each other after all."

Camri hadn't expected this. "What?"

"It's just that you both obviously have different goals in mind. Different things are more important to one than the other. I can't see that being a good foundation for marriage. Maybe this is God's way of showing you the truth before it's too late."

"The truth?" Camri looked at Patrick and shook her head. "The truth is that I love him. I couldn't bear to face life without him."

"And I love ye and feel the same way. I just wish ye could understand my heart when it comes to providin' for ye. I want to be the one to take care of ye—not yer brother."

She leaned closer. "I know that, and I'm sorry. I was just chiding myself for losing my temper. I'm not at all sure why I did. I suppose because I want to be with you . . . to take care of you and not have to be parted each day."

He put his arm around her and pulled her close. "And I feel the same way. Honestly I do. Believe me when I say that I want

153

there never to be another night when I have to walk away and leave ye."

Camri knew he was going to kiss her, and when his lips touched hers, she turned slightly and pressed closer. A sigh escaped her, which was followed by Caleb's hearty laugh.

She pulled away from Patrick. "What has gotten into you?"

"It was so easy to manipulate you two out of your argument. If only it were that easy with a jury, I might have become a prosecuting attorney."

Camri realized then what he'd done and had to smile. "Stuff and nonsense. One day you'll lose your heart to someone, and then you won't find it nearly so amusing." She leaned back against Patrick, comforted as he put his arm around her shoulder. "You'll see."

"Hold still, Kenzie," Micah commanded. "These scissors are razor sharp, and I'll end up cutting your finger if you don't stay still. Just let me get these last two stitches out, and then you'll be free of me."

"Ha! That's not very likely." She wanted nothing more than to flee to her room, but Micah was insistent that she allow him to finish what he'd started.

"The finger has healed nicely," he replied, ignoring her sarcastic tone. "You'll have a little scar, but you seem to enjoy wearing those."

"What?" She pulled her hand away after he removed the last stitch.

He shrugged. "You heard me. It seems to me that you don't care nearly as much about healing and feeling better as you do about having your scars to prove you've been through battle."

"You are daft." She shook her head. "You think that because

I'm not swooning over you like every other woman in the city, that it's because I feel sorry for myself and want everyone else to do the same?"

He grinned. "I don't quite have every woman swooning, but I think you put the matter into words well. I do think you enjoy feeling sorry for yourself."

"How dare you?"

"I dare because I can hardly draw any other conclusion. You mope around and avoid anything that might make you even slightly happy, and then tell me I'm daft for recognizing the matter for what it is."

"You know nothing."

He put away his things and closed his black bag. "I know you got your heart broken by a cad who didn't even bother to show up for the wedding. I know that must have been truly humiliating and devastating, but I also know that it's time for you to move on."

"Who are you to judge when I should move on?" Kenzie got to her feet at the sound of the front door opening. She had no desire to argue in front of the others. "I don't need advice from you on how to manage my heart."

"Well, it seems you need guidance from someone." Micah arched his brow and fixed her with a knowing look, as if daring her to prove him wrong.

Caleb entered the dining room and gave Micah a grin. "Well, it's good to see you two are talking again."

Kenzie gave a huff and left the room as quickly as she could manage. She flew into the hall, almost knocking down Camri. She could hear Caleb and Micah chuckling, and it only served to frustrate her all the more. Perhaps it was time to consider moving out on her own.

14

ousin George, please calm down," Kenzie said, doing her best to keep up with him as he ran in circles from one area of the factory to another. He was in a frenzy because there had been a fire, and as usual, he was convinced it was the act of his rivals.

"They want to ruin me. It's just that simple. I'm sure of it." The small balding man pushed up his glasses and turned on his heel. He shook a finger at Kenzie and Judith. "Mark my words. They will be the ruin of me."

"But, Mr. Lake, the fire is out, and the damage was minimal," Judith said.

He looked at her like she was crazy. Judith felt sorry for him, but his certainty of foes working toward his demise was so difficult to endure.

"Cousin George, you were telling me just last week that the wiring was showing signs of wear. I'm sure it was that which sparked the fire and nothing more." Kenzie usually had a way with her cousin, and Judith could only hope she would be able to calm him once again.

"Yes. Yes. The wiring was frayed, but an arsonist could have used that to his advantage. I tell you, they won't be happy until I'm destroyed." He looked at the clock. "You girls go ahead and leave. I'll tend to the cleanup and repairs myself. I need to think this through. There must be a way to ensure my protection."

Kenzie looked at Judith and nodded. "Very well. We'll be back bright and early tomorrow." She tugged on Judith's sleeve. "Come on. We might be able to catch the cable car after all."

The two girls raced to meet the crowded car, and only when they'd been dropped off a few blocks from home did they speak again of the situation at the Lake Boxed Candies Factory.

"I fear he'll go completely mad one day," Kenzie said as they began their trudge uphill. "Mother assures me he's always been like this, but I can't help but think it will take its toll and completely destroy him."

"He's always felt that someone was out to get him?" Judith couldn't imagine living in such anxiety.

"Yes. Apparently. No one really knows why."

"Does he . . . well, does he go to church? Does he have any faith in God?"

Kenzie shook her head. "I don't know. He is an extremely private person. Even when Mother wrote to tell him I was coming here, he telegrammed immediately to say I couldn't live with him, but he would find me some sort of accommodation. It was all so typical, Mother said."

As they neared the house, Judith spied an elaborate carriage parked outside. There were two beautifully matched black horses harnessed to it and a uniformed driver standing beside the carriage. She felt a heavy weight settle in her stomach. No doubt this had something to do with her grandmother.

"Oh dear," she murmured.

"Is that your grandmother's carriage?"

"I'm guessing so. I've half expected her to come here since I accidentally mentioned that I lived here. How I wish I'd said nothing."

"Well, it has been nearly two weeks since she saw you last. I expected her sooner."

"So did I." Judith shook her head and bit her lower lip.

Kenzie touched her arm. "You needn't let her bully you. Just remember, we are here for you, and we won't let anyone force you to make decisions that go against what you desire."

"I've tried to figure out what's best. I've even asked God for a sign. I just don't know which way to go. A part of me thinks it would serve everyone best if I did as she asked."

"But it has to be right for you as well as them." Kenzie turned Judith to face her. "Listen to me, Judith. No one can make you do what you don't want to do. I know Caleb and Camri will not allow that woman to force you into anything."

Judith let out a long breath. "I know, but it's time I figured this out. I've avoided making a decision because it was easier to do nothing. I've thought about it every day at work and dreamed about it in my sleep." She straightened and lifted her chin in a determined fashion. "I need to settle this now."

"Just make sure it's what you want and not what you think you owe someone else."

Judith nodded and started up the stairs. "A part of me has never wanted anything more than this. It's not that I don't want to know her. I do. I've always dreamed of having grandparents. I used to dream that one day we'd have a big family—lots of brothers and sisters and cousins and such. If dreaming could have made it so, I would have been awash with relatives."

"I had a lot of dreams myself," Kenzie said, shaking her head. "Sometimes dreams are best forgotten."

"But what if we aren't supposed to forget them?" Judith turned on the final landing. She paused before climbing the remaining steps. "What if we find our life—our calling—in those dreams? I can't believe wishing and dreaming is a bad thing."

Kenzie shook her head again. "People say it costs nothing to dream, but I beg to differ. I dreamed of romance and happily ever after, and it cost me everything."

Judith hugged her friend. "I'm so very sorry."

The redhead gave a hint of a smile. "That's why I know some dreams should be forgotten."

Glancing up at the door, Judith let out a long breath. "I suppose I might as well face this head on. Come on, Kenzie."

Entering, Judith heard voices in the main sitting room. The tiny foyer allowed her a place of momentary privacy. With great resolve, she unpinned her hat and set it atop the receiving table. She glanced down at her white shirtwaist and blue navy skirt. Thankfully the apron she'd worn at the factory had kept them fairly clean. There were, however, unmistakable smudges of soot on the cuffs of her blouse.

"Judith, is that you?" Camri called out.

Judith squared her shoulders and gave Kenzie a final glance. "Yes." She stepped into the room with a smile.

Just as she'd suspected. Ann Whitley sat by the fire. She was regal—queenly in her appearance. She wore an intricately designed walking-out suit of forest green. The large hat that crowned her white hair was designed from the same material and trimmed with pale yellow feathers that matched her blouse. Between her gloved hands, she held an ornate ebony cane with a gold handle. Judith found herself wondering if it were really gold or just made to look the part.

"I began to think you were never coming home," Camri said, smiling. "Your grandmother has come for a visit."

"Good afternoon. Or perhaps I should say *evening*." Judith smiled. "As you can see, I've just come from working at the candy factory." She toyed with the soot smudge on her cuff. "We had a fire, and that's why we're late."

Kenzie still stood in the doorway. "Cousin George was upset, so we stayed to calm him."

Camri shook her head. "What caused the fire?"

"Some frayed wires sparked when one of the machines was turned on or off. I don't know, really. Of course, Cousin George believes the worst."

"No doubt." Camri glanced at Judith's grandmother. "If you'll excuse us, I have something I need to discuss with Kenzie. It was very nice to see you again." She walked to the door and turned back. "Are you certain you wouldn't like some tea? Mrs. Wong makes the most amazing jasmine tea."

"No, thank you. I won't be staying all that long," the older woman assured.

Judith took a seat on the sofa opposite her grandmother. "I must say, this is a surprise."

"I apologize for coming without invitation, or even sending a card. It is ill-mannered, but I felt an urgency to do so."

"Urgency?" Judith leaned back.

"Yes. I know you are still trying to understand all that has happened, but I wanted to come and implore you to leave this place and your job and live with me." Mrs. Whitley held up her gloved hand as Judith started to speak. "Please, just hear me out."

"Very well." Judith folded her hands. "Continue."

Her grandmother glanced toward the opening to the hall. "Are we quite alone?"

"Yes. Camri and Kenzi went upstairs. I heard them on the steps." Judith frowned. "What is this all about?"

Her grandmother's expression relaxed a bit. "What I am about to share with you, no one else knows . . . save my doctor." She waited a moment, as if to let that sink in, then continued. "I must ask for your promise to say nothing."

"Unless my silence might cause harm to someone."

"No, it wouldn't." Her grandmother's expression seemed pensive. "It can only harm me."

"Very well." Judith had no idea what she was agreeing to, but decided it was best to give her pledge. "I promise."

Ann Whitley smiled. "Thank you. As you know, I'm not a young woman, and the years have taken their toll. That alone suggests urgency, but there is something more. My constitution is weak. There are issues with my body that . . . well, it's all very scientific, and I couldn't possibly begin to explain it all, but he called it diabetes. It has something to do with the sugar in my body. Sometimes there's not enough and sometimes too much. The doctor had me eat a diet of almost all potatoes for a time, thinking it might help, but it didn't. Then he advised me to eat large amounts of meat and sugar, yet I'm still having spells and wasting away. He says my time is limited because it has damaged my vital organs. I've said nothing to anyone until now."

"But why not? Surely your family should know."

The older woman shook her head. "They would only count the days until my demise—as if they aren't already."

"That's a terrible thing to say." Judith couldn't imagine anyone being so cold and indifferent to the old woman's plight.

"Perhaps, but true nonetheless. William is a simpleton when it comes to business. He ran through nearly his entire inheritance and only managed to maintain hold on a brief portion because I stepped in and demanded he accept help from my financial people. He lives off of my benefits, although his children do not know this. Bill is a strong individual, more like your father than his own. He's determined and self-sufficient, but he has much to learn. Even so, I know he has a taste for the best that money can buy. His sister, Victoria, is spoiled and indifferent as to how money comes her way so long as there is a never-ending source of it. She has her father wrapped around her finger and makes constant demands. They all love their money and crave more. That is why I know they look forward to the day I die. There-fore, I don't want them to know anything about my condition."

"I'm so sorry. I can't imagine them being so callous."

"Well, it is exactly that, and no doubt I have no one to blame for it but myself. However, the reason I'm here is because with my condition growing worse, I feel most desperate to plead my case."

"What case?"

"My case for having you move into Whitley House. You see, I lost you once so many years ago, and now that you are back in our lives, I don't want to waste another moment. I want to tell you stories about your parents and about our family history. I want, I suppose, to give you twenty-four years of information in whatever little time I have left." She smiled in that same way Judith had seen before. There was something that seemed forced, edging on insincere. It made Judith nervous. "Not only that, but I want to educate you in the ways of managing your money and knowing who you can trust."

"But I'm not interested in that. I came here solely to find the woman I thought was my aunt. Now that I know differently, I'm perplexed as to what to do. Moving into your house is a big decision—one that merits a great deal of thought." Judith brushed a piece of lint from her skirt and tried to put aside her fears. What if she said no and her grandmother died without

Judith ever having a chance to know her? What if hesitation cost her everything?

"My dear, I know you have your concerns and anxieties regarding such a move, but I assure you that should you come and not want to stay, I'll do nothing to stop you from returning here. I'll even write up a contract with you, and Mr. Coulter can approve it."

"I see." Judith hadn't considered that she might leave anytime she chose. Of course, she would have to speak to the others regarding whether she'd be welcome to return. Then again, Kenzie had mentioned something about finding another place to live, so maybe the two of them might strike a bargain.

"I won't insist on an answer today, but I would like one by the first of April." Grandmother got to her feet, leaning heavily on the cane. "Please consider it favorably, Judith. I long for your company."

"I must pray about it, and the first is only the day after tomorrow."

Her grandmother nodded. "Yes, I realize that. Please know that I am praying as well. Oh, Judith, you have no idea how many times I have prayed to have you returned to us. Your coming here was answered prayer."

Judith rose and nodded. Her grandmother's comment regarding her own prayers helped her feel less apprehensive. "I will give you an answer on Sunday, be assured."

"And you needn't return to that ghastly factory. I'll set up an account for you at the San Francisco First National Bank under the name of Judith Whitley."

"Please don't. I didn't come seeking you in order to get money like the other members of your family probably think. You may think that yourself, but it isn't true. I had no reason to believe you were rich."

"I know that." Her grandmother smiled, and this time it seemed to soften her entire expression. "That is why I insist on doing it. You are entitled to it. Your father left a fortune, which came to me upon the death of Edith and Cora. He had no way of knowing whether you were alive or would ever be returned to us, but he always hoped. Hence, that provision was in his will. That now makes his fortune . . . yours."

Judith sank back onto the sofa. It was too much to imagine that she could suddenly be heiress to an inheritance worth so much.

Grandmother gently touched her shoulder. "I know this is a great deal to take in, much less to understand."

"I came looking for a family . . . not a fortune," Judith murmured.

"Well, you have both. Now it's up to you to accept that fact and allow yourself to enjoy God's gifts."

That evening at dinner, Caleb noted how quiet Judith was. Camri had told him about Mrs. Whitley's visit. He knew Ann Whitley demanded her own way and probably intended to wear Judith down with her persistence. Even so, Judith had said very little about the visit, and Caleb felt, given the involvement he'd already had, that it would be all right if he questioned her about it.

"I understand your grandmother was here earlier," he said.

Judith looked up from her plate. She'd been doing very little eating. "Yes. She was here when Kenzie and I returned from work."

"I suppose she came to convince you to move into the mansion?"

"Yes." Judith frowned and looked down at her plate.

Caleb could see the situation was vexing her. "What did you tell her?"

Judith gave a slight shrug. "I promised her an answer on Sunday."

"Why so soon?" Kenzie asked. "You don't have to rush into anything. She can hardly expect you to make up your mind that quickly on a matter of such magnitude."

"She said if I moved in, she would let me leave anytime, should I become uncomfortable. She even offered to make up a contract that Caleb could approve."

"That was gracious of her." Caleb smiled as Liling refilled his coffee cup. The girl blossomed a little more each day since she'd been rescued from her life at the dance hall. "Thank you, Liling."

"I think she's very lonely and longs to reclaim some of her losses." Judith spoke in a quiet, even tone. "I can understand how she feels."

"But understanding doesn't demand action," Camri threw out. "At least not immediate action. You need to be comfortable with this move as well. Surely she would want you to be happy."

"Yes, but she's very old. I don't think I should waste any time. That's why I agreed to give her my answer on Sunday."

Caleb didn't like the idea of Judith being pressured into making the move. She was such an innocent when it came to the demands and decrees of those in positions of power. Hers had always been a simple life—a life without such concerns. Her parents, albeit not her true mother and father, had obviously loved her and cared for her as best they could. However, they could never have prepared her for such an outcome. There would have been no opportunity to warn her about such people without giving away the circumstance of her birth.

166

"I don't see how you can trust her," Kenzie said, tearing off a piece of dinner roll.

Judith dabbed her napkin to her lips, then placed it on the table. "If you'll excuse me, I need to lie down. This day has been too much, and my head hurts something fierce." She got to her feet.

"I can send Liling up with some headache powders," Caleb offered.

"Or she could fix you a hot bath," Camri countered.

"No, please. I just want to be alone." She hurried from the room before anyone could stop her.

Caleb frowned. He hated seeing her this way. "I suppose I shouldn't have been so hard on her."

"We were all difficult," Camri said, shaking her head. "Even if we didn't mean to be."

Kenzie put down her bread. "But she can't just go off and live with people she doesn't even know."

Caleb shrugged. "Why not? You all did it when you moved here. I suppose Judith sees this as no different."

———

Sunday passed in a blur for Judith. She remembered attending church, but the message had not been able to penetrate through her frantic thoughts about what to do. After two very restless nights filled with prayers begging God for wisdom, Judith knew she had to make a decision. Concern for her grandmother's health should have been the strongest influence on her decision, but instead she found herself thinking of Caleb. She couldn't go on living under his roof and feeling the way she did about him. It wasn't proper. She found herself daydreaming about him coming home and sweeping her into his arms. She dreamed at night that he had proposed marriage—declaring his undying love for her. She had come to San Francisco hoping to find her aunt, but instead she had fallen in love and lost her heart. She had very little left to lose.

Sundays were usually a day of rest. Often the time was spent outside if the weather was nice, but today was rainy and cold, so Judith kept inside—mostly in her room. Kenzie and Camri had both come to her at different times to talk about her grandmother. They wanted to reassure Judith that she didn't have to leave. But each time they argued for her to take her time and stay, Judith felt more convicted that she should go. Her grandmother might not have that long to live, and if she were to die without Judith taking time to know her better, the fault would be all her own.

Finally, late in the afternoon, Judith concluded that she must go. She at least had to give her grandmother a chance.

She found the others gathered around the table, discussing their plans for the week. Judith took her place and waited for the conversation to quiet.

"I have made my decision," she announced without flourish.

Kenzie looked at her for a moment, then shook her head. "You're going to her, aren't you?"

"I think I must," Judith replied, glancing at the others. "I've prayed on it, and it would solve many matters."

"But what if you can't abide it?" Camri asked. "What will you do then?"

"I . . . well, I suppose I shall have to find somewhere else to live."

"Nonsense," Caleb said. His expression bore witness to his worry. "You'll always have a home here, Judith. I would plead with you to reconsider, but I know that your mind is made up."

For a moment, she hoped he would plead with her. She imagined him coming to her—pulling her into his embrace and begging her to stay. She knew if he did that, she'd abandon thought of anything else and stay.

But of course, he didn't.

"Yes, my mind is made up." Judith barely murmured the words. "I'm going to leave in the morning."

15

*A*fter dinner, Judith telephoned her grandmother's house and spoke with Ramsay. She explained her decision and asked if he would let her grandmother know that she would come to the house in the morning. She'd no sooner hung up and returned to her room than Liling came to tell her that there was a phone call for her. It turned out to be her grandmother.

"I cannot abide these telephones, but I felt it was important to tell you that I will send a car for you right away. You needn't wait," Ann Whitley said.

"No, morning will be soon enough, Grandmother."

There was a long pause. "Very well. But first thing in the morning. Don't worry about bringing anything with you. I have arranged with various merchants to provide for your every need."

"That isn't necessary." Judith couldn't imagine such a thing, especially given the possibility that she wouldn't stay long.

"Oh, but it is. There will be social events, and you must have appropriate clothes and the accessories that go with them."

Judith frowned. She hadn't considered that her appearance might shame her family. "I hadn't thought of it that way. I wouldn't want to be an embarrassment."

"This isn't about embarrassing anyone. You are a Whitley, and as such, you deserve to be cared for appropriately. But all of that is unimportant at this moment. What matters is that I will have William send his car to pick you up. It won't take but a few minutes. As I said, I could even send him yet tonight."

"No, I need time. . . ." Judith couldn't explain her hesitation. "I want to spend one more evening with my friends."

"Very well, but the car will be there at eight o'clock sharp tomorrow morning."

And that was that. Her grandmother had arranged the matter without giving Judith any further say. Was that how it was always going to be? Judith stared at the telephone, shaking her head. Somehow, she was going to have to find the ability to stand up to the old woman.

On Monday morning, the Whitley driver knocked on the door at precisely eight o'clock. Judith had said good-bye earlier to Kenzie, giving her a letter of apology and resignation for Mr. Lake. He had hired a few extra girls for the Easter season, so hopefully he wouldn't be too upset. Kenzie made no pretense of approving of Judith's decision, but neither did she condemn her for it.

Now, however, as she said good-bye to Camri and Caleb, a part of her wished someone *would* condemn her choice. If they would just forbid her to go, Judith could yield to their demands. Instead, they were cordial and kind.

"Please let us know if you need anything or wish to leave," Camri said, giving her a hug. "You will always have us as your advocates."

"Yes," Caleb agreed. "I'll be over in a few days to check on you." He smiled. "Also to talk over the matter of your inheritance. Judge Winters mentioned that Mrs. Whitley intends to see your father's fortune settled on you immediately."

Judith nodded. She was glad to know that Caleb would at

least come to check on her. How she wished it was more for personal reasons than for business, but then, his lack of interest in her was one of the reasons she was leaving. She couldn't very well forget her feelings for him if she had to face him every day.

The ride to the Whitley estate gave Judith a few minutes of contemplation. Was she doing the right thing? Could she somehow become part of this family?

The driver helped her from the car and left her to face the others on her own. As he drove away, she felt tempted to bolt down the drive and return to Caleb's house. But then Ramsay opened the door, and Judith was ushered inside like the long-lost daughter she was.

Grandmother's happiness was evident. She smiled as she barked instructions at the servants. "Are you hungry, Judith? Did you have breakfast? Ramsay, please arrange a tray. Samuel, did you lay the fire in Miss Judith's suite?"

Judith turned in a circle, trying to follow her Grandmother's conversation. "I'm not hungry."

Her words were ignored. Grandmother was clearly focused on other things, and since she'd already arranged for a tray, Judith's hunger or lack thereof was no longer a concern.

"I'll give you a tour of the house later, but for now we'll go directly upstairs to your suite. I have the dressmaker there, and the others are gathered at the top of the stairs."

Grandmother slowly climbed the stairs to the left, and Judith followed her. The house was just as imposing as it had been that first visit. Judith couldn't imagine how she would ever find her way around it without a map.

Once they reached the top of the stairs, the old woman immediately called everyone to attention. Judith was stunned to find a small army awaiting her. She wasn't sure how her grandmother had managed to arrange for so much in the short time since Judith had called to say she was coming. There was not only a seamstress with three assistants, but a department store manager with two of his own hired girls and stacks of boxes, the owner of a shoe store with a vast assortment of footwear for her consideration, a milliner who had two young men to help with over a dozen hatboxes, and a woman who owned a store that specialized in undergarments and nightclothes.

For most of the morning, Judith found herself being measured for clothes that would be custom made for her. There were also ready-made items that needed to be tried on, as well as a few of Cora's things that were still somewhat fashionable.

"We will, of course, take daily outings to shop for any other items you might need," her grandmother said, seeming to enjoy the novelty of dressing Judith. "I've also set up accounts at each of the stores so that when I can't go with you, you'll still be able to shop for whatever you like."

"I'm sure I won't need anything for years to come," Judith said, marveling at the number of things her grandmother had already picked. There were parasols and hats galore, as well as perfumes and soaps. Along with those were undergarments, skirts, blouses, gowns, and shoes. There was nothing left out—as Grandmother kept reminding Judith, she was a Whitley now and had a certain appearance to maintain.

"And of course," her grandmother continued, "once you're settled, we'll have your suite made over in a fashion more suited to your preferences."

Judith looked around the massive sitting room that was attached to what had once been her parents' bedroom. The entire suite had been given to her and comprised not only the sitting room and bedroom, but a separate dressing room and bathroom. It was bigger than the entirety of Caleb's upstairs.

"There's no need for that. It's lovely. I wouldn't want to change it," she murmured. It was lavish and ornamental to such a degree that Judith could hardly imagine what kind of money had gone into its creation. Growing up, most of their furnishings had been handmade by her father. Here, the furniture was highly polished walnut crafted intricately with all manner of embellishment. The bed was a massive four-poster creation with a canopy of gossamer fabric in a dark shade of rose. The damask draperies and bedcovers were also done in hues of rose. "It's so beautiful."

"Your mother arranged it, but you may want to change it in time. After a few months or years, you may tire of it altogether and want something more suited to your own taste."

Judith tried not to react to her grandmother's comment. Months? Years? Would Judith really make this her permanent home? She thought of Caleb and felt the ache in her heart that had started when she'd made her decision to go.

Don't think about him. Just focus on what is at hand.

Judith's favorite part of the suite overlooked the gardens where she'd had tea with her grandmother. Draperies had been pulled back to reveal the double French doors that opened onto the stone balcony, where a small table and chairs had been placed. Judith could imagine sitting there for hours. Perhaps that would become her sanctuary.

By late afternoon, her grandmother sent everyone home and insisted that Judith rest. She introduced Sarah Linde, a rather plain woman in her thirties. "Sarah will be your lady's maid," Grandmother explained.

"My what?" Judith looked at the woman and then back at Grandmother.

"Your lady's maid. Sarah will be here when you rise in the morning and see to helping you with your personal needs. She'll dress your hair and help you with your clothing. She'll also tidy your room and oversee the cleaning and pressing of your clothes. During the day, she'll be available to help you change clothes and freshen up. We generally change clothes several times a day, and we always dress formally for the evening meal, which takes place precisely at seven. Should you desire writing paper or anything else, you have but to let Sarah know of your need, and she will accommodate you. I often have my lady's maid bring me something sweet just before bedtime. I find it settles my stomach. You might want to do that as well."

Judith wondered if she would ever be able to manage all the intricacies of life among the very wealthy. She was so used to doing for herself that it seemed completely out of line to ask someone else to take care of her in this way.

"Now, Sarah will help you undress and turn down your bed. It's generally our routine to nap for at least two hours in the early afternoon in order to recover from our morning duties and to be able to face those that will be upon us in the late afternoon and evening."

"Duties?"

"Most mornings we will either make calls or receive visitors. We will also use that time to attend to shopping if we so desire. We might enjoy lunch out on the town and then return home to rest. In the afternoons, we will on occasion have company. I frown upon it, but it is often a necessity. I prefer a quiet afternoon with tea around four or five, depending on what else might be happening. You'll adjust to our ways very quickly, I'm sure. After all, it's in your blood." Her grandmother smiled and made her way to the door. "I'll leave you in Sarah's capable hands."

Judith looked at the lady's maid. "I . . . well, I'm glad to meet you, Sarah."

The older woman nodded. "Let me help you disrobe."

It was most uncomfortable to allow someone else to undress her, but Judith stood obediently. When Sarah finally brought her a loose wrapper to wear, Judith let out a sigh of relief.

She hadn't thought it possible that she could fall asleep, but before she knew it, Sarah was waking her up and telling her that it was time to dress for the evening.

"I thought I was supposed to have tea with my grandmother," Judith said, stretching her arms.

"Mrs. Whitley said to let you rest. It's time for you to dress for dinner. You'll meet the others in the family's private drawing room. Then at seven, you'll go in to dinner. It's all very regulated."

Judith nodded, feeling a bit overwhelmed.

Sarah brought out a beautiful gown of lavender and held it up for Judith's approval. "Would you care to wear this, Miss Judith?"

It seemed so lavish, more suited to an evening out. "I suppose, if it's suitable. I'll trust you to help me not embarrass myself."

Sarah smiled. "I'm honored to do so."

After that, Judith once again found herself standing by while Sarah did the work of making her presentable. The maid was efficient, Judith had to admit. She styled Judith's hair in an elaborate arrangement before helping her into the gown. She did up the long row of back buttons, then helped Judith into beautifully embroidered silver slippers.

Judith felt like a princess in a castle. The one thing left was to find her way to the private drawing room. She hoped Sarah would handle that, as well.

"I don't suppose you can show me where I'm to go now?"

Sarah nodded. "I'd be happy to." She led Judith out of the suite. "You'll notice across the way is the other wing. That's where Mr. Whitley and his children's rooms are situated. This open sitting area is for everyone, and often your cousins spend late evenings here after Mrs. Whitley and your uncle have retired."

They descended the stairs slowly, and Sarah pointed out the way.

"The music room is where the family gathers before dinner. It's situated just across the hall from the dining room. You can enter either through the salon or via the hallway off the foyer," Sarah explained.

She motioned across the room to the right, where the sound of voices could be heard beyond the open pocket doors.

"She's probably lost her way," a young feminine voice said.

"Nonsense. She'll be here soon, so stop your whining," Grandmother replied.

Judith glanced at Sarah, who gave her a nod. After that, the maid quickly headed back the way they'd come. Squaring her shoulders, Judith lifted her chin and entered the lion's den.

"Ah, here she is now," Uncle William declared.

She was immediately struck by the formal attire of the others. She had worried that perhaps she was overdressed, but seeing the others made her relax. Bill threw her a big smile and nodded in approval.

"Judith, how lovely you look," Grandmother declared. "Come in and let me see you better."

Judith complied with her grandmother's wishes, trying not to gawk at the furnishings, which included a beautiful grand piano in polished ebony.

"I know you've met your Uncle William, but let me introduce you to your cousins. This is Victoria," Grandmother said, motioning to the young woman.

Judith turned to find Victoria's expression one of distaste. She was dressed in an elaborate blue gown with silver lace. So much lace, in fact, that Judith thought it all but swallowed Victoria up.

Although the girl looked less than happy to be there, Judith smiled. "I'm pleased to meet you."

Victoria gave a huff and marched to the piano, where she began to play a rather poor rendition of Beethoven's *Moonlight Sonata*.

"And this is your cousin Bill," Grandmother continued.

Judith was surprised when he stepped forward and took her hand. He was resplendent in his black tailcoat and pants, white vest, and bow tie. Lifting her hand to his lips, he said, "I am most delighted to acquaint myself with you, dear cousin." As he rose, Bill gave her a lopsided smile. "I shall enjoy getting to know you better."

William stepped forward. "You look lovely, my dear. I must say, I find it hard to get used to you being the mirror image of your sister. It's almost as if Cora were with us again."

"Cora was far prettier," Victoria said from the piano.

"Oh, Vicky, you should consider seeing a doctor for your eyes. They are identical, in case you didn't realize it," Bill said in Judith's defense.

Victoria pounded her hands down on the keys and stood. "Well, I would venture to say she can't play as well as Cora."

Judith bit off a sarcastic retort, but her grandmother seemed unwilling to let Victoria's challenge go unmet.

"Why don't you play for us, Judith?"

Victoria abandoned the piano and plopped down on an ornate settee. "Yes, please do, by all means."

Feeling a sense of purpose, Judith strode to the piano and took her seat. She drew in a deep breath to calm her nerves. Caleb's face came to mind. He always looked so pleased when she played, and so she played for him.

The instrument was the finest Judith had ever touched. The notes were rich and full and filled the air with such melodious wonder that it nearly brought tears to her eyes. She played the nocturne she and Caleb loved and devoted herself completely to giving her finest performance. When the final notes faded, she hesitated a moment, then stood to face her audience.

Grandmother smiled smugly, as if she'd known all along what Judith was capable of. Uncle William looked rather stunned, while Bill was smiling at her with obvious approval. That only left Victoria. Judith glanced at the young woman, who rolled her eyes and stood.

"I hate Chopin."

"If you could play it like Judith, you might reconsider," Bill said, coming to Judith's side. "That was the most beautiful music ever to come out of this piano."

Victoria gave another huff, which earned her grandmother's consternation. "Do mind your manners, Victoria. I won't have you acting the part of a hoyden."

"She doesn't have to act it, Grandmother," Bill shot back. "She is a hoyden."

"And you are making a fool of yourself by falling all over Judith's feet," Victoria countered.

"Stop it this minute," Grandmother commanded. "I won't have you two embarrassing me. Poor Judith must think you completely without social graces, Victoria."

It bothered Judith to be the center of attention and have no say. She wanted to prove herself strong and capable, but for the moment it seemed perhaps kindness, even humility, would serve her better.

She crossed the room to where Victoria stood. "I've always wanted to have cousins. I do hope we can be friends, Victoria."

The girl glared, narrowing her green eyes. "That will never happen. First, because I'm leaving shortly for Switzerland. Second, because even if you were the last person on earth, I wouldn't be your friend." She turned on her heel and headed for the door. "I'm going to my room. I don't feel well. Send up a tray."

Judith wondered if her grandmother would order Victoria back, but she didn't. Everyone, in fact, seemed more than content to let Victoria go. Judith considered commenting on it, but dinner was announced, and Uncle William went to assist Grandmother from her chair.

"Bill, you will bring Judith in," her grandmother instructed.

"With pleasure." He offered her his arm. "I'll be your friend," he whispered in a suggestive manner. "In fact, I'd like to be much, much more. Intimately more."

Judith couldn't hide her surprise. "We're cousins."

He chuckled and led her toward the door. "All of the royal heads of Europe are married to cousins," he replied.

His comment was still ringing in her ears when she settled into bed for the night. She could hardly believe his flirtatious nature. Even more surprising was that neither her uncle nor grandmother seemed to notice or care.

"But he isn't Caleb," she whispered. She thought of Caleb's smiling face, the way his eyes seemed to twinkle when he was truly amused. He had been gentle and tender when she'd been upset at the news of her parents. He was always so considerate and patient, helping her with her Bible studies if she had questions, listening to her concerns. How she longed to be near him right now.

She hugged her arms to her body. Here she was in a house with the extended family she'd always longed for, yet never had she felt so alone.

"Have I made a mistake in coming here, Lord?"

16

*C*aleb, you've been less than charming company this evening," Florence Brighton said, coming to stand beside him as he gazed into the blazing hearth. "I wouldn't have come had I known you'd be in such a mood."

"I presumed you came at the invitation of Mrs. Charles to view her latest painting," Caleb replied. "That was the reason for this gathering, after all."

She considered him for a moment, then shook her head. "Something about you is different. Ever since you returned from your ordeal, you've been quite changed. I suppose it's all of that religious nonsense you were spouting a few weeks ago."

Caleb thought about her comment. He knew he was different from the carefree man he'd been before being shanghaied. His experience had left him with a desire to see justice served and protect the less fortunate. Men like Ruef and Daniels had made this city a nightmare for many, and Caleb longed to see things made right. Then too, he was still trying to figure out what God wanted him to do with his life. Was he to preach full-time or continue in the law with Bible studies on the side? As

Judge Winters had pointed out to him not long ago, he could serve God through his legal practice as well as from a pulpit.

"It wasn't nonsense, Florence, but the fact that you see it as such has changed my opinion of you," he said.

Her expression betrayed a momentary loss of confidence. "I'm sure I don't know what you mean."

"I've long loved God and sought to do His will, but as I told you, my experience facing death has given me a sense of urgency to know my true purpose. I'm determined to take spiritual matters more seriously."

"You were always serious when it came to spiritual matters. I've never met a man more tediously devoted to his faith who wasn't wearing priest's robes. Honestly, Caleb, you really should learn to be less serious." She leaned closer. "I could help you." Her expression suggested far more than a proper lady should imply.

He shook his head. "When it comes to matters of faith, Florence, I could never do that. God is far more important to me than anything else."

She tilted her head and shrugged. "Have it your way, but it isn't a way that will include me." She left him in a swirl of diaphanous silver fabric and sparkling diamonds.

He watched her make her way to a group of men he considered friends. She mentioned something, then glanced his way. Most of the people in the group laughed. No doubt he was the focus of their amusement, and this signaled to him an end to the evening.

Caleb made his way to his hosts. He commended them for their good taste in art, then thanked them for the evening. They protested his early departure.

"You've not even been here an hour," his hostess said, glancing at her husband. "Surely we can entice you to stay."

"I'm sorry, but I must go. Please forgive me." Caleb didn't wait for their approval, but made his way outside, where a footman ordered his car. By the time he reached home, Caleb's disposition had soured considerably, and his head ached.

Mrs. Wong met him at the door, ready as always. She took his hat and outer coat and never questioned him as he headed down the hall in silence. Once in the privacy of his study, Caleb shed his coat and vest and undid his tie. He had intended to do some work, but instead he paced around the room like a restless animal.

What's wrong with me, Lord? Why am I so out of sorts? I feel like I'm missing something. I pray to know Your will for my life, but nothing seems right. I know You directed me to help with the Ruef matter, yet even that offers little satisfaction. Am I supposed to cast it all aside and take up a church? Am I supposed to give away all that I've inherited to the poor? I'm willing, Lord, I just don't know what You're trying to show me.

He plopped into a chair in front of the fire. He was grateful for the warmth, as the night had grown chilly. He studied the flames and considered his future. God had always spoken to his heart through the Bible and even other people. Perhaps he just needed to listen better. Maybe his worry and frustration had stuffed up his ears.

"I thought I heard you come in," Camri said, coming into the room uninvited. "You're home early, aren't you?"

"Are you keeping a record of my comings and goings?" He hadn't meant to sound so disagreeable, but he offered no apology.

She sat in the chair beside him. "Do you want to talk about it?"

"Talk about what?"

"Whatever has you so upset. You're not at all yourself. You haven't been for days."

Caleb started to tell her to mind her own affairs, but when he turned to speak, he could see the genuine concern in her eyes. He let out a heavy sigh. "If I knew what was bothering me, I'd tell you. Honestly, I'm not sure it's even just one thing. Nothing seems right. I feel like I'm displaced. I keep asking God what He'd have me do, and I feel that I'm doing it . . . yet something is missing."

She smiled. "Perhaps that something is in truth . . . someone."

He narrowed his eyes, trying to guess her meaning. "Someone?"

"You've been fit to be tied since Judith left. I know you're as worried as the rest of us about her well-being, but I have a feeling that it's something more for you."

"Of course, I'm worried. I feel responsible. After all, I was the one who put her in touch with Mrs. Whitley. I know she didn't want to go. I'm still not sure why she did. She could have spent the days with her grandmother and gotten to know her that way while still living here. She certainly didn't need to put herself under that woman's control."

"And that's the only reason you're worried?" Camri asked with a gentle smile.

Caleb wrestled with his heart. He knew he'd come to care for Judith, but he'd tried to convince himself that it was nothing more than brotherly concern. "I'm not sure I take your meaning."

"I think you do. You have feelings for Judith."

He jumped up. "Of course I have feelings for her. I already said that. She may be miserable with the Whitleys. She's never lived that lifestyle, and Mrs. Whitley has in mind to replace her dead family members with Judith. She'll be under tremendous pressure to become someone she's never been." He began to pace in front of the fire. "Judith is a sweet girl. She's also naïve.

People like Mrs. Whitley will put demands on her that she won't be able to refuse. She'll be changed."

"And that troubles you?"

He stopped and looked at Camri. "Yes. Yes, it does. She's a gentle soul with a heart of gold. She's just learning to put her trust in God. I doubt Mrs. Whitley overly concerns herself with such matters. She probably puts her trust in her bank balance."

Camri got to her feet. "Caleb Coulter, I've never known you to be so judgmental of a person you hardly know. I think this has very little to do with any of the reasons you've stated. I think the problem is that you're in love with Judith and you won't allow yourself to admit it."

He stared at her, openmouthed. He'd always known his sister to speak her mind, but her thoughts this time were like a slap in the face.

She touched his cheek. "You are a good man, Caleb, and Judith is, as you say, a gentle soul with a heart of gold. She's worthy of your pursuit, so why are you letting her slip away?"

He started to deny his feelings, then shook his head. "I don't know. I've never found myself in this situation before. I'm not sure I know what to do."

Camri stretched up on tiptoe and kissed his cheek. "I'm sure in time you'll figure it out. Hopefully before you make yourself and the rest of us too miserable."

———

Judith sat across from her grandmother, enjoying a delicious luncheon of crabmeat salad, croissants, and an iced drink made with fruit the likes of which she'd never before sampled. The morning had been spent visiting several of society's grand dames, and then Grandmother had insisted on taking Judith shopping.

"I do hope you've enjoyed the day," Grandmother said. The old woman looked tired but continued to orchestrate their every move with great attention to detail.

"I have, but I hope you aren't overdoing it." Judith took a sip of her drink and smiled. "This is amazing. What's in it again?"

Grandmother chuckled. "Mango, pineapple, oranges, and strawberries. They crush them all together and blend them with sugar water infused with flowers. I think perhaps we should have Cook prepare them for us at home. What do you think?"

"I think that would be marvelous. I love it. I'd never even tried pineapple or mango before coming to California." She glanced around the busy restaurant and marveled at the scene. Just the week before, she had been working at a candy factory, watching the clock closely during her lunch so that Mr. Lake wouldn't chastise her for being late back to work.

"I promised to tell you today about how your mother and father met. Would you like me to do that now?"

"Yes, please." Judith had been anxious to learn more about her family since her arrival at the Whitley house days earlier.

"My husband and your mother's father were dear friends. They decided when Edith and Lila turned thirteen that they would arrange a match for Edith with our Nelson. It was discussed that our William might marry Lila, but your grandfather felt it necessary to settle her elsewhere, in order to honor another financial obligation. Lila was arranged to marry some railroad baron's son, but I don't recall which one."

"They sold her to be married?"

"After a fashion," Grandmother replied. "It is the way of things with moneyed families. Your grandfather had an agreement with the railroad baron, which included marrying the families together. Generally speaking, the couple would join their fortunes."

"I thought arranged marriages tapered off in the 1800s."

"Hardly. Your cousin Victoria is arranged to marry a prominent man. It was set when she was just fourteen—five years ago. Once she completes finishing school in Switzerland, they are to be married."

"That sounds terrible." Judith envisioned her poor cousin with a man she didn't love.

"It's not at all bad. After all, for your mother and father, the arrangement was made all the sweeter because they fell in love. It often happens. It will no doubt happen for Victoria, and in time for you."

Judith shook her head. "But I don't intend to be arranged. I want to marry for love."

Grandmother gave her a patient smile. "That might have been acceptable when you were a Gladstone and your prospects were limited, but now you are an heiress. Believe me when I say that I've already had offers for your hand."

It was impossible to hide her shock. "I won't marry a stranger."

"Of course not," Grandmother replied. "He will be someone with whom I'm thoroughly acquainted. He will be of upstanding character, and his fortune will match your own."

"Grandmother," Judith began, trying to pick her words carefully, "we've only just met, and I'm trying hard to learn about my family and the ways of your society." She wanted to squirm under her grandmother's fierce gaze, but Judith was determined to hold her own. "I will not consent to be matched to anyone, and if that is a requirement for your love and hospitality, then I will move back to the Coulter house immediately."

Ann Whitley stared at her without a hint of change in her expression. Judith wondered if she'd caused the woman's heart to suffer attack, because her face seemed to pale a bit. Perhaps it was one of her diabetic spells. Nevertheless, Judith tried to appear unconcerned. Caleb had warned her that Mrs. Whitley was used to being in control and knew very well how to manipulate the situation to her benefit.

Finally, the older woman nodded and smiled. "My dear, I have no desire to see you married off any time soon. You may rest assured that there will be nothing done to set an arrangement. I have made it clear to those who've expressed interest that you will be under my care and tutelage for some time to come."

Judith wasn't all that happy with this answer, but at least she wasn't going to push the idea of marriage. "So you said that my mother and father fell in love."

The crisis seemed to be momentarily averted, and Grandmother continued. "Yes. They were delighted to marry. Once Nelson began to court your mother properly, they were soon head over heels for each other. I couldn't have been happier."

"But my—Lila . . . she didn't want to marry the railroad baron's son?"

"No. She was quite a handful, that one. She was constantly seeking her own way. Your grandmother once confided in me that she had considered sending Lila to a very strict girls' school back east. Apparently from the time the girls were old enough to have an opinion, Lila's was constantly contrary."

Judith shook her head. "That isn't at all the woman I knew. She was always congenial and loving. She and my father . . . they were very much in love. She told me that she'd never love another."

"I am glad if Lila found true happiness, but I hold no love for her. She destroyed this family with her actions. You have no idea the devastation. There was hardly a smile or laugh in this house for a decade. Poor Cora endured much of our misery and fears. She grew up with a mother who wept at the oddest times and a father who wouldn't let her be left alone even at night.

She was fifteen before Nelson agreed to put her governess in a separate bedroom."

"They must have been so afraid of losing her." Judith ached at the thought of her parents' suffering.

"We all were. Especially since there was absolutely no trail to follow. We felt so helpless. Here we had all the money in the world, but it couldn't buy us what we wanted most."

Judith nodded. "Money can't buy the most important things in life. Mother used to say that all the time. Now it takes on new meaning."

"She was a heartless fool."

Judith couldn't hide her displeasure. "I know that what she did was wrong, but she loved me. I can't just forget that, even after knowing what she and my father did. You should at least take comfort in knowing that they were good to me—that we were a happy family."

"I can't take comfort in anything Lila and Homer did. They destroyed the people I loved. I know it's hard for you to understand, and I don't blame you for feeling as you do. You had no way of knowing what had happened. That's one of the reasons it's so important to me to share all of my memories with you. I want you to have them for your own so that you will know your true family." Her grandmother seemed to have had enough of this sad topic. "I've just had a thought. Let's finish here, and before we head home, we can stop off at the dressmaker's and see what progress they've made on your wardrobe. We can also have a look at Victoria's wedding gown. I'm having it made for her from the finest silk."

"You're having it made? Doesn't she have anything to say about it?" Judith braved the question. She was still feeling out of sorts with the old woman.

Her grandmother shook her head. "No. I'm the matriarch of

this family, and everyone abides by my wishes. In time you will understand the benefit of putting your trust in my wisdom."

Judith set her linen napkin aside. It didn't appear that maintaining control of her life was going to be quite as simple as stating her desire to do so. Ann Whitley was used to running the affairs of her family and household, and Judith was just one more person to control. She wanted to know her grandmother—to know her uncle and cousins too—but what if the price to be paid was too high? What if that desire cost her everything?

She was glad to get back to Whitley House for an afternoon of rest. Her grandmother had talked on and on at the dressmaker's about styles and fashions she thought perfect for Judith. The dressmaker showed them progress on gown after gown, promising to have the first five delivered in time for Easter. They were beautiful dresses, ones that Judith would probably have chosen for herself, but the fact that her grandmother had made the decision left her less than enthusiastic.

Sarah met her at the suite and immediately helped Judith into one of the wrappers. She took the pins out of Judith's hair. Judith had learned that unless a question needed to be asked, Sarah remained silent. Judith supposed it was a part of her training and yet another of the things that was done this way because that was the way Mrs. Whitley wanted it.

By the time Sarah had Judith's long blond hair brushed out, Judith was weary of the day.

"I lit a fire," Sarah said. "The room seemed chilled."

Judith nodded. "Thank you. You're very considerate."

"It's my job."

Judith realized that nothing any of the staff did was done out of kindness or love. It was nothing more than a job to them. They were paid to be considerate. It made her feel all the more alone.

"If there's nothing else, I'll let you rest." Sarah waited for Judith's dismissal.

"There's nothing else. Thank you."

Sarah nodded and exited without another word.

With a sigh, Judith went to the French doors that led to the balcony and peered out. She wanted to just relax there rather than go to bed, but she saw that Bill and Uncle William sat discussing something at one of the tables below. The conversation seemed rather heated. Perhaps it was best just to go to bed.

Sarah had turned down the covers as she always did, but at the sight of movement beneath the bedding, Judith froze. Only a moment passed before a snake peered out from beneath the sheets. Judith gasped and jumped back as the snake slithered out, seeming not to notice her. However, once it caught sight of her, the snake immediately coiled and began to rattle its tail.

Judith had dealt with more than her share of snakes in the past. After her first encounter as a young child, when her mother had killed the snake for her, Judith's father had taught her how to chop the head off a rattlesnake. Of course, she wouldn't find a hoe handy in the elaborate suite. But she did notice the fireplace poker and tongs. She moved with caution away from the bed, keeping an eye on the snake. It would be better to call for help, but she didn't want to leave the snake free to roam. She remembered Uncle William and Bill below, and after retrieving the poker and tongs, she moved to see if they were still in the garden. They weren't. Nevertheless, she opened the doors so she could put the snake outside.

The snake was still coiled on the bed, but it no longer rattled. He seemed to watch her movements as if to judge her threat level. Judith had only to move closer, however, and it would again become defensive.

"Lord, I need Your hand to guide me."

Her father had taught her that the most important thing was to move slow and control the head as soon as possible. Once that was done, she could take hold of the beast by the tail and move it. It would still require great care.

She took slow steps, the tongs in her right hand. The snake wasn't pleased to have her return. Thankfully, it wasn't very large, and Judith managed to slowly come at it from the side. She used the poker in her left hand to distract it, moving slowly and steadily. The snake continued to rattle, but even when she brought the tongs closer, it didn't strike. Drawing a deep breath, Judith prayed silently and caught the snake just below its neck with the tongs. She squeezed the tongs tight and dragged the snake from the bed, catching its tail with the poker.

Once she reached the balcony, Judith draped the snake over the stone balustrade and delivered two heavy strikes against its head with the poker. It wriggled for a few moments, then finally went limp. It was dead.

She let out her breath, realizing for the first time that she'd been holding it. She wondered what she should do with the carcass, as she didn't like the idea of leaving it for Sarah to clean up. There seemed to be nothing to do but see to the matter herself. She made her way back through the suite, dead snake hanging from the tongs.

Judith knew her way to the front door, so that seemed to be the best solution. Hopefully she'd spy Ramsay on the way, and he could advise her as to where she should dispose of the snake or perhaps even take it from her to deal with himself. But Ramsay seemed to be otherwise occupied, so when Judith reached the door, she decided she would walk around back to the stable area. Surely someone there would be able to point her in the direction of the rubbish bin.

One of the stable boys was just wheeling out a load of manure and soiled straw as she came around the corner of the house. His eyes grew wide at the sight of the snake.

"He's dead," she assured and continued her approach. "I just need to know where I might dispose of him."

The young man shook his head. "You're sure he's dead?"

"Absolutely. I killed him myself." Judith smiled. "But he's getting to be rather heavy. Where can I take him?"

"If he's dead, you can just put him here on top of the manure."

Judith nodded and gave the snake a toss, which caused the young man to jump back. She didn't give it another thought. "Thank you."

She made her way back to the house. The episode had rather energized her, and now she had no desire to take a nap. Especially not until the sheets were changed. Thoughts of the snake made her smile despite the danger. Rich or poor, it seemed all houses had their problems with dangerous pests.

CHAPTER

17

aleb sat at Henry Ambrewster's desk and tried to focus
on the papers in front of him. He hadn't planned to
spend the day in their old offices, but as a favor to one
of their practice's longtime clients, Caleb felt an obligation. For
weeks now, he had intended to close the office and release the
secretary. He couldn't see it being important to keep the office
if he went into ministry work. But that decision hadn't been
made. No matter how much Caleb prayed about the matter, it
just didn't seem God was pointing him to the pulpit. But if not
preaching—then what? He felt strongly that he should minister
God's love, and didn't that mean preaching the Gospel, as well?

He looked at the papers in front of him and tried to force
himself to double-check the figures and information. It should
have been a simple matter, but for the life of him, Caleb couldn't
keep his focus on the work at hand. Instead, he thought about
his future . . . and Judith.

Ever since Camri had suggested he was in love with Judith,
Caleb had been unable to think of anything else. Deep within,
he knew Camri had hit upon something, but he wasn't yet able

to accept the truth of it. He hadn't planned to fall in love with anyone. He knew that one day he would, but he figured it would be some time yet before he grew serious about anyone. He had been looking for God's direction for his life—his career. How had it happened that he'd lost his heart to Judith Gladstone? No, Judith Whitley.

He sighed and gave up on his work. He called his secretary and handed him the file. "Would you please go over these papers? My mind is on other things, and I don't want the client to pay the price for my distraction. If there are any problems, just correct them."

"Of course, Mr. Coulter," the young man said, nodding. He took the file and gave Caleb a hesitant look. "Will there be anything else?"

"No." Caleb got to his feet. "I'm going to head home. When you're done with that, give Mr. Sanders a call and have him come in on Monday to look things over and sign the contract."

"I will. Have a good evening, Mr. Coulter."

Caleb nodded and headed out. As he passed through the outer office, he grabbed his top coat and hat. He made his way to his car and tossed his coat in the back. It had been a rainy spring, but today the weather had warmed considerably. Hopefully the nice weather would extend into the weekend.

He drove down California Street to the west, knowing it would take him within a block or two of the Whitley estate. He toyed with the idea of just stopping in unannounced to check on Judith. No doubt Mrs. Whitley was keeping her busy, and he hated to think of Judith being forced to do things against her will.

"Why can't I stop thinking about her? Is this truly love?"

With all that had happened to him over the last year, Caleb supposed he shouldn't be surprised that this life-changing event could come upon him as well. Still, what of Judith? Did she care about him that way? She'd certainly never given him an indication of feeling anything more for him than friendship. Perhaps she did care for him, but probably only as her friend's brother. Then too, he had allowed her to live at his home. Perhaps she only felt gratitude.

Poor Judith. He shook his head, thinking of all she might have to contend with. Mrs. Whitley was a formidable woman. In his conversations with Judge Winters, Caleb had realized that Mrs. Whitley seldom allowed anyone to oppose her. At least not with any hope of winning. Judith was tenderhearted and naïve. He could just imagine the old woman telling her some sob story about how she didn't have many years left. It would be just the kind of thing that would prompt Judith to act. That was probably why she had made such a quick decision to move into the Whitley mansion. Hadn't she even said something about her grandmother's age?

He reached home and parked the car. For some time he just sat there, contemplating everything going on around him. Camri was to marry Patrick. Ruef's criminal activities were being dealt with, and soon they would hopefully see the man imprisoned. Once that was resolved, what was Caleb going to do? His thoughts refused to fall into any order. Just when he figured out a way to make sense of things, something else came to mind and negated the solution.

"Ye just goin' to sit here all night?" Patrick Murdock asked.

Caleb startled. He found Patrick watching him with a look of concern. "Sorry, what?"

"I've asked ye three times if ye were all right. Ye didn't seem to be hearin' me." Patrick smiled.

"I've just had a lot on my mind." Caleb got out of the car, then grabbed his coat.

"I've got a good ear if ye're lookin' for one."

Patrick had proven to be a good friend. Since Caleb had represented him in court and saved him from what was sure to be a murder conviction, Patrick had been at his side. Now he planned to marry Camri, and soon they would be family. Even so, Caleb wasn't sure he wanted to discuss Judith and his feelings with anyone just yet.

"I spoke with Judge Winters today," Caleb offered instead of confession. "He said he's got an appointment to talk to Ruef. He feels that we can force the issue regarding your business and house. Apparently, Henry's brother-in-law Frederick Johnston was helpful. After Camri told me he had been helping Henry, I suggested the judge speak with him and see if he was of a mind to help in our pursuit of seeing justice done. Apparently one thing led to another, and Johnston shared some information that he felt we could use to push forward your claims."

"'Tis wonderful news indeed. For sure yer sister will be dancin' a jig once she hears about it."

Caleb laughed and led the way up the stairs to the house. "Don't be too hard on her. She's stubborn and willful, but extremely loyal—to a fault, even. She'll fight to the death for you now that she's in love with you."

Patrick shook his head. "I'm sure I don't deserve such love."

"Does anyone really deserve love? That's the wonder of Jesus. He came and ministered to the folks around Him—loving the unlovable—healing those who did nothing to deserve His concern. Then He let some of those same folks nail Him to a cross. All because of love. Love we didn't deserve."

"Aye, for certain that's true, but Jesus is Himself God and so it's different than a fancy woman like Camrianne fallin' in love with a poor Irishman."

As they reached the front door, Caleb turned to Patrick and grinned. "Personally, I think she's gone soft in the head."

Patrick roared with laughter. "Aye. No doubt ye're right."

Mrs. Wong opened the door and looked at the two laughing men for a moment before smiling. "You happy to be home, Mr. Caleb?"

He nodded. "I am, Mrs. Wong. I truly am. However, I'm even happier that my sister has found such an agreeable man to wed. She'll need a strong man like Mr. Murdock to keep her in line."

The Chinese woman's smile faded. "You keep Miss Camri in a line?"

Caleb shook his head. "No, I'll explain it later."

"What will you explain?" Camri asked, coming down the stairs.

Caleb looked at Patrick. "Ask your beloved. I'm sure he'll be able to tell you better than I can."

He left the two of them in the hall and, after handing Mrs. Wong his top coat and hat, headed to his study. He was still smiling as he took a seat behind his desk and picked up the newspaper to read the events of the day. It looked like S.N. Wood & Co. was having a sale on men's suits and trousers. They were offering the latter for three dollars and fifty cents each. It might be a good idea to check into it. Caleb knew his wardrobe was getting well-worn. He supposed society would expect him to choose a higher-end company or even a private tailor for such things, but he had no pretenses of being someone he wasn't. He flipped through the pages, glancing at stories related to happenings abroad. The Emporium had an ad selling their men's suits for fifteen dollars. He had always liked their tailoring better, so perhaps he wouldn't worry about going to Wood & Co. after all.

"Caleb?" Camri called from the door. "Patrick has something to ask you."

Pushing back the paper, Caleb leaned his elbows on the desk. "Come on in. I was just contemplating the purchase of a new suit or two."

"You could definitely use them," Camri said. "Your old ones are so out of date and show considerable wear."

"Perhaps you can go shopping with me tomorrow."

"Well, tomorrow is what we'd be here to discuss. I forgot to tell ye," Patrick said, holding up several pieces of paper. "I was given four tickets to the Sutro Baths. I thought bein' as tomorrow is Saturday, we might all go and make a day of it."

Caleb nodded. "I've heard it's a wonderful place of amusement. Although I've never found the time to go."

"I've been there, but it's been some time," Patrick admitted. They both turned to Camri, but it was Patrick who asked. "What about ye?"

She shook her head. "No. When we were here visiting before, there wasn't time, and I certainly had no interest when you were missing," she said, looking at her brother.

"So what of it? Why don't we get Kenzie to go with us and make it a foursome?" Caleb could see that Camri was considering the proposition. He thought he'd push a little to convince her. "I could use a diversion, and I'll even buy us lunch. You know they have all sorts of places offering food, and there's entertainment and arcades. We could just make an entire day of it."

"What of your shopping for suits?" Camri asked.

"It'll wait until Monday."

"All right, then," she said, nodding. "Let me go ask Kenzie if she wants to join us." She hurried from the room.

"Well, for sure that went over better than I'd figured. I thought it would probably be impossible to be gettin' yer sister to have a little fun," Patrick said, taking a seat in front of Caleb's desk.

"Oh, Camri isn't opposed to a little fun now and then. She is rather singularly focused at times. I suppose you know she's applied to teach at one of the area colleges."

"Aye. She told me about it. I figure it might well be in my best interests to encourage her, that way she'll be occupied with something other than plannin' our wedding and naggin' me to set the date."

"I have to admit, I thought the same thing. Apparently there are some classes in women's studies, whatever that is, and she's quite determined to be a part of it. I encouraged it, hoping you wouldn't be against the idea."

Camri returned. "She won't go. She says she has promised her Cousin George to help him with some project. What if I give Judith a call?"

Caleb felt his breath catch. Before he could say anything, Patrick was nodding. "Go to it, then. I think it'd be a fine thing. She's probably ready to get away from those strangers, and a day with ye would give her a chance to bare her soul and tell ye all the details."

Camri didn't need to be told twice. "I'm sure Caleb would enjoy having her along."

Patrick turned to Caleb as Camri exited the room. "Oh, and why would that be?"

"Never mind. My sister is just up to her old tricks again. Trying to run the world and master everyone's life for them."

———

Judith was surprised when Ramsay came to call her to the telephone. Her grandmother kept the phone in one of the smaller drawing rooms, as she abhorred the thing and wanted it well out of view and away from her regularly inhabited rooms.

"This is Judith Whitley."

"Judith, it's Camri."

A smile cut across Judith's face. "I'm so glad to hear from you! I miss you all so much."

"Well, that's why I'm calling. Patrick got four tickets to the Sutro Baths. It's a place for swimming and other amusements. We wondered if you would join us—Patrick and Caleb and I."

"Oh, that sounds like great fun. When?"

"Saturday."

"As in tomorrow?"

"Yes," Camri replied. "Can you come? We'll drive over to pick you up. The place opens at seven, so Caleb thought we should go early. Then, when things start getting overcrowded, we can go have some lunch. He's going to buy."

"Tomorrow sounds wonderful. I would love to come with you."

"Judith." Her grandmother's stern voice sounded from the doorway. "What are you doing?"

"Camri, I'll see you in the morning. I need to speak with my grandmother now." Camri bid her good-bye, and Judith hung up the phone. She turned to see her grandmother frowning at her. "Camri called to see if I could join them tomorrow for an outing. I told her I would."

"But I have plans for you tomorrow. Call back and give her your apologies."

Judith had been doing her grandmother's bidding all week and knew she needed to take a stand. "No, Grandmother. I've already arranged to go with them. I'm sorry that you made plans without consulting me first, but I want to go with my friends."

"I won't have it." Grandmother swept into the room like a reigning queen. "You must call and give your regrets."

"Could we sit and talk for a moment?" Judith asked, moving to a small chair by the fireplace. She sat without waiting for her grandmother to reply.

Ann Whitley was clearly uncomfortable being dictated to, but nevertheless she hesitated only a moment. "Very well." She gave a sort of exasperated sigh and sat in the chair across from Judith. "What is it you wish to say?"

"I want you to know that I appreciate all you've done for me. However, I am not going to allow you to plan out my life as you have done with the others. That's not how I was brought up, even if it was how I should have been brought up. I have friends whom I care a great deal about, and that isn't going to change just because I now also have family."

"I see." Her grandmother raised her chin ever so slightly. "I suppose you do not care for us as you do for them."

Judith shook her head. "That isn't the point at all. I care about all of you, but I won't be dictated to by either side. If you want me to be a part of this family and get to know you, then you must allow for my wishes as well."

"I suppose my desires are of no concern."

"I didn't say that." Judith could see how manipulative the old woman could be. She'd watched in silence all week as Grandmother had played the other members of the family like finely tuned instruments.

"Well, it seems it must be, or you wouldn't hurt me this way."

Judith got up. "I suppose then, that I must pack my things and return to the Coulter house."

"What?" By the look on her face, it was clear Ann Whitley hadn't expected this turn of events.

"Grandmother, I want very much to stay here and know you better—the others too. However, I must be allowed to make some of my own plans. I gave up working a job that I enjoyed because it grieved you. I've let you play with me like a doll, arranging my wardrobe and taking me to teas and other gatherings. However, I won't give up my friends."

She saw a moment of indecision in her grandmother's expression. Then the old woman got to her feet and nodded. "Very well. I agree that you will be allowed to make some of your own plans so long as you agree to participate in mine as well."

"I'm happy to. Didn't I tell you I would go to the various parties your friends are having for Easter?"

"Yes. Yes, you did." She nodded.

"And so I will. There is no reason I can't go along with my friends tomorrow and still accompany you next week. Now, if you'll excuse me, I need to change for dinner."

———

Ann Whitley watched her granddaughter exit the room. She smiled to herself. She liked the girl's spirit and willingness to stand up for herself. The others in the family bent easily to her will. They knew she held a vast fortune in her control, and each hoped to inherit their portion—if not someone else's as well. If she despised anything about her son and grandchildren, it was this. Bill would stand up for himself from time to time, but of late, even he was more compliant. She'd even heard him mention being ready to consider marrying. Just last year, he'd taken the reins of their shipping industry. He was proving to be quite capable, although profits were still somewhat diminished. Ann had been at him recently to consider some of the young ladies she thought suitable. Perhaps she could plan a mate for him while she was also considering one for Judith.

Judith had declared she wouldn't be arranged in marriage, but the child didn't know her own mind. She didn't understand that men would start to call on her with great frequency now that she was an heiress. Ann could allow for an outing or two with her friends, but she would not allow Judith to marry just anyone.

Ann walked to one of the windows and pulled back the drapes. The skies were growing dark. She thought of this property and house and how her husband had built it to please her. And it had pleased her. It was perfectly situated amidst other opulent homes and had perfectly groomed gardens. It was a clear indication of power and money, and Ann liked that she belonged to the elite Nob Hill society.

She let the drapes fall back into place and turned back to look at the small drawing room. She'd never cared for it. The fireplace always seemed to smoke, and in the summer the room was much too warm. Perhaps she'd have it redone. There were all sorts of new novelties that might be utilized to help make it more appealing. Perhaps she could even interest Judith in helping her. After all, she had to find a way to keep the girl occupied and under her control. At least until Judith learned what it was to be a Whitley.

"She's more self-determined than I'd expected," Ann mused aloud.

Judith's strength reminded Ann of herself. She had never tolerated anyone dictating terms to her, and it would seem Judith was cut from the same cloth. It pleased Ann to no small degree to see this trait in her granddaughter. Still, it would have to be carefully molded in order to be useful to Ann.

She smiled again. "Perhaps there's hope for this family after all."

CHAPTER 18

The Sutro Baths were unlike anything Judith had ever seen before. There were seven saltwater pools with toboggan slides and overhead rings and trapezes. A band played music to entertain and enliven the mood, while hundreds of people gathered to enjoy the waters or watch others from overhead.

Judith's fascination for swimming in an indoor pool had gotten the best of her. Growing up, she'd not had a lot of opportunities to swim, but when she had, it had been in a pond, with only her mother and father for company. Coming here had seemed like a good idea—something fun to do with the day, but now that she was here, she wasn't so sure.

Holding up the navy blue bathing suit, she frowned. "I don't think I can do this."

Camri held up hers too. "I was thinking the same thing. For all my progressive thinking, I'm not sure I can give myself over to running around half-naked in front of the entire city."

Judith breathed a sigh of relief and lowered the suit. "I'm so glad you feel the same. I didn't want to spoil everyone's fun. I've never been one to dress at all daringly." She smiled. "I doubt I'll ever be one of those women who wears trousers either."

Camri looked over the suit again. "It's so thin, and you can't very well wear undergarments with it." She gave a little shudder. "I truly can't imagine Patrick or even Caleb would want to see us like that in public." She put her suit down on the bench. "I'll go find them and explain."

"We might as well go together." Judith left her suit atop Camri's. "I wouldn't want them to think I wasn't willing to face them, nor that this was just your idea."

Camri laughed. "I think they both know you're of strong character. After all, you went to live with complete strangers."

"Not once, but twice." Judith shrugged. "I don't know if that shows strength or a bit of the ridiculous."

Camri looped her arm through Judith's. "Well, never mind what it is, I'm proud of you. You must have had misgivings, and yet you've overcome them all to learn about your family. I admire that. Perhaps now that you don't have to worry about working, you might even want to go to college."

Judith had heard this from Camri on more than one occasion. She was convinced that an advanced education was critical for women. Judith didn't have the heart to tell Camri that the idea of going to college made her stomach churn.

They left the dressing room and found the guys standing in their swimming attire, deep in conversation. Judith was embarrassed to look at Caleb's well-muscled physique and lowered her gaze to the floor as Camri boldly approached the men.

"What's this?" Caleb asked. "You're neither one dressed."

"It would be more appropriate to say we're neither one undressed," Camri began. "Judith and I don't feel at all comfortable wearing what little they provide for swimming."

Caleb chuckled. "Patrick and I were just discussing that.

We're not very comfortable with it either. We noticed several young women who were less bashful, and frankly . . . well, suffice it to say we were trying to figure out how to forego swimming without disappointing the two of you. It would seem God already made provision for that."

Judith glanced up, careful to look only into Caleb's eyes. "Thank you for understanding."

"We'll go change, and then we can tour some of the exhibits upstairs. There's far more than just swimming available. Why don't you wait for us on the promenade near the elevator?"

While Judith and Camri waited for the men, they looked down on the pools of swimmers, marveling at some of the acrobatics being performed.

"I would never have imagined such tricks," Judith said, watching a man dangling from a trapeze. "I'm just as content to watch from afar."

"Me too. I do love to swim. Chicago sits right on Lake Michigan. It's one of the Great Lakes."

"I think I remember that. Those are the big lakes up north— five of them, right?"

Camri nodded. "Yes, and the first letter of each spells out HOMES."

"Yes. I do recall that. My mother told me she'd seen each of them." Sorrow washed over Judith as she thought of the woman she'd known as her mother. It was impossible to think of her as anything but her mother. Lila Gladstone was the woman who had comforted Judith in the night when a bad dream made sleep difficult. Lila and Homer Gladstone were the parents who had taught her most everything she knew. They didn't cease to be her mother and father just because they'd stolen her away. Yet she couldn't seem to forgive the lie.

"Are you all right?" Camri asked, touching Judith's sleeve.

"I think so. I was just thinking about my folks. What they did was so wrong, yet they're the only parents I'll ever have."

Camri offered her a sympathetic smile. "It can't be easy. You came here searching for an aunt and found your entire world turned upside down."

"I don't know what I would have done without you and Kenzie. Caleb too. I've sometimes regretted leaving your company."

"Well, you're always welcome to return. You know that. We miss you. Some of us more than others," Camri said in a teasing tone.

Judith frowned. "What do you mean?"

"It isn't important." Camri squeezed Judith's arm. "Just know that you are missed. Oh, look. There are our fellows."

Caleb and Patrick approached, still buttoning their suit coats. "We got dressed as quickly as we could," Patrick said, shaking his head. "'Tis sorry I am for suggestin' this bit of fun."

"Don't be." Camri took his arm. "It wasn't your fault. None of us thought it through."

Judith smiled and nodded. "She's right. However, I'm excited to see the exhibits. I read that Mr. Sutro brought back stuffed animals from all over the world."

"He did, and hopefully they're all fully clothed. Although I thought my knees were rather dashing."

The others laughed at Caleb's comment, but Judith felt her cheeks grow hot. How could he not know the effect he had on her? Dashing knees, indeed.

"I want to go read up on Mr. Sutro," Camri said, pulling Patrick down the hall. "We can all meet up for lunch at the Cliff House."

"What time?" Caleb called after her.

"Noon."

Judith watched them disappear into the crowd of other strolling visitors. She glanced at Caleb and found him watching her. The expression on his face was one she couldn't quite read.

"Is something wrong?" she asked.

He smiled and shook his head. "I was just thinking of how much I admire you for your modesty." He took her arm. "Now, what would you like to see first?"

They toured all over the building, enjoying the arcades and displays. Mr. Sutro had spared no expense, bringing in tropical plants from far away to decorate the walkways and pavilions. The indoor gardens thrived, giving off glorious scents along with their sensational colors.

At the Panorama of the World, Caleb introduced Judith to her first view of exotic animals—leopards, hyenas, and monkeys, to name a few. The time passed quickly, with Caleb explaining certain exhibits in great detail while admitting less knowledge on others. They even stopped to play a game or two. It was at a particularly challenging game of knocking down bottles with a baseball that Caleb won Judith a small stuffed bear. It had a tag around its neck that read, "Sutro Baths."

"Strange name for a bear."

Caleb smiled down at her. "You could always rename him. Maybe after a favorite pet."

"No, I'll call him Sutro." She smiled and cradled the bear close.

They met up with Patrick and Camri at the Cliff House for lunch after hours of exploring. Judith gazed over the menu and finally suggested the others pick for her. The luxurious meals were expensive, and she wasn't at all comfortable choosing. It was only after Caleb had put in an order for fresh seafood and steamed asparagus that Judith remembered the bank account her grandmother had set up for her, as well as the cash in her purse. She could afford to buy her own meal—even furnish meals for the others. Her life had changed in so many ways, and even now she couldn't quite comprehend it.

Judith found the view from the restaurant exhilarating. Looking out over the Pacific Ocean, she wondered about the lands far beyond. Until last year, she'd never ventured more than twenty miles from home. Now it seemed she'd gone a million or more.

As they ate, they chatted about the day and all that they'd seen. Finally Camri opened the topic of Judith's new life.

"So how is it, being Judith Whitley?"

Judith gave a shrug. "Sometimes confusing. Sometimes endearing. My grandmother is demanding, as we knew she would be. She wasn't happy that I chose to spend the day with you instead of her."

"How did you ever convince her?" Camri asked.

"I had to be firm. I threatened to pack up and leave. I kept remembering things you and Caleb had said about her manipulating me. It wasn't easy, but I knew she wasn't taking my desires seriously and that it was time to prove myself capable of action."

"Good for you! I'm so proud of you," Camri said, raising her glass to Judith.

"As am I." Caleb smiled. "It wouldn't have been nearly as nice a day without you."

Judith's heart picked up speed. She wondered if the others could see how Caleb's nearness and comment affected her.

"I . . . well, I don't think Grandmother means to be difficult—it's just been her way all her life. Even so, she's been very kind and more than generous. She spoils me and indulges me with every possible thing I could ask for."

"Well, you deserve it," Camri replied. "What have you learned about your parents?"

"They were an arranged marriage." Judith thought back to

all she'd been told. "However, they fell in love. Grandmother said that my mother—that Lila was unhappy at the prospect of an arrangement of her own. She had fallen for one of the cowboys who worked for her parents. Apparently, my grandparents had a large horse farm, and that's where my father worked. Grandmother still believes in arranged marriages. She has arranged for my cousin Victoria to be married to a much older man."

"What does Victoria have to say about it?" Caleb asked.

"Nothing. Grandmother told me she intended the same for me, but I told her I would only marry for love." Judith made the mistake of looking into Caleb's eyes. If only he knew that she'd already fallen in love—with him.

"Your grandmother will just have to get used to the idea that not everyone is willing to do things her way." Camri pushed back her plate. "Today's women are entitled to pursue careers or marriage based solely on their own desires."

"Oh, go on with ye now," Patrick said, shaking his head. "Ye'll be filling Judith's head with all sorts of nonsense, and then she'll be having to fight her way out."

"Nonsense? We'll soon have the vote, and then we'll see how much nonsense it is. When women are making the choices for president and our other representatives, then men will have to accept that our opinions are not to be taken for granted."

"I doubt anyone would ever be takin' yer opinion for granted." Patrick grinned and gave Camri a wink.

"Well, I don't suppose Ann Whitley is used to anyone, man or woman, standing up to her, much less refusing to do things her way," Caleb said. "I hope you'll stand strong, Judith. Don't let her force you into situations that go against your beliefs."

"I promise you, I won't allow for that. Although, my grandmother does revere God. I was glad to learn that much. She attends a large church, and I've promised to share in the Easter events with her and the rest of the family."

"Tell us about the others," Camri insisted. "What's your uncle like?"

"I don't think he much cares for me." Judith shrugged. "Grandmother tells me that he all but lost his fortune in bad business decisions and squandering. She's had to give him a stipend to live on while some of his investments mature. However, my cousins know nothing of their father's folly."

"That seems unlikely," Caleb said. "Your uncle's son is twenty-three or so, isn't he?"

"Yes. Bill is quite nice." Judith couldn't help but smile. "However, he's also a bit of a pest. He's always around and seems desperate to impress and charm me. Whereas his sister will have nothing to do with me. Victoria hates me. Probably because I've taken her grandmother's attention, although given Grandmother's demands, I can't imagine anyone minding less of her attention."

"What does Bill do for a living?" Caleb asked.

"He's been put in charge of the Whitley shipping interests. Grandmother instructs him and demands he spend time training under her financial advisors. He resents it, I can tell, but he does what he must. I'm sure he knows who butters his bread. However, he's never said a word about his father being in a bind. I honestly don't think he knows. Grandmother has told him it's to his benefit to heed her demands. She told me flat out that she promised him that she'll turn the entire shipping business over to him if he proved himself to be loyal."

"Given that all of her businesses are worth millions, I would think that a strong incentive," Caleb said, leaning back.

"I think I'd like to take a walk on the beach," Camri said, looking at Patrick. "What about it, husband-to-be? Would you care to escort me on a stroll?"

"And would I really be havin' any say in the matter?" he asked, grinning.

Camri cast her napkin aside. "No. No say whatsoever."

Patrick laughed and got to his feet. "What about it, Caleb? Would ye two care to join us?"

"No. I think if Judith is agreed, I'd prefer to stay here and enjoy some coffee and maybe dessert. They have an amazing chocolate torte."

Judith nodded, eager to sample some of the luscious-looking desserts. "You know how irresistible I find chocolate."

Caleb frowned. "And here I thought it was my company you enjoyed so much."

Judith quickly ducked her head, lest he see her surprise. Of course she enjoyed his company—even more than chocolate. Well, at least marginally. She grinned. If only he knew what thoughts went through her head.

"We'll leave you to enjoy your dessert, then," Camri said as Patrick helped her from the chair. "We won't be long."

They left the restaurant, and Judith found their absence made Caleb's presence seem all the more intimate. It didn't matter that the restaurant was filled with chattering patrons. It was as if she and Caleb were alone on an island.

"I'm glad they've gone," he said, surprising her. "Now I have you all to myself."

Their waiter came to the table. "Would you care for dessert?"

"Absolutely. We want the chocolate torte and coffee."

"Very good, sir." He slipped away as quickly as he'd come.

"I've had so much rich food these past days that I'm sure to grow fat." Judith gazed out the window, smiling. "However, I can't say no to chocolate."

"You would be beautiful even if your waistline expanded,"

Caleb assured. "But I'm more concerned about your happiness. I hope you have that and much more."

"I suppose I've found a way to be content." She stroked the linen napkin on her lap. "I wonder, however, if you might answer some questions for me."

"Anything."

"Well, I'm rather . . . not confused, exactly, but concerned."

"What's wrong?" He leaned forward. "You know you can talk to me about anything. Is it about your family?"

She shook her head. "How does one know if they're really and truly saved from hell?"

Caleb's expression revealed his surprise. "Whatever has caused you to ask that at a time like this?"

"We can talk about something else, but I have no one else to ask."

"It's not a problem," he said, reaching out to touch her arm. "Forgive me."

"I suppose it's because I've had so much time on my hands. Not that Grandmother doesn't keep me occupied, but at night, I lie awake and ponder these things. I've had conversations with my grandmother and even my cousin Bill, but neither seem as interested in God as you and Camri are. Bill believes that if God is love, then He surely will not send anyone to hell. In fact, he isn't even convinced that there is a hell."

"I've known others who thought the same, but to me it's obvious. After all, God sent Jesus—His only Son—to be crucified for our sins. Why would He do such a painful thing if there was no consequence to sin? There is a depth to God's love that we cannot understand, but just as any other loving parent, He disciplines His children and gives them choices to make. If we reject His love—that's our choice, but the results are eternal."

"I believe that. I told Bill as much. I explained that I made a

218

commitment to accept Jesus as my Savior. I even arranged with Pastor Fisher to be baptized. He just laughed and suggested it was nothing more than ritual that Christians put themselves through as a part of their religious training."

Caleb smiled. "I'm inclined to think that people turn to those excuses to avoid having to make a choice regarding God. In Romans it says, 'That if thou shalt confess with thy mouth the Lord Jesus, and shalt believe in thine heart that God hath raised him from the dead, thou shalt be saved. For with the heart man believeth unto righteousness, and with the mouth confession is made unto salvation.'"

"I have made those confessions, and I do believe." Judith shrugged. "However, I felt something within me that led me to believe it was absolute truth. Is it possible that some folks never feel the same?"

"The Holy Spirit is the one who convicts and directs. Some people have put up an absolute barrier between them and God. They don't think it's necessary to recognize there is a God. I think when they hear or see others who have devoted their lives to God, it's a reminder of what they are missing. They see us comforted and happy in our relationship with God, and the void in their own life seems all the bigger."

"That makes sense to me."

"God's ways are those of order, even if they seem mysterious. As Christians, we truly have only to seek answers from God, and He will give them."

The waiter returned with their coffees and tortes. Judith looked at the large piece he placed in front of her. "This looks amazing, but I'm not sure I can eat it all."

"What you can't eat, I will," Caleb promised, already digging into his piece.

Judith poured a liberal amount of cream into her coffee,

then swirled the contents with her spoon. Caleb's words were comforting, but she still wanted to know more.

"So if I pray about the matters on my heart—for instance, my future—God will show me the way?"

Caleb chuckled. "I've been wrestling with that very same concern. Since my return from Hawaii, I thought perhaps God wanted me to go into the ministry. I attended many theological classes in college and have studied the Bible in great detail. I've led others to God and helped encourage and pray with a great many, and yet I still have no idea exactly what I'm supposed to do."

"Truly?" She found his confusion almost a comfort. If someone like Caleb Coulter wasn't completely certain of God's direction, then perhaps she wasn't doing everything wrong.

"Truly. I think maybe I've been mistaken in the way I've been looking at it."

"In what way?"

He shrugged. "Well, I've supposed that the only way to truly serve God is from behind a pulpit, but I know better. God can use us in any job, at any time. Serving Him requires a willingness to yield my way and will for His. It doesn't require I be a pastor. So I'm trying hard to see where God can use me best."

Judith nodded. "I think I understand. It's not always—"

"Judith, whatever are you doing here?"

She looked up to find Bill Whitley standing beside their table. He leaned down and gave her a kiss on the cheek before straightening to give Caleb a once-over.

"Grandmother said you were out with friends," Bill said, "but this looks like more of a date."

"I'm having lunch with my friends. Camri and Patrick went for a walk, and this is Caleb Coulter."

Caleb's gaze was guarded and contemplative. It was clear he

didn't trust Bill. Perhaps he was worried about whether or not her grandmother had sent her cousin to summon her home. At least, that was Judith's worry.

"Caleb, this is my cousin, William Whitley the Second. We call him Bill."

"At least, my friends do," Bill said, putting out his hand. "How do you do, Mr. Coulter?"

"Very well, Mr. Whitley."

Bill moved behind Judith and put his hands on her shoulders. "Judith has become important to us. Our family has long searched for her, and now that she's returned, we're rather concerned about where she goes and whose company she keeps. I do hope you understand."

Judith stiffened. "Did Grandmother send you here to follow me?"

Bill chuckled. "Of course not." His grip tightened enough to be uncomfortable. "She has others to do that."

Judith gasped. "Grandmother is having me watched?"

"Most likely. She keeps track of us all." Bill released her and stepped to the side. Bending down he kissed her cheek again. "I hope I haven't spoiled your day. I must return to my friends, but we can speak about all of this later tonight. Maybe just before . . . bed." He straightened and smiled at Caleb. "I'm glad we had a chance to meet, Mr. Coulter."

"As am I," Caleb replied. His tone was irritated.

Once Bill had gone, Caleb leaned forward. "There's something about him that I don't care for. He seems quite . . ." He let the words fade into silence and gazed at his coffee cup.

"Spoiled?" Judith asked, hoping it would remove any doubts of her interest in Bill's affections.

Caleb looked up and nodded. "For a start."

CHAPTER

19

*A*nn Whitley finished her tea, then motioned for the footman to remove her breakfast plate. "Judith, remember, tomorrow we'll be meeting with my lawyer regarding your inheritance."

Victoria glared at her cousin. Ann knew the spoiled girl despised Judith for the competition she represented. She'd never cared for Cora either and was always seeking ways to get the other girl in trouble. Ann would have to keep an eye on Victoria to ensure she did nothing to cause Judith harm. Many times Victoria had done things to Cora. During one particularly nasty argument over a dress, Cora had taken a tumble down the stairs, breaking her arm. Victoria swore it was an accident, that she hadn't pushed Cora, but Ann knew otherwise.

Fixing Victoria with a stern gaze, Ann made her feelings clear. "Victoria, I will not brook your nonsense." The girl straightened, and her expression went blank. "You are soon to be a married woman, and it would serve you well to at least act like a grown-up." Ann didn't miss the flare of temper in the girl's eyes but chose to ignore it. "We will meet promptly at nine in Mr. Whitley's office," she said to Judith. "Sarah will show you where it is."

"You did remember to invite Caleb to join us, didn't you?" Judith asked.

Ann nodded. She didn't like that Judith was still so dependent upon her friends. "I have sent word to him, but I do hope in time you will come to trust my direction. I have only your best interests at heart."

"Mother, you can hardly expect Judith to put her trust in you after only knowing you for such a short time." William motioned to the footman. "I'll take more coffee." The footman nodded and quickly served him. "I'm sure Mr. Coulter and Judith's other friends represent the familiar to our Judith."

"Yes, well, our Judith needs to realize that as her family, we will always seek to benefit and assist her." Ann smiled at Judith. "We Whitleys look after each other. We always have."

"Grandmother is right. We are your family," Bill interjected with a wink.

Ann had noticed Bill going out of his way to charm Judith. Perhaps he had thoughts of romancing her. It was something Ann had already considered for the pair. It would keep the family money in the family. However, marrying Bill off to another family of means would inject new money and support to the Whitley coffers.

"I must go write some letters," Ann said. The words were barely out of her mouth when William jumped up to assist her from her chair. Bill rose too.

"I have some papers to go over," Bill announced. "I'll be in the library if you need me."

Ann paused. She wasn't convinced that Bill and Judith should advance their relationship to marriage, but perhaps she should encourage their closeness. If Judith could see Bill as a confidante, then so much the better.

"Bill, I think it might be nice if you and Victoria took Judith out this evening. Perhaps dinner with some of your friends."

"I can't go," Victoria said, getting to her feet. "I have to oversee my packing. I leave Sunday, you know."

"Yes, but you have the rest of the week for that." Ann fixed her granddaughter with a firm expression. "It would be good for you to get to know Judith better."

"I think it's a capital idea," Bill replied. "I'll make arrangements right away."

Judith looked surprised by the suggestion, but offered no protest. Ann smiled. Perhaps she was coming to understand how things were done.

<hr>

Judith didn't know what to think about her grandmother's arrangement of her evening. She hadn't had anything else going on, but neither had she any desire to spend the evening in the company of the sullen Victoria.

Making her way outside, Judith took refuge in the gardens. The fog had lifted, and the flowers glistened in the sunlight. For a long time, she strolled along the path, praying and thinking about her day at the Sutro Baths. Camri had said several confusing things. She implied that while Judith was missed in their household, one person missed her more than the others. It was almost certain she meant Caleb, but Judith couldn't very well ask for confirmation. Had he said something to Camri? Maybe Kenzie had confided Judith's feelings to Camri, and in turn she shared them with Caleb?

Pausing to look out across the gardens, Judith spied two servants working at the far end to plant new flowers. She had heard her grandmother order them to see that there were always flowers in bloom, even if they had to plant new ones. It appeared Grandmother would impose her will even on nature.

However, of all that the Whitley estate could offer, Judith liked it best here. It was tranquil and generally void of people. She looked forward to later in the summer, when everything would be in full bloom without the imposition of her grandmother's servants.

"There you are," Bill said, coming to join her.

Judith smiled. "I didn't know you were looking for me."

"I wanted to let you know that our plans are made. We'll leave for a nice dinner out on the town around six. Then we'll go to a musical performance. Afterwards, we can enjoy some dancing at one of my favorite clubs."

"That sounds like a very full evening." Judith tried not to look unhappy. "You do realize, however, that you don't have to do this just because Grandmother wishes it."

He laughed. "I do. Perhaps I'm the only one besides you who doesn't tremble when the dragon breathes fire. However, in this instance, I happen to find her suggestion very agreeable."

"I know she just wants me to feel part of your world. I don't mind so much for myself, but I do hate for others to feel obligated. Your sister, for example."

"Victoria is unimportant. She has never been a happy person, and as far as I know, she has never willingly liked anyone."

"Not even Cora?"

"Especially not Cora. She was Vicky's rival for attention, and my sister made her life miserable. At least until Grandmother threatened to send her to a permanent boarding school."

"How sad. They could have been great friends."

Bill shrugged. "It's her loss, and her misery is her own fault.

Frankly, the sooner Grandmother has her married off, the better for everyone."

"So you approve of arranged marriages?"

"Not exactly, but where my sister is concerned, I'm just glad that someone is willing to take her off our hands." He grinned. "Now, enough about Vicky. I'll expect you to be ready to leave at six. Wear something elaborate and expensive."

Judith laughed. "Everything in my wardrobe is elaborate and expensive. Do you have a favorite color?"

He considered that for a moment. "I should very much like to see you in red."

"There is a lovely burgundy evening gown, as I recall. Will that do?"

"Absolutely. I shall look forward to seeing you in it." He started to walk away, then turned back. "I promise you that this evening will more than meet your expectations."

Judith smiled. He couldn't hope to understand that she had no expectations for the evening. He was kind, however, and right then she could use a friend.

When the large upstairs clock chimed six, Judith stepped from her room and made her way downstairs. Sarah had arranged her hair in curls high atop her head and trimmed it with gem-studded hairpins. Around Judith's neck, Sarah had placed a beautiful choker of pearls. Judith had never had any jewelry of her own, but Grandmother had insisted on presenting her with some of the Whitley pieces. Pieces that had originally been given to Judith's mother.

Bill stood in the foyer, waiting, and his expression left her no doubt of his pleasure at her appearance.

"Judith, you are beautiful. I knew red would suit you."

She smiled. He was once again stylishly dressed in his tails and tie. His straight blond hair had been parted and slicked back.

Ramsay appeared with her cloak. Bill took it from him and put it around Judith's shoulders. "No one will be able to hold a candle to you this evening," he whispered against her ear. He took his top hat from Ramsay. "The car is waiting, so let us be off." He took hold of Judith's elbow with his free hand.

When they were finally settled and on their way, Judith let herself relax a bit. She couldn't help but wish it were Caleb at her side, but for now she would find a way to enjoy her cousin's company.

"I suppose Victoria couldn't be persuaded to come?" she asked.

"Actually, I made it clear that she shouldn't come," Bill replied. "I told her I wouldn't allow her to accompany us if she intended to be difficult. She told me she couldn't possibly care less about what I wanted or did, and that she had no intention of joining us."

"I'm sorry if I'm coming between the two of you." Judith frowned and looked out the window. "Is it far to the restaurant?"

"Nothing is far from us in this town," he answered. "I hope you like Italian food."

She gave him a smile. "I don't know that I've ever had it. I lived quite isolated in Colorado."

"I suppose Lila and Homer did that to keep you from being found."

She had always believed it was due to the less expensive land being farther removed from town, but what he said made sense. "I can see the location they chose for our home was probably due to that very thought."

"They no doubt knew they'd be sent to prison if they were ever found."

"Do you really suppose the family would have allowed for that kind of scandal?"

He seemed surprised by her question. "Grandmother wouldn't have seen that as scandal. She would have seen it as justice."

The car came to a stop in front of a four-story brick building with red awnings. The restaurant's sign read *Fior d'Italia, est. 1886*.

Bill jumped out before the driver could open the door. He came around and assisted Judith. "This is one of my favorite places." He glanced over at the driver. "Come back for us in time to get us to the concert at eight."

Judith allowed him to take her arm and guide her into the restaurant. His large hand encircled her just above the elbow, and his grip was tight. She didn't particularly care for his possessive hold, thinking it quite different from the way Caleb held her arm.

They were immediately led to a secluded table. The host snapped his fingers, and just as quickly, uniformed men appeared. One was the wine steward, Judith soon learned, and the other their waiter.

"Since you've never had Italian food, I shall order for both of us," Bill said. He spoke in what Judith could only imagine was Italian to the wine steward, who nodded and quickly left.

Judith glanced around the busy restaurant. There were a great many elegantly dressed people enjoying their dinner amidst the beautiful furnishings and candlelight.

"We'll start with the *cozze e vongole con vino e aglio*, then bring us the *lasagne bolognese al forno*. We have to make our concert by eight, so be quick about it," Bill commanded.

The waiter nodded and vanished without another word.

"I suppose you will tell me what we're eating." Judith smiled. "I didn't realize you spoke Italian."

"I speak Italian, French, Spanish, German, and a bit of Portuguese. But of course, I'll explain what I've ordered. First, we'll have some clams and mussels in garlic. Then you're in for a treat. Pasta with cheese and a meat sauce all layered like a torte."

"It sounds delicious."

The wine steward returned and showed a bottle to Bill. He nodded, and the steward opened the wine. Judith didn't say anything about her lack of interest in the wine. She didn't want to make Bill uncomfortable, so she once again gazed off across the restaurant at the happy diners. She could well imagine coming here with Caleb. Did he like Italian food?

"You look deep in thought."

Judith looked at Bill. She couldn't very well explain her thoughts about Caleb. "Where are the others?"

"The others?"

"Yes, Grandmother mentioned me meeting your friends."

Bill chuckled. "I didn't want to share you."

"But why?"

"Silly goose, because I wanted to be alone with you. In case you haven't realized it yet, I'm quite smitten with you."

Judith tried to remain calm. "Bill, I'm flattered, but you hardly know me."

He put his hand to his heart with a wounded expression. "You don't have to know someone very long to realize how you feel about them. Have you never heard of love at first sight?"

She swallowed the lump that rose in her throat. "Of course I've heard of it." She could hardly bring up the fact that she'd fallen in love with Caleb in the same fashion.

"Well, what else need I say? You've commanded my every thought since the first moment we met. I hope you'll give me a chance to show my devotion to you. I know it may seem silly, but you are already more important to me than anyone else in the world."

"I . . . I don't know what to say."

"Then say nothing. Just indulge me. Let me court you and show you how much you mean to me."

"Bill, we're first cousins." She considered telling him about her feelings for Caleb but decided against it.

"As I mentioned before, that needn't be an issue. If the crown heads of Europe can marry their cousins, I see no reason that it should stop us. Besides, it's perfectly legal."

"Then why is it so frowned upon?"

Bill laughed. "Who can say? The world is full of fools who insist on telling others how to live."

The waiter served the mussels and clams, along with a basket of crusty bread. When he once again departed, Bill raised his wine goblet. "Let's drink to true love. Given time, I'm convinced you will find me the most ardent of suitors."

Judith shook her head. "I don't drink alcohol, Bill. I'm sorry."

He lowered his glass. "It would seem there's a great many things you don't do." He shrugged. "But if I can prove my love for you by showing tolerance, then I will. Perhaps you'll even allow me to be your instructor in some of the unfamiliar ways of your new life."

She didn't know what to say at that. The look he gave her made her feel bare and exposed. She reached for her water glass, determined to hold her own. Unlike her formidable grandmother, who bullied and demanded, Bill used charm and seduction as his weapons. She would have to be on her guard.

The evening passed with Bill sharing stories of their grandmother and her commanding ways, as well as tales of her sister.

"Cora was a very serious person, but at times we coaxed laughter out of her. She loved music, as you already know, but here's something you might not have heard. Cora was very fond of sailing."

"Sailing?" Judith tried to imagine what that would be like. "I've never been."

"I shall remedy that as soon as possible, and you'll see for yourself why she loved it," Bill replied, nodding as the waiter refilled his wine.

After a while, Judith found herself relaxed. She enjoyed the stories Bill told. In the details of his memories, she caught a glimpse of the family she might have known. By the time they left for the concert, she was happy that it was just the two of them.

It startled her to realize some time later, as the orchestra struck up a piece by Handel, that she hadn't really thought about Caleb for most of the evening. This particular song, however, brought him to the foreground of her thoughts. Could there ever be a future for them? After all, he certainly couldn't look down on her social standing—not now that she was a Whitley. With Grandmother's vast fortune and fashionable taste, Judith could surely hold her own in the company of people like Florence Brighton.

As they made their way from the performance, Judith talked easily about the music. "I'm extremely fond of Chopin, but aside from him, Bach and Handel are my favorites. Thank you for bringing me here."

Bill led her to where cars were lined up to receive their passengers. "I'm glad you enjoyed the music. I could see by the look of delight on your face that you were quite happy."

She nodded. "Music has always been important to me. I find my solace there."

"I wish you might try to find your solace in me."

His comment took her by surprise. "How did we go from Bach and Handel to this?" she asked.

Bill helped her into the car and joined her before answering. "I can't help it, Judith." His expression grew serious. "I am in love with you. This evening only served to prove to me that this love is beyond a doubt the real thing." He pressed closer. "I love you."

Judith clasped her gloved hands together. "You've made your feelings clear, so let me be just as honest. I cannot return your feelings. I simply don't feel that way about you."

He moved without warning to pull her into his arms. Judith pushed him away as he tried to press a kiss to her lips. "Bill, please stop. You aren't going to change my mind by trying to force your affections on me."

He fell back against the car seat, dejected. "I'm sorry, Judith. Please forgive me. I just felt overwhelmed by the need to show you how much I adore you."

Judith could see the misery on his face. "I don't want to mislead you, Bill. I had a very nice time with you this evening, but there will never be anything more between us than friendship. I hope you understand."

He nodded. "I suppose I shall have to be satisfied with that. I wouldn't hurt you for the world."

She smiled, feeling that all was back in its proper place. "Thank you, Bill. I'm grateful for your friendship. It keeps me from feeling quite so alone in that big house."

"I don't suppose you'd still like to go dancing?"

Judith shook her head. "I'm exhausted and would prefer to remember that beautiful music as I fall asleep." In a passing streetlight, she could see the disappointment on his face. "But maybe we could go another time. It would be nice to see the kind of places you enjoy and meet your friends. And I loved hearing your stories tonight. I feel I know my family a little better now."

"I'm glad to have pleased you in some way." He straightened

his cuffs. "I'd be happy to take you out again and regale you with my memories. Grandmother will have us busy the rest of the week with various dinners and such, so perhaps next week we might venture out again."

"That sounds just fine."

He turned to gaze out his window. He was clearly unhappy, and there was nothing she could do to ease his discontent. She turned to look out her own window. She had little desire to be with Bill or meet his friends. Every minute with him only served to remind her of how much she longed to be with Caleb.

Why couldn't things be different? Why couldn't it be Caleb trying to steal a kiss and pledge his undying love? She sighed and closed her eyes. Love at first sight, it would seem, was far more painful than pleasurable.

CHAPTER

20

*J*ust before nine o'clock, Caleb was ushered into an office in the Whitley mansion. The room was large and filled with extravagant displays. Clark Whitley had been known for many things, among them his love of hunting. He had gone on multiple safaris abroad, and the trophies from his trips were prominently displayed in the room.

"You must be Caleb Coulter," an older, stately man declared. He came forward and extended his hand. "I'm Mathias Pettyjohn, the Whitley family solicitor."

"I'm pleased to meet you. I represent Miss Judith Whitley's interests."

The man gave him a weak handshake and a tolerant smile. "Yes, well, Miss Whitley's future interests will be handled by me at the request of her grandmother, Mrs. Ann Whitley."

"If Miss Whitley agrees to that, I will offer no objection." Caleb returned the lawyer's smile. "If she is not in agreement, however, I will not allow her to be forced into such an arrangement."

Mr. Pettyjohn took a step back as if Caleb had struck him. He had no chance to comment, however, because Mrs. Whitley and Judith appeared at the door. Caleb's breath caught at the sight of Judith. She was more beautiful than he remembered, and he'd just seen her.

"I'm glad to see you are both prompt," Mrs. Whitley said, sweeping into the room.

Judith hurried to Caleb's side. Her elegant day dress of pale pink and lace seemed delicate and appropriate for her beauty. "I'm so glad you came. Thank you."

Caleb grinned. "I will always come when you need me." His heart seemed to pound all the harder. Could she hear it?

Mrs. Whitley gave a soft harrumph. "Let us get right to business. Mr. Pettyjohn, you may take the seat behind Mr. Whitley's desk. We will sit here in front of you while you speak on the matter of Judith's inheritance."

Mr. Pettyjohn nodded, then picked up the satchel at his feet and made his way to the desk.

Caleb offered Judith his arm and escorted her to a high-backed sofa done in red leather and framed in mahogany. He sat down beside her, feeling almost giddy at her nearness. He had missed her more than he'd allowed himself to believe.

Mrs. Whitley sat in one of two matching wingback chairs. She seemed out of sorts at the chummy way Caleb and Judith acted. It made him all the more determined to remain at Judith's side.

He smiled at Mrs. Whitley. "That is an impressive desk. Ebony, I believe?"

"Yes." She looked at him for a moment, then shrugged. "Mr. Whitley had it made from a tree he came across while in Africa."

Mr. Pettyjohn cleared his throat. "If you are ready for me to begin, I will get right to the heart of the matter."

"Yes, please do. I have a headache, so the sooner we are concluded, the better."

Mr. Pettyjohn nodded and drew several papers from his satchel. "As I mentioned before, Mrs. Whitley, the matter of Judith's inheritance is rather well documented. Her father, Nelson Whitley, made provision for Judith should she be found. As you know, upon his death and the death of his wife and daughter Cora, the entirety of his estate was left to you with the provision that should Judith be found and there be no question to her identity, his fortune would then go to her."

"There is no question as to her identity," Mrs. Whitley stated. She looked at Judith and smiled. "She is an identical twin of her sister, as I'm sure even you can attest to."

The lawyer nodded. "Yes, the resemblance is uncanny. There is no doubt she is Judith Whitley."

"And was the question of her identity the only condition upon which the release of the inheritance would be made?" Caleb questioned.

Mr. Pettyjohn nodded again. "With exception to her age. She was to be of legal majority. Otherwise her inheritance was to be held in trust by her grandmother until she turned twenty-one."

"She is twenty-four, so there is no question of that condition being met," her grandmother declared. "I have no desire to keep her fortune from her, but I do wish her to be willing to allow me to help direct her in its use. She knows nothing about the businesses, stocks, bonds, and so forth that Nelson invested in and owned. As I understand it, she grew up in poverty and has no understanding of any such financial dealings."

"It is understandable that the child—er, the young woman will be in need of guidance—of a teacher," Mr. Pettyjohn confirmed.

"I agree," Caleb said, looking at Judith. "But I believe the choice of teacher should be Judith's."

"She can hardly know what's best in such a matter," Mrs. Whitley said, raising her chin.

"You all speak of me as if I weren't here," Judith interjected. "I do understand that I need help in this. I'm happy to take your guidance, Grandmother, but I would also like Caleb to be a part of this as well."

"You scarcely know Mr. Coulter," the older woman protested, "and while I have had his situation looked into, he is hardly used to handling a fortune of the size you are to inherit."

"Mrs. Whitley," Caleb interjected, "I feel confident that we can work together to a mutually agreeable outcome. I have no desire to commandeer Judith's wealth nor to see her led astray. I don't even desire to usurp your authority in matters of your family's investments. However, I am a lawyer and a friend. I can offer Judith my opinion and support."

The grand lady stiffened. "She has Mr. Pettyjohn for legal opinions."

Mr. Pettyjohn nodded enthusiastically.

"Stop it!" Judith held up her hands. "Grandmother, we have spoken about this before. I won't be dictated to. I want very much to be a part of this family, but I will not be held hostage. Caleb is my dearest friend and a fine lawyer. I trust and admire him more than anyone on this earth."

Caleb felt his chest tighten at her words of defense. When she looked at him and smiled, it was nearly his undoing.

"I want Caleb to have access to all of the supporting documents related to my inheritance," Judith continued. "If that is unacceptable to you, then I will pack my things and return with him to my previous home."

He was so proud of her. She had been such a mousey thing when he'd first met her. Shy and demure, almost fragile. Now, however, Judith was able to stand her own ground, and Mrs.

Whitley, while clearly frustrated, also seemed to have a certain admiration for her granddaughter.

"There is no need for dramatics, Judith. I simply want to guard you from . . . well, let us say from those who might seek to benefit themselves. I do not believe Mr. Coulter is one of those people, however, and so I will not object to his being involved in this matter." She held up her hand. "So long as you allow me to speak my mind and help you."

Judith settled back. "Of course, Grandmother. I wouldn't have expected otherwise."

The meeting went on for another hour, with Mr. Pettyjohn giving a brief list of properties, industries, stock, bonds, and other investments that made up the bulk of Judith's inheritance. She was now a very wealthy young woman, and Caleb could easily see Mrs. Whitley's concerns.

When they reached the end of the meeting, Mr. Pettyjohn promised to have copies of the will and other details brought to Caleb by courier later that day. Mrs. Whitley announced that she had some personal business to discuss with her lawyer, so Caleb led Judith from the room.

Once they were in the hall, Judith took his hand. "Come, I want to show you the gardens."

He held fast to her hand, surprised but no less delighted at her touch. "I'm proud of how you handled yourself in there."

She looked up and smiled. "I couldn't have done it without you. Thank you for coming here and being my defender."

"You hardly needed one. You're very capable of dealing with your grandmother. It's clear she respects that, even if she doesn't like it."

"I've had to constantly remind her that it's easy enough for me to pack up and leave. Especially now that I have a bit of money to my name."

"A bit?" He chuckled. "That's an understatement."

She led him across the hall and into a sitting room that Caleb had not yet seen. Without stopping, she drew him to the open French doors and outside. "Next to the music room, this is my favorite place," she announced. "I like to come out here and just walk the garden paths and pray."

Caleb glanced around and smiled. "It is lovely—peaceful too. I can see why you like it."

Judith dropped his hand, and the loss was immediate. Caleb frowned. Maybe he should just tell her what was going through his mind. Tell her that he'd come to care for her in the way a suitor might, rather than just a friend. But what of her money? Would she think he was making his declaration simply because she was an heiress?

"Grandmother has given me everything I could ask for. I have an entire wing of the second floor to myself. She's encouraged me to make it over in my own colors and styles, but I think it's just fine the way it is. My mother—Edith was the one who decorated it, and I feel somehow connected to her in keeping it as it is."

"I can understand that." Caleb kept pace with her and battled his emotions. "I know I've asked you this before, but . . . are you happy?"

Judith stopped and turned. Her expression was puzzled. "I don't think I would exactly call it happiness. I was much happier living at your house with Camri and Kenzie . . . and of course you and Mr. and Mrs. Wong and Liling. We were like a little family." She shrugged. "My uncle doesn't seem to know what to make of me. I always feel like he's seeing a ghost when he looks at me. My cousin Victoria hates me and makes no pretense about it, while her brother Bill declares himself madly in love with me. Love at first sight." She seemed suddenly uncomfortable and began to walk again.

Bill was in love with her? That hardly made sense. From what Caleb had learned, he was a notorious bachelor. He was known to escort as many as five different girls in a week to various functions. Now he declared himself head over heels in love with his cousin?

" . . . but so long as there aren't any more snakes in my bed and Grandmother learns that she can't run my life, I suppose happiness will eventually come."

Caleb was the one who stopped this time. He caught Judith's arm. "Snakes? What are you talking about?"

"I was just as surprised as you sound. We often dealt with rattlesnakes back home, but I hadn't expected to find one in a house of this grandeur."

"A rattlesnake was in your bed?" A wave of fear washed over him. "Judith, that isn't natural. It doesn't happen here."

"Well, it did. I'm not making this up. I was in my room, ready for my afternoon rest, when I saw something moving under the covers and the snake appeared."

Caleb shook his head. "What did you do?"

She gave a little laugh. "I did what my mother and father taught me to do. I captured him and killed him."

"You?"

She looked at him as if it were the most natural thing in the world. "Yes. There was hardly time to get anyone else, especially without leaving the room, and I wasn't about to lose track of where he was. I took the fireplace tongs and poker and managed it all quite easily." She paused, and her brow furrowed as her eyes narrowed. "What do you mean that it doesn't happen here?"

"I mean that snake was put there by someone who meant to do you harm. I'm sure of it. Snakes don't just slither into the houses of the very wealthy." He took hold of her shoulders.

"Judith, someone was obviously trying to scare you off." *Or kill you.* He left the latter unspoken.

"Probably Victoria. She hates me. Apparently she hated Cora too. Grandmother said she and Cora were always rivals. She probably meant it to scare me and make me leave. She doesn't want me here, that's for sure."

"Did you tell your grandmother about the snake?"

"No." Judith didn't try to move away from him. "I had forgotten about it. I know that sounds silly, but I've killed a great number of rattlesnakes, and this one was just one more. When I went down to dinner that evening, it never came to mind."

Caleb didn't think. He pulled her close and held her tight for a moment. She could have been killed. Might be killed yet. Someone wished her harm. That much was certain.

"Umm, Caleb," she barely whispered.

"Yes?"

"You're squeezing the breath . . . out of me."

He let her go. "I'm sorry. I shouldn't have done that, but the thought of you coming to harm was more than I could bear. You're in danger here. Maybe you should come home with me."

"Danger?" She shook her head. "It was probably just a joke. Although, I can't imagine Victoria having anything to do with a snake. Of course, she probably paid one of the servants to put it there."

"It doesn't matter who put it there or how they did it, this is serious."

Judith nodded. "I see that now." She bit her lower lip.

"I couldn't bear it if something happened to you. Camri and Kenzie would never forgive me. Are you sure I can't convince you to come back with me? I know your grandmother would be furious, but we can tell her why."

"No. If Victoria was responsible, it will just make her hate me all the more. I have a key to my rooms. I'll start locking my door. That way only Sarah will be able to get in. She's my lady's maid and certainly has no reason to hate me."

"You don't know that, Judith. You can't be sure who is responsible. Keep this in mind: If you die, then everything goes back to the way things were before you came. The fortune stays with Mrs. Whitley, which in turn no doubt will go to her son and his children. This could be about nothing more complicated than greed."

*J*udith sat at the garden table, glancing overhead. The skies were cloudy, but thankfully the rain held off. She leaned her elbows on the linen tablecloth and pressed her fingertips to her temples, silently praying for her headache to cease. Ever since Caleb had convinced her that someone meant to harm her, she had been unable to shake the vice-like grip that pressed against her head.

Caleb had said that most likely someone wanted her dead due to greed. The thought so upset her that she'd been unable to eat much at the lavish supper party they'd attended the evening before. Even this morning at breakfast, her food had sat like a brick in her stomach.

"Why are you sitting out here all alone, and with rain threatening?" Bill asked, joining her.

Judith lowered her hands and forced a smile. "I like the gardens."

He pulled out a chair and sat down at the table. "I've ordered coffee. I do hope you'll join me."

"I suppose I can, but what brings you here? I thought you had business down at the shipping offices."

"I did." He shrugged. "I met with my managers and told them what I expected, then brought home the books to review here."

"I see. I suppose that is one of the privileges of being the owner." She smiled and brushed back an errant strand of hair.

"Being a Whitley has its privileges in every way, but I think you're already coming to see that."

She shook her head. "It seems to me that there are far more headaches to being a Whitley than privileges."

He laughed and patted her hand. "I'm sure it's daunting when you aren't used to it. Ah, here comes our coffee."

A footman brought out a tray and placed it in the center of the table. "I'm sorry, sir, but I didn't realize Miss Judith would be joining you. I'll bring another setting."

He left in a hurry while Bill picked up the silver coffeepot. "I believe if you look under that cloth, you'll find some of Cook's cinnamon rolls. He's a phenomenal baker, but I think his sweet rolls are the best."

Judith lifted the cloth, and as he said, there were several iced rolls. "They smell wonderful."

"They are. You must have one. Why don't you help yourself while I pour the coffee?"

The footman brought another cup and saucer as well as another serving plate. Judith occupied herself with sampling the roll while Bill prepared their coffee.

"Do you take cream and sugar?" he asked.

"Yes, please." She picked up her fork and took a bite of the roll. She was relieved that Bill wasn't bringing up his love for her. Hopefully he understood her position and would be a gentleman about it.

"Do you like the cinnamon roll? I think the icing is my favorite. Cook puts some kind of creamed cheese in it."

"It's very good, but I'm afraid I've not been very hungry."

"I noticed that you ate next to nothing at breakfast. You aren't coming down with something, are you?"

"I don't think so." She touched her hand to her head. "Although I do have a headache." She hadn't considered the possibility that she might be ill. She took the cup and saucer he handed her and sipped the coffee. The warm liquid seemed to settle her stomach. "This is good."

Bill smiled and tasted his own. "It is. Grandmother buys a special blend from South America."

"I've only ever had the tea." Judith took another sip, then put the cup back on the saucer. "Bill, I wonder if I might ask you a question."

"Of course. Anything." He sat back and drew his cup to his lips.

"Well, I wondered . . . and please don't think badly of me for asking, but why is Victoria so hateful toward me? I've done nothing to deserve her bitterness."

He shook his head. "Don't give Vicky any thought. She's a spoiled brat. She always has been. She was Mother's little darling who could do no wrong. Grandmother didn't approve of the way our mother dealt with Vicky and made that clear."

"How old was Victoria when your mother died?"

"Only four. It was difficult for her. I was just eight."

"I'm sure it couldn't have been easy for either of you."

"No," Bill replied, his expression saddening. "It was a tremendous loss in my life." He took a long drink.

"I'm sorry to bring up painful memories. It's just that this entire matter has me perplexed. Grandmother said that Victoria didn't like Cora either. You said as much in your stories too."

247

"No, Victoria didn't like Cora, despite Cora liking her very much. I think she thought of Vicky like a new baby doll. Of course, she adored your little brothers. Mothered them something fierce. But I think she favored Vicky." Bill shrugged. "However, I believe Nurse always made it clear that Cora was her favorite, and Vicky couldn't abide that."

"Was she the same nurse who was there when I was taken?"

He considered the question for a moment. "I can't be certain, but she might have been. It would account for her favoring Cora. Still, she wasn't around for long. Shortly before our mother died, she was dismissed."

"For what reason?"

"Vicky, of course. She told our mother that Nurse had done horrible things to her. Tied her to a chair and forced her to take some awful medicine. None of the rest of us were around to witness it, but Mother believed Vicky and insisted the woman be fired."

"And without any proof, she was let go?"

"The proof was Vicky's word against hers." He cocked his head slightly to the right. "You must understand, in this family, a Whitley's word will always hold more weight than anyone else's."

"I see." Judith could well imagine that Victoria learned this early on and used it to her advantage.

A wave of dizziness washed over her. She closed her eyes as the pain in her head increased.

"Are you all right?"

"It's probably nothing." She opened her eyes, relieved that the world had righted itself.

"There is a bit of influenza going around. Someone mentioned it last night at the dinner. You might have a touch of that."

"I hope not. I don't want to ruin Easter for Grandmother. She has a great many plans for me."

"Indeed she does, and Easter is only the beginning. She's planning to host a debut for you next month. It will be quite the rage, and everyone in the city will be vying for an invitation. Watching San Francisco's social elite work to earn our grandmother's favor can be highly amusing."

Judith tried to smile, but the dizziness was back. "I'm sorry, Bill. I think I'll retire to my room. I wouldn't want to expose you if I've managed to catch-sick."

She got up and held on to the table for a moment while the world spun.

Bill stood and took hold of her arm. "I'll help you upstairs."

"Oh, that isn't necessary. I'm sure I'll be all right." She turned to leave, but her knees gave way.

Bill caught her and lifted her into his arms. "You aren't all right." His expression was filled with grave concern. "I'll get you upstairs and then have Ramsay ring for the doctor."

He carried her into the house, and Judith felt so weak that she did nothing but close her eyes and hold on to him.

"What's this?" Grandmother asked.

Judith opened her eyes. "I'm afraid I'm not well."

"She might have that influenza that's going around," Bill added.

"Oh, dear. I'll have Ramsay get the doctor. Bill, you put her right to bed, and I'll ring for Sarah to see to her."

He nodded and headed for the stairs. "What did she think I was going to do, deposit you on the steps?"

Judith couldn't help but smile. "She lives to order people around."

Chuckling, Bill started up the stairs. Judith looked down, feeling even more dizzy. She prayed he wouldn't drop her and held on a little tighter.

"Don't worry. You don't weigh anything at all. I won't lose my grip." He smiled down at her. "Besides, this is rather pleasant. I like holding you."

She didn't have the energy to argue with him. Her head hurt worse than ever, and the dizziness was coming in regular waves.

Sarah met them at her suite door. "Mrs. Whitley said you were sick."

Judith nodded. "I'm afraid so." She handed Sarah the room key. "Here."

"What's that for?" Bill asked. "Why have you locked your room?"

"It's a long story. I'm afraid I'm not up to the telling."

His brows knit together, and his eyes narrowed, but he said nothing. Judith wondered if he would tell Grandmother what she'd done, but her physical miseries didn't allow her to dwell on the matter.

Within twenty minutes, the doctor arrived and examined her. He was an older man—probably as old as Grandmother. He poked at her and listened to her heart, then looked into her eyes and throat before stirring up some sort of concoction in a glass of water.

"You need to drink this," he instructed.

Judith found it difficult to even hold the glass, but she did as he commanded, then fell back against the pillow. The room tilted back and forth in rhythm to the pounding pain in her head.

"I wouldn't worry," he told Grandmother, who had refused to leave Judith's side. "I'll leave some of these powders for her. Give her tea and toast, but nothing else until I see her tomorrow." He took the glass from Judith and placed it on the nightstand.

"Can she have sugar in her tea?" Grandmother asked, looking down at Judith. "She enjoys her tea with sugar."

"Of course. I think that's just fine. I find sugar can have

curative powers." The old bearded man put his instruments back into his black bag.

Judith was glad when Grandmother instructed Sarah to show him out. She instantly fell asleep.

———

Camri pulled on her gloves. "Caleb saw Judith Monday, and she was fine, but I haven't heard anything from her since. When I called, they wouldn't let me talk to her, so I don't think we have a choice."

"I know, but couldn't we wait for Caleb?" Kenzie asked.

"I know Caleb wanted to go yesterday, but his business with Spreckels and Judge Winters has kept him busy all week. I would have asked Patrick, but he's been working night and day on the warehouse."

"I suppose we might as well go, then."

Camri secured her hat with a long pin. "I feel we must. Something may be wrong, and we certainly don't want to wait."

"I can't imagine her not contacting us," Kenzie said, adjusting her hat.

"Well, I'm glad you're coming with me. I know you must be tired after working all day, but I'd rather there be two of us. Strength in numbers, you know."

Kenzie gave a slight nod. "I have the rest of the week off for Good Friday and Easter. Cousin George was planning to use the time to go over all the wiring in the factory. He's such a worrywart. But I suppose we're all doing a great deal of fretting."

"Perhaps, but I don't think it's unmerited in our case."

Camri knew from Caleb that Mrs. Whitley was becoming more and more demanding of Judith. She knew too that Judith had threatened to up and leave if Mrs. Whitley didn't allow her more say. A woman like Mrs. Whitley wouldn't like being dictated to, and if Judith continued to hold her ground, Camri feared Mrs. Whitley might very well seek to impose her will upon Judith.

She and Kenzie walked the hilly distance to the Whitley mansion in silence. Both were worried and knew that speaking about it would only make matters worse. Camri thought of the first time they'd met Judith at the railway station in Denver. She was so quiet and confused by the city. Camri feared she might never have found her train, much less her way in San Francisco, had it not been for their help.

Camri rang the bell, and after a lengthy wait was about to ring again when the butler opened the door.

"We're here to see Judith," Camri declared.

The butler frowned. "Mistress Judith is ill, as is Mrs. Whitley and Master Bill. I'm afraid we cannot allow anyone to visit. The doctor has ordered no visitors. He believes it could be highly contagious."

Camri shook her head. "What's wrong with them?"

"The doctor is uncertain."

"If that's the case, then perhaps there isn't the risk he suspects."

The butler gave her a blank look. Camri could see that he wasn't going to allow them entry and that further arguments weren't going to sway him.

"Very well. I'll check on her tomorrow." She saw Kenzie open her mouth to speak, but Camri smiled and pulled her away from the door. "Don't say anything," she whispered.

They were halfway down the drive before Camri let go of Kenzie's arm. "I think they're hiding something."

"Then why didn't you insist we be allowed in?"

"They're a powerful family. No doubt they have more than enough servants to keep us out. I think we need to tell Caleb what's going on and let him handle it. Maybe he and Micah can come. After all, Micah is a doctor, and Caleb is Judith's lawyer. Caleb can insist and no doubt gain entry."

"I hope you're right."

"I can't imagine that he would let the matter go. He cares very much for Judith, whether he'll admit it or not."

"He does?" Kenzie looked at her in wonder. "That's good, because Judith is head over heels in love with him."

"How do you know that?"

"She told me. It was love at first sight. She completely lost her heart."

That brought a smile to Camri's face. Her biggest concern was that Caleb's feelings would never be returned. "Well, that's a huge relief. I can't believe I didn't see it. I mean, I've always thought she would make someone a wonderful wife. I probably even considered the two of them to be well suited, but this is welcome news."

"So long as she recovers. What if Judith is desperately ill?" Kenzie asked. "There has been an awful lot of sickness going around."

Camri nodded. "Once we get Caleb and Micah involved, we're sure to get to the bottom of it."

22

W'e're here to see Judith." Caleb met the butler's blank stare. "This is Dr. Fisher, her personal physician, and as you know, I am her lawyer. I insist we be allowed to see her."

"I cannot admit you, sir. The doctor is concerned about the contagiousness of the illness."

"But I am a physician," Micah protested. "I take these risks all the time, and Mr. Coulter is aware of the situation."

Caleb frowned at the butler. "I can return with an order from the court." He wasn't entirely sure that could be done, since it was Good Friday, but he felt compelled to threaten it nevertheless.

"That won't be needed," another man said, coming to door. "Ramsay, go about your work. I will show the gentlemen to Judith's room. I'm her uncle, William Whitley."

Caleb considered the stocky but fashionably dressed man. William Whitley bore the trappings of wealth, but his demeanor was far less intimidating than most of those Caleb had met.

255

"Thank you, Mr. Whitley. I'm concerned about Judith's health, and Dr. Fisher has treated her before. He's familiar with her, and it would be a relief to us, her friends, to have him confirm your physician's diagnosis."

"I can understand that." William led them upstairs. "My own son, Bill, was sick for a couple of days, but he's much improved. I'm hopeful the same will be true for Judith."

"And your mother?"

William stopped at the top of the stairs. "My mother is quite old, and the doctor informs me she wasn't in the best of health even prior to this. Of course, she didn't bother to tell us. She has to have her secrets." He started walking again and led them to the left. "This is Judith's suite." He knocked on the door.

A maid dressed in a uniform of black and white appeared. "Yes, Mr. Whitley?"

"Judith's lawyer and physician have come to see her." He turned to Caleb and Micah. "This is Judith's maid, Miss Linde."

She pushed up her gold-rimmed glasses. "Please come in."

Caleb could see evidence of the Whitley fortune in the furnishings and art. This room had once belonged to Judith's parents, as he understood it.

Sarah crossed to Judith's bed. "Miss Judith, your lawyer and doctor are here to see you."

Caleb was alarmed at how pale and sickly Judith looked. Her face was gaunt, and there were dark circles around her eyes. He wanted nothing more than to pull her into his arms and carry her away to safety.

"Judith, my dear," Caleb said, bending over her, "I've brought Micah to see what he can do for you."

"Caleb." She barely whispered his name. "I'm sorry to be a bother."

He smiled and brushed back her lifeless hair. "You aren't a bother."

Micah examined Judith, listening to her heart and asking her questions. Caleb found himself holding Judith's hand, not even realizing he'd taken hold of it until he was pressing it to his cheek.

"How did this come upon you, Judith?" Micah asked.

"I had a headache . . . and nausea, and then it got worse with dizziness and body pain. The other doctor said influenza is going around, and. . . ."

"There have been some cases," Micah agreed. He looked at Caleb. "Maybe we could move her to the hospital so I could run tests."

"No."

Caleb and Micah turned to find William Whitley at the door. "Bill has already recovered, and I'm certain our Judith will as well. My mother has strictly forbidden her to be taken to the hospital. She says such places are where people go to die, and she won't have it. I won't have it either. My wife died in a hospital fifteen years ago. The things they put her through . . . well, it was hideous." His expression was sorrowful.

"It's not entirely up to you to decide," Caleb said, standing. He still held fast to Judith's hand.

"I understand your misgivings about hospitals," Micah said, "but you must remember that the hospital of the 1800s is hardly the hospital of today. Today's hospitals are vastly improved and boast operating theatres that save more lives than they lose. We can run tests on the blood and—"

"No. I won't allow her to be tortured." The older man shook his head. "She's not worsening, so I believe she's on the mend. I will bring in a nurse, if that gives you additional comfort, and you may come whenever you like, but I won't allow you to take her to a hospital."

Caleb let go of Judith and shot across the room. He grabbed Whitley by the lapels of his suit. "And I won't have you—"

"Caleb!" Micah was immediately at his side. "Calm down. Judith is stable for the time. Let's check on her again later this evening—if that would be acceptable to you, Mr. Whitley?"

The older man looked terrified, and Caleb felt a rush of shame. He let go of the suit. "I'm sorry, Mr. Whitley. I'm just worried about Judith."

William Whitley nodded and took a step back. "It's all right. I understand." He looked at Micah. "You're both welcome to return. I give you my word that you'll be allowed to visit her whenever you like."

Micah smiled. "Good. Then I will return around six. Meanwhile, would you like me to look in on your mother as well?"

He shook his head. "No. Mother would never hear of it. She'll probably be cross with me for allowing you to visit Judith. She's rather set in her ways."

Caleb rolled his eyes. "That's putting it mildly."

William gave a hint of a smile. "It is, but I'm trying to be a respectful son." He was clearly used to cowering under her rule, and Caleb couldn't help but feel sympathy for him.

Micah went back to Judith and gathered his things. "Come say your farewells, Caleb, and we'll be off."

Caleb didn't want to leave Judith, but he knew social rules would not allow him to remain at her bedside. He fought back words of protest.

"Judith?"

Her eyes fluttered open. "Caleb?"

"I'm here. Look, Micah and I have to go, but we'll be back this evening."

"Don't go," she barely whispered. "Please."

Caleb looked at Micah. How could he leave when she was pleading with him to stay?

"Judith, you can't expect Mr. Coulter and the doctor to remain at your bedside indefinitely," Whitley said, coming closer.

"What's this, then?" Bill Whitley called from the doorway. He wore a dark blue dressing gown, and his hair was mussed, as if he'd just awakened. "Vicky told me we had company."

"It's nothing you need to worry about," his father replied. "Mr. Coulter and Dr. Fisher came to check on Judith."

Caleb found the young man watching him intently. Knowing that Bill had declared himself in love with Judith didn't endear him to Caleb. Not one bit.

"I understand you had this ailment," Micah said, moving toward Bill.

"I did." Bill smiled. "I'm mostly recovered now, however. I'm sure it'll just be a matter of days until Judith and Grandmother are on the mend."

"Did you have the same degree of sickness?" Micah asked.

"I did. It was something fierce. I hurt all over, especially my head. And when I tried to eat, I threw it all back up. Dr. Barringer said it was typical of influenza. It seems sleep was the best thing for recovery."

Micah turned back to the elder Whitley. "Do me a favor. I want to speak to Dr. Barringer about this matter. Until then, don't give her anything more by mouth. No medicines or teas. Not even water. It'll just be for a few hours, but I want to try a new medication when I return, and she needs to have a completely empty stomach. Understand?"

"Of course," William declared. "I'll let her maid know."

"Good. I feel certain we'll have Judith on her feet again soon." Micah smiled and gave the older man a nod.

William wrung his hands together. "She must get better. We've only just had her returned to us. My brother would never forgive me if I didn't do everything in my power to help her."

"But your brother is dead and gone." Caleb shook his head. "He's far beyond caring about such things."

"You don't know my brother," William replied. "And if his ghost doesn't haunt me for my failures, then Mother would surely do the job. And in truth, I doubt I could forgive myself."

Caleb could see he was sincere. Any misgivings Caleb might have had about Judith's uncle were lessened considerably.

"Father is right. We'll do whatever we can to see her well again," Bill added. He gazed at Judith with such concern that even Micah was apparently moved.

"I'm touched at how much you both care. I feel better knowing she'll have constant supervision," Micah said. "We'll be back soon, and hopefully we shall find her improved."

William called for Sarah and gave her strict orders for Judith before leading Caleb and Micah back downstairs. He spoke in hushed tones with Micah all the way. It truly appeared his concern for Judith and his mother was genuine.

Caleb thought of the rattlesnake and his fears that William might be trying to rid himself of Judith. But he didn't seem capable of such things. Maybe it was Bill or his sister. They had as much to lose as their father did.

On their way back to Caleb's house, Micah was quiet. Caleb thought perhaps he was upset at Caleb's violent reaction.

"I'm sorry for losing my temper. I hope you aren't holding it against me," Caleb began. "I just didn't like the way he seemed determined to keep us from caring for Judith."

"I couldn't hold that against you. You're in love with her," Micah said with a chuckle. "I would expect nothing less."

"Love?" Caleb glanced at Micah, then quickly looked back at the road. "Why do you say that?"

"Good grief, man, the way you held her hand. The way you spoke to her. If you don't propose and marry her, you're an idiot."

"I'm so afraid she's going to die."

"I am too, but I can't figure out what's wrong with her. That's why I would have liked to have seen her grandmother as well."

"What do you suspect?" Caleb could hear the worry in Micah's tone. It didn't bode well.

"I don't know, but there are clear indicators that it isn't influenza. She has no fever, for one thing, and her pupils are dilated. Of course, that could be due to the medication given to her by Dr. Barringer. I will consult with him before we head back."

"Is that why you were eager to go?"

Micah nodded. "I need to know more before I can figure out what's really going on."

"Poor Judith," Camri said after hearing all that Caleb had to tell. "Isn't there something we could do? Perhaps sit with her to give the rest of the staff a break?"

"I suppose we could ask," Kenzie said. "I don't have to be back at work until Tuesday. Cousin George called earlier and said he was taking an extra day to work on the machines. I'd be happy to sit with her."

"You'd make a wonderful nurse, I'm sure," Micah said with a wink. "But let me consult with Dr. Barringer first. I shouldn't be gone long. Want to walk me out, Kenzie?"

Kenzie looked away, clearly annoyed.

Camri shook her head. "You two are such a bother."

Micah laughed and left.

Caleb looked at his sister and then to Patrick. "You said you had something to tell me when I was leaving with Micah earlier."

Patrick nodded. "I wanted to report to ye on the warehouse, but it can wait."

Caleb shook his head and took off his suit coat. "No, it'll help me to have something else to consider."

"Well, then, I've removed the damaged portions of wall and replaced them. I'll be puttin' in some additional supports as well. I'm thinkin' we should be havin' a plumber come in to consult with me, as well as an electrical man. Both of those things will cost plenty. Especially if Ruef catches wind of what we're doin'."

Caleb tossed his coat over the back of a chair. "Talk to Judge Winters about it on Monday. He knows men who have come over to our side of things. I'm sure he can point you in the right direction."

"Aye. I'll be seein' to it after the holiday." Patrick glanced at Camri, who was pouring herself a cup of tea. "And ye should be knowin' that yer sister has ideas for the furnishin' of the place."

"She's always got an idea about something." Caleb plopped down in his favorite chair by the fireplace. Despite telling Patrick he needed to focus on something other than Judith, he didn't want to think about the warehouse. The entire project seemed so unimportant with Judith's life hanging in the balance.

"I have some very good ideas." Camri crossed the room with her teacup and saucer in hand. "I've made some calls. I've found us an industrial-sized stove for a greatly reduced price. It's not new, but it's in perfect condition. It will be exactly what we'll need for the kitchen."

"So buy it, then. I told you that you could arrange to purchase whatever was needed and have me billed."

"And so I have," Camri replied. "I arranged to have it delivered tomorrow."

"How did you manage that with it being Easter weekend?" Caleb asked.

"Not everyone cares that it's Easter," she replied.

"But we do, and therefore I think it inconsiderate for us to put others to work on a holiday."

"I tried to tell her the same," Patrick said, taking a seat on the sofa. "But ye know yer sister."

"Indeed, I do." Caleb looked at Camri, who sat sipping her tea as if nothing were amiss. "So the stove will be delivered tomorrow. Is that all you wished to tell me?"

"Well, not exactly. I've been busy all week making calls." She smiled and put the cup and saucer on the table to her left. "I've arranged for two dozen cots, three tables, and eighteen chairs to be delivered Monday. There will also be several crates of blankets, pillows, bedding, dishes, and three bathtubs."

"Only three?" Caleb couldn't keep the sarcasm from his tone.

"Well, until we speak with the plumber, I thought it best to wait. I'd like to have six separate bathrooms installed. I arranged for six toilets to be delivered, but then Patrick pointed out that we know nothing about the sewer lines, so I thought perhaps I should wait on doing more."

"And what is all of this costing me?"

Camri smiled. "The receipts are all on your desk. You said there was plenty of money and not to worry about the cost, so I didn't."

Patrick laughed. "Never tell a woman not to worry about the cost. Especially yer sister. It's expensive taste she has, and soon ye'll find her orderin' china and silver tea services."

"Don't be ridiculous, Patrick. I'm only purchasing the minimal that I believe will be useful to us. It's just to get us started.

I've still got to arrange for cupboards for the kitchen as well as iceboxes."

"I can build the cupboards," Patrick offered. "No sense payin' a fortune for somethin' fancy. Besides, I thought we were still waitin' for some sort of approval from the Board of Supervisors."

"All the permits and approvals have been put in Judge Winters' hands. We can check with him on Monday and see what he's managed to come up with. I think since Frederick Johnston has come on board to help us, along with all the other support we can muster from the men working to end Ruef's control, there won't be too much trouble."

"I hope not," Camri said, smiling. "I'm so excited to see our project completed. I even noticed that the property just to the south of ours looked abandoned. Maybe we could speak to someone about it."

Caleb shook his head. "Slow down, Camri. Let us accomplish one thing at a time. Frankly, until I know more about Judith's condition, I have little interest in any of this." He got to his feet. "I'm sorry."

He walked from the room and made his way to his office. Once there, he sat down at his desk and buried his face in his hands. For the first time in a great long while, he actually felt close to tears.

"Lord, please help us—please help Judith."

CHAPTER

23

*S*ince you mentioned the incident with the snake," Micah
said later that day, "I've been inclined toward a thought
regarding Judith's condition."

"You think she's been bitten?" Caleb asked.

"No. I'm wondering if she's been poisoned."

"But her grandmother and Bill took sick as well."

Micah shrugged. "You mentioned Victoria Whitley hating
Judith. Perhaps she hates her grandmother and brother as
well."

Fear spread through Caleb like wildfire. "Then we have to
get her out of there. We'll take her by force if necessary."

Micah held up his hands. "Calm down. Listen to me. That's
why I told them to give her nothing by mouth."

"So you don't have some new medicine to offer?"

"No, but if someone is slipping her poison in her tea, then
being without it for several hours may show us some improve-
ment. If it's poison, it's being administered in small doses over
time to affect the look of sickness rather than sudden death.
It would be much harder to explain sudden death in someone

as young and healthy as Judith. But even if it isn't poison, the medication Dr. Barringer left for her has properties that cause symptoms of its own. I want to examine Judith without its effects."

Caleb paced like a caged animal. "I still think it would be better to remove her. We could take Patrick with us. He could probably take on anyone who might try to stop us."

"I don't know that it's come to that. Besides, if she's being poisoned and we remove her, it might just happen again when she returned."

"I won't let her return."

"Caleb, we need to take this one step at a time. We don't even know that she's being poisoned or is in any real danger. It could be just as Dr. Barringer believes—an influenza of some type. We need to remain calm."

"I don't feel at all calm."

"Look, after speaking with Dr. Barringer, I'm fairly certain Mrs. Whitley's condition is grave. He told me he's tried to convince William to move her to the hospital, but he won't allow it. The doctor plans to speak to William again this afternoon. I thought we could go earlier than six and hopefully arrive before he left. With his encouragement and support, we might be able to move them both."

"All right. When do you want to go?"

Micah looked at his pocket watch. "I'd say in an hour. Dr. Barringer said he'd be there around four thirty. He should still be there at five."

Caleb wasn't sure he could stand to wait until five. If someone was poisoning Judith, he wanted to act swiftly.

"We need to say nothing about the idea of them being poisoned," Micah warned. "Whoever is doing this—if it is poisoning—will only find another way of attack. We need some proof. If we can lay our hands on some of the tea Judith's being given, then perhaps we can test our theory."

"I never should have let her go." Caleb went to his study window and looked out on the day. "None of this would have happened if we'd made her stay."

"And how would you have done that? Locked her in her room? She's a Whitley, Caleb. She has every bit as much right to live there as the others, and she wanted to go."

Caleb turned back to face him. "I'm not sure that she did. I think she felt obligated. I'm convinced Mrs. Whitley gave her some story about being old and needing to spend time with Judith before she died."

"And that would be valid." Micah's words were matter-of-fact. "Dr. Barringer said her body is extremely weak. Her heart and kidneys have been damaged from diabetes. He's treated her for years, and the problem has only grown worse. She wasn't doing well even before this illness."

"You couldn't have convinced me of it, the way she conducted herself."

"Be that as it may, she hasn't much time, according to her doctor. Perhaps not even a full year. And now, given this illness, her chances are worse yet. She doesn't have the ability to fight back the way Bill and Judith can."

Caleb began pacing the room. "Well, hopefully we can get Judith and Mrs. Whitley out of there without too much fuss. I don't want to have to bang down doors on Easter weekend, but I will if I have to. I'll gather more men, and we'll storm the place if need be."

Micah stepped in front of him, halting his frantic movements. "We need to go about this in a calm and civilized manner. You won't help her by acting like a wild man."

Caleb nodded, but it was hard to control his feelings. He loved

Judith. He knew that now beyond any doubt, and he couldn't bear the thought that someone wanted to hurt her.

At five o'clock, the Whitley butler ushered Micah and Caleb into the house. Micah inquired as to whether Dr. Barringer was still there.

"He is, sir. He's with Mrs. Whitley."

"I'd like to consult with him before he leaves. Would you let him know?"

"Of course, sir." The butler gave a curt nod. "Shall I show you to Miss Judith's room?"

"We're able to make our own way there, if you like," Micah replied.

Caleb remained silent for fear he might say something that would create trouble. He still felt their presence wasn't entirely welcome and feared that someone might force them to leave.

"Very good, sir. You'll find Miss Linde is with her, and she's doing better."

"Thank God!" Caleb exclaimed and moved past the butler without waiting for anything further. He took the steps two at a time and found Bill seated on one of the sofas in the large open room at the top of the stairs.

"Mr. Coulter. I didn't think you were returning until later this evening." Bill got to his feet. He was dressed now and properly groomed. He looked like he was about to go to a garden party.

"Dr. Fisher wished to consult with Dr. Barringer while he was here." Caleb forced a smile. "You look completely recovered. I'm glad."

"Yes, well, I've always had a strong constitution."

"And what of your sister? Has she managed to stay well?"

"Victoria is too mean-spirited to take sick." Bill glanced over his shoulder toward the east wing of the house. "Besides, she's leaving tomorrow. Bound for Switzerland. She wasn't sure she should go, with Grandmother so ill, but Father assured her she must. Grandmother expects it and would no doubt be infuriated if Vicky did otherwise."

Caleb nodded. Having Victoria gone would be good. If she was the one causing trouble, then the problems would end with her departure. At least he hoped that would be the case. She could have paid someone on the staff to help her. If that were true, the trouble could go on and on even after Victoria was safely in Switzerland.

"Shall I accompany you to see Judith?" Bill asked.

"No." Caleb turned. "I know the way."

He crossed the room and stepped through the open doorway into Judith's suite. Sarah sat beside the bed, and to Caleb's surprise, Judith was propped up and speaking.

"Caleb," she said, smiling. "I'm so glad you came back." She looked at Sarah. "You can go now. I'm sure if I need anything, Caleb can manage it."

The maid nodded and got to her feet. She smoothed down the white apron she wore. "You have only to ring if you need me."

Caleb took the vacated chair and waited until Miss Linde was gone before speaking to Judith. "You look better."

"I feel better. I think the medicine Dr. Barringer was giving me made me sleep all the time. I didn't care for it at all."

For a moment, Caleb could only gaze upon her face. Her color had improved, but the darkness still circled her eyes. "Micah's come too. He's speaking right now with Dr. Barringer. Apparently your grandmother is still quite ill."

"I know. Bill said I should prepare myself for the worst." Judith bit her lip and shook her head. "I don't want to lose her after just finding her."

Caleb took her hand. "I know." He glanced toward the door and lowered his voice to a whisper. "Micah thinks you may have been poisoned."

"What?"

Her expression betrayed her fear, and Caleb wished he'd been gentler in telling her. "I'm sorry. I didn't mean to just blurt it out like that." He got up and walked to the door. Bill was nowhere in sight, so he hurried back to Judith's side. "I told Micah about the snake, and after he examined you, he admitted that it didn't seem like influenza to him. He talked with Dr. Barringer, and later when he came to speak to me, he told me he had concerns that perhaps you'd been poisoned."

"Bill and Grandmother too?"

"I'm afraid so."

Judith relaxed a bit, but she held fast to his hand. "But who would do such a thing?"

"My first thought is your cousin Victoria. But who's to say? I want to get you out of here—your grandmother too. Micah thinks she should go to the hospital, and he's trying to convince Dr. Barringer."

"This is terrible, Caleb. If it's true, then it means someone here is willing to commit murder. But why?"

"Money or jealousy." He squeezed her hand. "But don't worry about that. We need to get you on your feet. I want to take you home, where you can recover."

She cocked her head slightly and gave him a strange look.

Caleb worried that he'd offended her. "I didn't mean to sound as though you had no say in the matter."

A smile replaced her expression. "They won't like that."

"No, I'm sure they won't."

Micah bounded into the room with his large black bag. He threw Judith a smile. "You look better."

"I am, but I'm very thirsty. Sarah said you didn't want me drinking anything or eating."

"And she was right." Micah opened his bag and pulled out a bottle of liquid. He opened it and handed it to Judith. "This will give you some energy and hopefully help with your thirst."

Judith sampled it and smiled. "Thank you. It's good. What is it?"

"Soda water, lemon, and sugar. It's a concoction that a friend of mine bottles and sells. There's nothing harmful in it, unlike some of the other bottled sodas." He drew three more bottles from his bag. "I brought these for you, and I don't want you to drink anything else."

She nodded and whispered, "Caleb told me that you're worried I've been poisoned."

"I am. We must be meticulous in what you eat and drink over the next few days." He drew out a small box and handed it to Judith. "Here are a few of my mother's oatmeal cookies. If you feel up to it, you might eat one or two. I'll take the others back with me and bring you something else in the morning."

"But why can't we just take her home with us?" Caleb asked.

"I was just speaking with Dr. Barringer and Mr. Whitley. I've finally convinced them to move Mrs. Whitley to the hospital, but I think Mr. Whitley would change his mind if we suggested Judith go as well. He already feels hesitant going against his mother's wishes regarding the hospital, but I think he realizes how grave her condition is. However, he was adamant about Judith remaining here, since she's doing so much better. I think if we keep her eating only what we bring her, then we'll know for certain whether someone has been poisoning her."

"But how can you keep them from slipping something into the bottles?" Caleb asked.

"Judith will open them. She'll insist on doing it herself and not drink from the bottle unless that's the case. Understand?" he asked, looking at Judith.

She nodded and nibbled on one of the cookies. Caleb was encouraged by her willingness to eat. He met her gaze. She was so beautiful, even in her sickness. He wanted to declare his heart right then and there, but Micah had other plans.

"I'm going to listen to your heart and lungs, Judith."

She handed Caleb her cookie and soda. Micah examined her while she waited in silence. Caleb still didn't like the idea of leaving her. Perhaps he could convince Whitley to let his sister come and stay with Judith. Of course, if they agreed, they would expect Camri to take meals with them, and what if they started poisoning her as well?

"You are improved, but only slightly," Micah declared. "I'll come again in the morning and see how you're feeling. The next twenty-four hours should tell us a great deal."

"But it's Easter," Judith protested. "You should take the day with your family."

Micah smiled. "I've come to think of you as family, so no arguments. Can you eat a bit more?"

Judith took the cookie from Caleb. "I can and will. I want to do whatever I can to put this behind me."

"Just remember what I've said. Eat and drink nothing else. Nothing," Micah instructed.

Bill entered the room and smiled at the trio. "It's good to see you so improved, dear Judith." He frowned. "What is it that you're eating?"

"A special concoction I had made for her," Micah answered before Judith could speak. "I also want her eating nothing else. She has some bottled tonic that she can drink, but otherwise no teas or even water. I want to ensure that she makes a full recovery."

"What a strange idea," Bill said, shaking his head. "I know

some people claim that soda drinks can act as healing medications, but I was unconvinced."

"This is brewed by a trusted friend." Micah got to his feet. "Now, I must go. I promised to help Dr. Barringer with your grandmother."

Bill nodded. "That's what I came to tell you. They are ready to move her, and I believe they could use your help." He looked at Caleb. "Yours too."

Caleb glanced at Judith. He didn't want to leave her but knew he must. "I'll come to see you tomorrow and bring Camri too."

"I'd like that." Judith finished her cookie and reached for the bottle Caleb still held. "Thank you for coming to check on me. It helps just having you here."

Micah paused at the door. "Remember what I said about the drinks, Judith. Only open them when you are ready to drink the entire bottle. Otherwise you will compromise the effectiveness." He nodded at Bill and exited the room.

Judith couldn't believe how much better she felt by morning. She was still weak as a kitten but no longer dizzy, and her head didn't feel as if it would explode. She considered the possibility of someone poisoning her. It seemed outrageous. Why should anyone feel threatened by her? Of course, Caleb said it was probably all about the money—money that William and his children would have had if she weren't in the picture. However, the lawyer had already drawn up all the papers. She'd even signed additional paperwork that allowed Mr. Pettyjohn and Caleb to transfer many of her father's previous holdings into her name. So with all of that complete, why would anyone continue to try to harm her?

"Good Easter morning to you!" Bill said, sailing into the room without so much as a knock.

Judith glanced around, wondering where Sarah had gone. "Good morning."

He gave her a silly grin. "I got you this. I remember how much you love chocolate." He handed her a box of Ghirardelli candies. "Happy Easter."

Judith smiled. "I do love chocolate, and it was kind of you to remember."

"Well, open them up and have at it," he encouraged.

She started to do just that, then remembered what Micah and Caleb had said. She shook her head. "No, I should wait until after Dr. Fisher comes to check on me." Bill frowned, and she quickly added, "Then I shall dive in with great abandon."

His smile returned. "Well, Father, Vicky, and I are off to church, and then we'll stop by the hospital to see how Grandmother is faring. Father will probably want to have something to eat while we're out, because after that we're taking Vicky to catch her train. It'll be late in the afternoon before we're back, but I'll check on you the moment I return. Maybe help you eat some of those chocolates."

Judith fingered the edge of the box. "I'll be happy to share."

He chuckled. "If the good doctor comes and allows you to go ahead, feel free to start without me. In fact, I insist. After all, it's your Easter gift." He gave a slight bow and left the room as quickly as he'd come.

Judith looked at the box. Perhaps just one or two chocolates wouldn't hurt. After all, it wasn't something anyone here had made. This was a box of store-bought chocolates.

But even as temptation washed over her, she shook her head. Micah had said to eat nothing but what he'd brought her, and he'd promised to see her first thing this morning.

"I can wait that long." She put the chocolates beside her on the bed.

"Can I get anything for you, Miss Judith?" Sarah asked, entering the room.

"I'd love a little fresh air. I'm starting to feel like myself again. Hopefully when Dr. Fisher comes, he'll deem me well and let me get out of this bed. If so, I intend to sit on my balcony and read."

The maid smiled at her. "Very good. I'll open the French doors, and then you should at least feel the breeze. Then, if you don't need anything else, I'll tend to some personal things."

"You go right ahead, Sarah. I'm going to sit here and read my Bible until the doctor comes."

It was nearly half an hour later when Micah appeared at her door. "Your butler said it was all right to come up. It seems the rest of the family have gone for the day."

"Yes. They went to church and then to take Victoria to catch her train. Bill told me it would be late afternoon before they returned." She glanced beyond Micah at the empty doorway. "Caleb didn't come?"

Micah smiled. "He wanted to, but he wanted to take care of something first. I've no doubt he'll come see you at the first possible opportunity."

Judith met his amused gaze and felt her cheeks warm. She remembered Caleb holding her hand and putting it to his cheek— to his lips. He cared for her. At least that was what she remembered, but maybe it was just the sickness wreaking havoc with her mind.

Micah came to her bedside and frowned as he caught sight of the chocolates. "Don't tell me you've been eating those."

"No. I was very obedient. Bill brought them to me this morning. I told him I had to wait until you came to say whether or not I could have some. He might join me for a few pieces, if so."

"I don't think it would be wise to eat them. They're rich, and they might be too much for your system to handle just yet." He picked up the box. "They appear newly purchased." He set his bag on the bed, then opened the lid and looked down at the candy.

"I suppose so. Bill said it was an Easter gift. He was so happy that I'm recovering." She shook her head. "You totally made me forget about Grandmother. How is she?"

"Not good, Judith. I wish I could give you better news. She's very frail. Her heart is weak, and her kidneys have all but shut down." He put the lid back on the chocolates.

Judith tried not to succumb to her sadness. "Is there anything we can do that isn't being done? Obviously money isn't a problem. If we need to purchase something, Caleb knows more about my funds than I do, and he could help you."

Micah shook his head and took her pulse. After a moment, he finally spoke. "We're doing everything we can. She has a disease called diabetes. It destroys the internal organs. There's no cure, not even any decent medication, although there are some promising finds. I'm sad to say they won't be developed soon enough to help your grandmother.

"I *am* glad to say your pulse is stronger. I believe you're over the worst of it, but given how quickly you've turned around, I truly believe someone was poisoning you. I don't like to think that way, and I don't accuse lightly."

"Then they poisoned Grandmother too." She felt tears come to her eyes. "I just don't understand how people can be so evil. I've done nothing to anyone here."

He shrugged. "Nothing but take away their dream of inheriting a fortune. Caleb had a long talk with Mr. Pettyjohn. He wasn't eager to reveal the truth, but eventually he did admit that William made some very bad investments and hasn't recovered. Mrs. Whitley is basically providing for William and his family."

"She told me. Wouldn't that make it all the more important to keep her alive and well?"

"Not at all, Judith. If she dies, then they will inherit. I suppose whoever is behind the poisoning believes that if you also die, then everything will go to your uncle."

She nodded. "That was the arrangement I agreed to for now. I told Caleb I wanted him to create another will for me, but we haven't had time to go over it."

Micah finished her examination, then glanced at the box of chocolates again. "Judith, would you allow me to take several pieces with me? I'd like to see if they can be tested for poison."

"Of course. Take the whole box."

"I should, but if Bill happens to be the one doing this, then he'll wonder why the entire box of chocolates has disappeared. Maybe this way, you can tell him you've already opened the box. When he sees some of the candy missing, perhaps he won't question why you won't eat anymore. If he starts eating the candy, it's probably a good sign that the pieces aren't poisoned. However, remember, he too was ill, and it's possible someone else had access to the candy before he brought it to you."

Judith looked at the box. It might as well be another rattlesnake. The danger was there, but there was no way of knowing the degree. Hopefully, Micah could find out.

"Happy Easter," Camri said when she arrived to visit Judith later that afternoon. Patrick was with her, as well as Kenzie.

"Aye, Happy Easter," Patrick said. "Ye're lookin' as though ye're feelin' a mite better."

"I am." Judith strained to look beyond the big burly Irishman. "Where's Caleb . . . ah, and Micah?"

Camri smiled. "I thought you might notice my brother's absence. He planned to be here, and he may yet join us. He had an emergency meeting to attend. Apparently, there is a big conflict with Ruef and the Board of Supervisors over whether or not to allow underground cables for the trolleys versus overhead. It's been an ongoing problem, and Rudolph Spreckels and James Phelan are determined to force the issue."

"On Easter Day?"

This merited a shrug from Camri as she joined Judith, who sat in a chintz-covered chair in the sitting room of her suite. "I don't know all of the issues, but it seems that Spreckels is determined to file papers tomorrow morning. There's some sort of deadline."

Judith tried not to appear disappointed. "Ah, well, duty calls. Did you have a lovely church service?"

Kenzie sat on a chair beside Judith. "It was very nice. I think every woman in the congregation sported a new hat."

"Aye," Patrick agreed. "They were so large and pinned with so much frippery that it was hard to see Pastor Fisher in his pulpit."

Camri laughed. "He's right. There were a great many hats."

"Did you wear new dresses and hats?" Judith had planned to wear one of her new gowns for the holiday. Instead, she sported a lacy white robe and nightgown.

Kenzie shook her head. "I wore my pale green and peach gown. My mother used to say it was sinful, the way people got new clothes and gussied up for Easter Sunday. The focus shouldn't be on us, she said. So I couldn't bring myself to buy anything new."

"Our mother used to say something similar," Camri admitted. "She told us that we should be looking to the beauty of the resurrection and what Christ had done—not our neighbor's apparel."

"Well, I'm sure you were both beautiful." Judith knew better than to ask what Caleb had worn, but she couldn't help but wonder. He looked so dashing in formal wear, but she also liked the navy blue double-breasted suit that he often wore to church. She pushed the thought aside. "Aren't you going to sit?" she asked Camri.

"No, Patrick and I can't stay long. We're heading to the cemetery. Ophelia's new headstone was laid last week, and we want to inspect it and make sure they did it right." She bent over and gave Judith a hug. "I'm so glad to see that you're feeling better. We truly feared we might have lost you."

"You might have, had Caleb and Micah not been insistent on seeing me. Once Micah forbid me to eat anything but what he brought me, I rallied rather quickly."

"So they said." Camri looked at Kenzie and then back to Judith. "That's why I hope you'll understand what I have to say next."

Judith took in the grave expression on her friend's face. "What is it?"

"Well, we know that your grandmother is in the hospital, and that leaves you here alone with the people who were probably responsible for your illness. We want you to consider leaving this place."

CHAPTER

24

*J*udith was sitting on the balcony, watching the sunset and thinking about Camri's insistence that she leave Whitley House, when Sarah announced that Bill and his father had returned home. The men wanted to know if they might come see her.

"Of course." Judith put aside the book she'd been trying to read and straightened her robe. She felt swallowed up in lace and ribbon. If one judged wealth by the amount of fancy trim on their clothing, she was certain to impress. "Are they . . . alone?"

Sarah looked at her and frowned. "Yes, do you not remember that they took Miss Victoria to the train station?"

"I knew that. I just wondered if anyone else had come to visit."

"No, miss." Sarah left the room, shaking her head as if Judith had completely stumped her.

Judith did her best to hide her disappointment. She could hardly make a scene wondering why Caleb hadn't come to call. It was well past the hour for normal visiting, and she'd seen nothing of him, but it was hardly something she could discuss with Sarah. Nor with her uncle and cousin.

"You are looking much improved," Uncle William said, joining her on the balcony. "But it's getting rather chilly."

Judith nodded. "I was just about to come inside."

Bill came up behind his father and beamed a smile at her. "I believe your Dr. Fisher knows what he's doing. You look amazingly well."

"I feel nearly recovered." She did her best to relax and not think about the fact that either of these men might have been responsible for her illness. "Were you able to see Grandmother at the hospital?"

William nodded, and his expression betrayed his worry. "She's very ill. She asked about you, however."

"Do you suppose I might be able to go see her tomorrow?"

"That depends on your doctor's wishes. I told Dr. Barringer that Dr. Fisher would continue to provide your care. It seems his treatments have worked wonders. I might even inquire as to getting some of that bottled tonic for Mother."

Judith reached for her book. "I'll ask him when he comes if he'll provide some, and if I might visit Grandmother. Did Victoria make her train?" She stood, and Uncle William took her arm.

Bill spoke before his father could reply. "She did, along with two of her friends who are going to the finishing school with her. They are all three being accompanied by a very severe governess who will no doubt keep them from having a single moment of fun." He grinned. "Just deserts where Victoria is concerned."

William helped Judith into her sitting room. "Now, Bill, that's hardly called for. Your sister can be difficult at times, but she's soon to be married and has a great deal on her mind."

"That's a decent excuse for now, but what about the other nineteen years of her life?"

Uncle William shrugged. "Let's not speak of it now. Instead, let's focus on Judith. You're looking the picture of health, and if your doctor approves you visiting your grandmother tomorrow, I will drive you there myself."

"Thank you, Uncle William." She motioned to the chintz chair. "I'll sit there by the fireplace. Sarah promised me a fire this evening."

"I see it has been laid. No doubt she'll soon come and light it," Uncle William said, stepping back as Judith took her seat.

"If not, I'll tend to it myself," she assured him.

"Nonsense, child. You're a Whitley. Those tasks are beneath you," her uncle said matter-of-factly. "Now, if you'll excuse me, I long to get out of these clothes and relax. I instructed Cook that we would dine casually in our rooms this evening. If there's something you want in particular, just let Sarah know."

"I'm still on restrictions. Dr. Fisher left me with his prescribed food. He will be by to see me in the morning again to let me know whether or not I can resume regular eating."

"I suppose that means he didn't allow you any chocolate. He must believe in torture," Bill said, shaking his head. "Well, hopefully you'll be set free tomorrow. For now, I believe I'll follow Father's example and go change. If you like, I could come back later and we could play a game of cards."

Judith shook her head. "I'm rather tired and plan to make an early evening of it. I'm hoping the additional rest will see me completely restored by morning."

"Of course." Bill leaned down and kissed the top of her head. "Good evening, sweet cousin."

Uncle William drew close and bent to kiss her cheek. "I'm so delighted that you are better. Mother would never have let me hear the end of it had anything happened to you."

Micah agreed that Judith might visit the hospital Tuesday. Caleb wanted to accompany her, but ongoing issues with Ruef kept him from being able to go. According to Caleb during his brief visit on Monday, Spreckels was filing papers today to incorporate the Municipal Street Railways of San Francisco. Spreckels was determined to prove that underground cables were not only more economical in the long run, but would enhance the city's beauty. Judith was disappointed by Caleb's focus on business and his brief stay, but kept it to herself. She knew it was important to him to see Ruef put in his place along with the other grafters.

"Are you warm enough, my dear?" her uncle asked.

Uncle William and Bill treated her like a delicate flower as they rode with her to the hospital. She thought them both rather silly but allowed for their ministering. Uncle William tucked a heavy wool blanket around her, while Bill handed her his scented handkerchief, explaining that the hospital odor was quite unpleasant.

"You forget that I grew up on a ranch, Bill. I know all about unpleasant smells." Nevertheless, she kept his handkerchief in order to avoid arguing the point.

"You must realize," Uncle William told her, "that your grand-mother is very ill. The doctors are doing all they can, but they don't hold out much hope."

Judith had talked at some length with Micah the night before. He had gently encouraged her to prepare herself for her grandmother's death. She nodded. "I understand, Uncle."

The thought saddened Judith more than she could have imagined. She hardly knew the old woman, but it didn't matter. Ann Whitley was her own flesh and blood. She had never given up hope of one day finding Judith, and now that they were reunited, it seemed a cruel joke that they should be again separated.

At the hospital, William and Bill were overly attentive. Bill thought they should get one of the patient wheelchairs so Judith didn't have to walk far. William thought perhaps they should just walk slowly and sit down often to rest.

"I feel fine. I'm sure I can walk the distance." Judith fixed the two men with a look that she hoped made her determination clear. It seemed to do the trick, because neither man offered further argument.

"We arranged a small private room," her uncle said as he led her down a long corridor. "We wanted Mother to have peace and quiet. It's just at the end of the hall." When they reached the room, he paused. "Are you sure you want to do this?"

Judith had no more patience. "I'm certain. Now please stop worrying."

Her uncle nodded and opened the door to the room. The dim light revealed a single iron bed, a night table, and a chair. There wasn't even a window.

"This is so stuffy and dismal," Judith murmured.

"I wonder where the nurse is?" her uncle asked. "I paid for someone to be with her around the clock."

Judith moved to her grandmother's bedside and took her hand. She frowned at the sight of the frail woman. Her gray-white hair was down around her shoulders, making her face seem even paler.

"Grandmother, it's Judith. I've come to see you."

The old woman opened her eyes. She looked at Judith for a moment, not seeming to comprehend who she was.

Judith drew the wrinkled hand to her heart. "Grandmother?"

Recognition dawned. "Judith. You're alive."

"I am. I'm much better, and you must get better too. I'm so

glad you let them bring you to the hospital where you could get proper treatment."

"Bah," the old woman murmured. "They're all fools. I came here to die."

"Mother, you mustn't speak in such a manner," Uncle William admonished.

"Don't tell me what I mustn't do. I want to speak to Judith alone." She paused and took several strained breaths. "Leave us."

Bill, who stood at the end of the bed, shrugged. "I know when I'm not wanted." He smiled, but Judith could see by the way his eyes narrowed that he wasn't pleased.

Grandmother waited until both men had gone before speaking again. "Judith, I haven't much time. We must speak frankly. Close the door and then sit."

Judith frowned and released the old woman's hand. She closed the door to the room, then came back to take a seat beside her bed. Despite what Micah and everyone else seemed to believe, Judith had to hope her grandmother might recover. "You can get better, Grandmother. I did."

The old woman smiled. "You are young and full of strength. I'm relieved to know you are better, but there's nothing they can do for me . . . and we mustn't spend our time arguing the point."

"I understand your feelings, but I will continue to hope. God can heal your body if He chooses. Now, what is it you wanted to talk to me about?"

"William . . . the others . . . I know it may sound strange, but . . . my passing will cause some grief."

"Of course they will be grieved." Judith shook her head. "We will all be grieved."

"No, it's more than that." Grandmother said. "It's about the future and . . . what they expect."

"But what has that got to do with me?"

"Mr. Pettyjohn can better explain . . . or perhaps that young man of yours. I . . . altered my will."

Caleb had already told her that Grandmother intended to leave half of her fortune to Judith. It was so much more than Judith could even fathom. Her father's fortune alone made her a very wealthy woman. Richer than most, in fact.

"The new will is in place. It was witnessed . . . and signed the day you were told about your fortune. It was . . . the same day . . . I had you sign that temporary will."

"I don't know what to say, Grandmother. I have no need for more of the family fortune. If it's going to cause grief and bad feelings, then I'd rather not have it."

"You have no say in it. It's yours. William . . . is a fool who will not alter his course in order to benefit his family. I see no reason to further aid him in his folly. However, I've left him enough that if he . . . will heed my advice . . . he will live comfortably. As for Bill . . . he has great potential. I've left him the shipping industry, which if . . . if he's willing to work at it and take counsel . . . he'll continue to be wealthy. Victoria . . . she will receive a portion of money . . . as already dictated by her marriage contract." It was clear the old woman's energy was failing.

"You should rest, Grandmother."

"No, you need to know. The rest is yours. Everything . . . the house . . . the industries your father . . . and grandfather worked to create, as well as everything your mother inherited from her parents."

The full meaning of what her grandmother had said began to sink in. "Everything?" she murmured. "But, Grandmother, the house . . . it's their home. I cannot take that from them."

"Then don't. Allow them to live with you there."

Judith thought of the fact that someone there had tried to poison her . . . had put a rattlesnake in her bed. "I don't intend to live there, Grandmother. It isn't a home to me, especially if you aren't there."

The old woman smiled and reached for Judith's hand. "I'm glad for the time we've had. This . . . isn't what I wanted for us . . . but I believe God has at least arranged to bring you back to me so that I can bless you with all that you should have grown up with."

Tears came to Judith's eyes. "The only thing I want is more time."

Grandmother nodded. "And it's the only thing my money cannot buy you."

———

Caleb finally dropped into bed that night just after the hall clock chimed one. He was relieved that Judith was on the mend and that she'd decided to move back to his little home. Now that Henry Ambrewster's house had sold, Caleb was already thinking about the future. A future with Judith.

He'd wanted to speak to her about his feelings on Monday, but his visit had to be cut short. Ruef was starting to feel the interruptions to his normal operating methods. The Home Telephone Company, a consortium owned and financed by those who weren't obligated to Ruef, had challenged the exclusive franchise held by Pacific States Telephone and Telegraph Company, who were clearly operating under Ruef's guidelines. Then, issues of the city's water supply and operations came under scrutiny. The Spring Valley Water Company, backed and protected by Ruef, was doing its best to maintain control despite arguments that what they provided was inadequate for the fast-growing city. Proposals for a large reservoir had been presented by those who recognized that the city's supply of water would never be able to meet the future demands of a large-scale emergency. Fire Chief Sullivan had pleaded with the Board of Supervisors to see the need. He had pointed out how most of the city's cisterns were in disrepair and unusable. Most were empty of water, and many had even been filled with dirt and trash. The Board, however, under Ruef's directions, had ignored the problem for years. Now those in positions to challenge their decisions were rising up to make demands of their own.

Like dominoes falling in line, one problem after another was demanding the attention of those who would see Ruef and his cronies defeated. The time to act was now, and Caleb knew it better than most, but there was also his desire to declare his love for Judith and propose marriage.

He felt confident her answer would be yes. So much was unspoken between them, but his heart was certain of her feelings. As he fell asleep, Caleb made up his mind to notch out time the following morning to see Judith and tell her how he felt.

He was sure that he'd only just fallen asleep when something woke him. A sound vibrated through the house, like a locomotive coming into a station. It built and grew louder, and then the vibrating turned to shaking. The entire house seemed to shudder.

"Earthquake!" He threw back the covers and tried to get out of bed, only to be thrown to the floor. The entire room seemed to jump up and down. Caleb struggled to stand, but lost his footing time and again. He'd experienced smaller earthquakes in the past, but nothing like this.

All around him, things fell to the ground. Paintings from the walls, bric-a-brac from the mantel. Caleb strained to see the time, but his clock seemed to spring to life and jump from the dresser. It shattered in pieces on the floor.

Overhead, the light fixture swung dangerously from side to

side, and to Caleb's amazement, the furniture seemed almost to dance across the floor. He thought of his sister and Kenzie, as well as the Wongs. He couldn't do anything to help them.

The shaking and noise went on longer than any earthquake Caleb had ever experienced. Worse still, the up and down movement was joined by a side to side motion. It gave Caleb the sensation of being at sea. Would it never end?

———

Judith awoke to the entire room falling apart. She heard the glass in her French doors shatter as the roof seemed to give way and crack above her. She was momentarily mesmerized. What in the world was happening? She tried to reach for the lamp, but it fell away from her as the nightstand pulsated with the rest of the room.

She had experienced smaller earthquakes, but this one was so much stronger. She had no idea what to do. She tried to sit up, but the force of the shaking was such that she could hardly move. Around her, the walls seemed to rip apart as if they were paper being torn by some giant hand.

It was the end of the world. She was certain of it. The end of the world, and she was once again all alone.

You aren't alone, Judith.

The words seemed to come from deep within her. She thought of the faith she'd come to—of God's promise to never leave or forsake her.

Cracks opened in the plaster walls. A piece of her ceiling fell to the floor at the end of her bed. Through the hole in the roof, she could see the early morning sky with only the slightest hint of predawn. The broken French doors swung back and forth, pounding against the walls and debris, while all around her, the Whitley mansion crumbled.

The assurance that God was with her gave her comfort, as Judith had little doubt that she was going to die. How strange that she had just regained her strength after nearly succumbing to illness or poisoning, only to be buried alive—killed by the very house she was soon to inherit. A sense of regret settled over her as the madness continued. Regret for the wasted time and lies her parents had told her. Regret for never knowing her real parents and sister.

Her biggest regret, however, was never telling Caleb that she loved him.

CHAPTER

25

*W*hen the shaking ceased, an eerie silence filled the air. Judith glanced around the room. She was cut off from the world by the debris that had fallen around her. For a moment, she didn't move, almost afraid that if she did, the shaking might start up once again. The skies were growing light, but her room was too dark to be able to see all the dangers.

"Hello? Is anyone out there?" She called for her uncle and then for Bill and Sarah. No one answered.

She scooted to the edge of the bed and looked down at the floor. Shards of glass and splintered wood lay mingled with pieces of plaster. There wasn't a clear spot to step, but amazingly, her shoes still sat just where she'd left them the night before, on the other side of the nightstand. Sarah had promised to put them away, but Judith had told her not to worry about it. She glanced at her nightstand. Most everything had fallen off of it, and what little was left, she easily pushed aside. She then scooted onto the stand and swung her feet down to reach her shoes.

After this, she tested the floor in front of her. It seemed

sturdy enough. She heard things shifting outside and dropped into a crouch beside the bed when something large fell in her sitting room.

"Is someone out there? I need help!"

No one answered.

Judith felt her way along the bed. The route to the hall door wasn't going to be easy. She turned to see if she might be able to get to the balcony, but that route was also impossible. The roof had fallen in completely, blocking that escape.

She began to push aside lighter pieces of furniture, wood, and plaster. If the rest of the house was in this state, it would be a wonder if anyone else had lived through the earthquake, much less thought to see if she was all right.

When she reached the sitting room, Judith caught the first whiff of smoke. Was the house on fire? She tried to move the large beam that had fallen against the door, but it was far too heavy. Crouching down, she tried to crawl under it, but too much debris was in the way.

She moved out from under the beam as she heard something else crashing down. The Whitley mansion was falling apart. She had to get out.

"Help me!" she cried out. "Someone help me!"

To her surprise, she heard movement outside her barred door. "Is that you, Judith?" It sounded like Bill.

"It's me! I'm trapped in my room."

"Are you hurt?" he asked.

"No. Just stuck." She was relieved to know that someone else was alive.

She could hear him doing something outside the door and presumed he must be trying to get it open. Judith put her back against the blocking beam and pushed with all her might. It shifted slightly, and Bill managed to push the door in. However, as he did this, plaster rained down on them, and another portion of roof collapsed against the beam.

The debris knocked Judith backward to the ground. Something heavy fell against her leg and pinned her to the floor.

"Help me, Bill. I can't move it." She tried to sit up, pushing at the piece trapping her leg, not even able to see what it was for all the dust.

Bill climbed over the pile of rubble at the door and stared down at her. Judith could just make out his shadowy figure.

"What are you waiting for?" she asked.

He chuckled. "I was just marveling at how easily everything has come about."

"I don't understand. Come help me." She continued trying to free her leg, but it only caused her pain.

Bill remained where he was. "My father is dead. I found him on the floor of his room. Part of the chimney collapsed on him."

"That's terrible. I'm so sorry, Bill."

"I'm not. And now here you are, trapped, and the house in flames—"

Judith shook her head. "If the house is on fire, why are you just standing there?"

"Because, my dear cousin, I intend for you to die."

She stopped working to free her leg. "What?"

"I tried to get rid of you before—first the snake and then the poison. At least the latter has probably finished off the old lady, but I've no idea what happened to the snake."

"I took care of it." She felt rage build within her. "I killed it."

"Indeed? You have some strange skills, dear cousin."

Judith sickened at the realization that Bill truly intended to let her die. "How could you? I never did you any harm. Neither did Grandmother. You wouldn't have had the good life you enjoy so much had it not been for her."

"Ha! Hardly that. That old dragon did nothing but breathe hellfire and brimstone on everyone. She insisted the world do exactly as she demanded. I hate her, and I'm glad she's going to die. Perhaps she's already dead. Maybe the earthquake finished her off just as it has brought you to your end."

Judith had no idea what to do, but her panic was rapidly building. Bill was the only one alive to help her, and he'd just confessed that he wanted to see her dead.

"You have no reason to hate me, Bill. I've done nothing to you."

"Nothing but take my fortune. I overheard Grandmother tell you that she left you everything. I also know that you signed a will that returned everything back to the family should you die. So you must die."

"You can have it all, Bill. If you were listening to us talk at the hospital, then you know that I don't care about any of it. I only wanted a family." The skies were growing lighter, and Judith could make out Bill's twisted expression.

"Family? This has never been a family. We're more a gathering of opponents—each determined to overcome the aggressions of the others. I'm glad to see the last of it."

"You still have your sister."

"Vicky won't be a problem, and if she is, then she knows what I'm capable of." He straightened and sniffed the air. "I believe the gas is leaking. How fortuitous. That and the fire will see an end to this place and to you."

He climbed back over the debris. "It might have been different if you'd accepted my proposal of marriage. Then the money would have been mine, and I wouldn't have had to kill you . . . at least not right away."

"Bill, please, help me. You can't just leave me here."

He laughed. "That's where you're wrong, cousin. I can and

I will." He left her room, laughing. "The house is soon to explode, so you'll excuse me if I don't remain to chat."

Judith shook her head at his madness. How could anyone just leave another human being to die?

———

"Is everyone all right?" Caleb asked, taking a head count. "It looks like we're all here."

Mrs. Wong stood holding a kerosene lamp. "Gas turned off and no fire. We are all good."

Caleb nodded. "The house seems to be in one piece, but it's impossible to tell how bad it is. I don't know if it's safe, but I suggest we get dressed as quickly as possible and then meet outside on the stairs. We can take stock from there."

They scattered in different directions, with Caleb following Camri and Kenzie back upstairs. He dressed in record time and pulled a large satchel out from under his bed. The floor was littered with broken glass, and pieces of it stuck into the leather as he drew out the bag. He didn't worry about it, however, instead cramming several things into the satchel and then making a dash for the first floor. He hurried to his office and opened his safe. He drew out all the papers there, as well as money he'd put aside, and shoved those into the bag as well.

As he made his way back down the hall, Camri and Kenzie were coming down the stairs. They were doing their best to finish dressing and keep hold of their purses.

"Come on," Caleb said, taking Camri's arm.

He was almost to the front door when someone turned the knob several times. Caleb was about to call out when Patrick kicked in the door.

Everyone looked at him in shock, but it was Kenzie who

began to giggle. Caleb couldn't help but smile, and Patrick looked rather embarrassed.

"We would have opened the door for you," Caleb finally said.

"Beggin' yer pardon, Caleb. I'll be fixin' that for ye, of course." He went to Camri and pulled her into his arms. "I'm so glad ye're all safe. The world's in pieces out there."

"How bad is it?"

"Bad. Fires are startin' everywhere. Buildings have collapsed, and streets have split open wide. It's like the end of the world." He looked at Caleb over Camri's shoulder. The fear in his eyes was something Caleb had never seen in the big Irishman's face. Not even when he faced the possibility of a death sentence for a murder he hadn't committed.

"Judith!" Caleb shoved his bag at Kenzie. "There's money in here, as well as important papers. Would you mind?"

She shook her head. "Not at all. Are you going to Judith?"

"Yes." He headed for the door and stopped. "Will the car make it through?"

Patrick shook his head. "It's doubtful."

"It's all right. I'll run it."

"Caleb, be careful," Camri called. "We don't want to lose you."

He didn't even look back. "I have to find out if she's all right. I have to bring her home."

He ran as fast as he could, but the life of a lawyer had caused him to grow soft. His legs burned and his lungs fought to draw in enough air. As he topped the first hill, he could see the fires sprinkled across the lower neighborhood. Smoke was muting the rising sun and turning the sky the color of blood. As he gazed upon the destruction, it was easy to see that the fires were spreading fast.

After running another few blocks, Caleb pushed through

the gates to the Whitley estate. At first it appeared to be in one piece, but as he drew closer, he could see that the walls were cracked, windows shattered, and there were places where the roof had caved in. The front door stood ajar, as if to welcome him inside.

Caleb entered the foyer and saw the disastrous mess. The large gild-framed mirror had splintered into a thousand pieces. The overhead chandelier now lay on the floor, crystal shards mingling with the broken bits from the mirror. The far side of the room, including the right-hand staircase, was engulfed in flames.

"Is anyone here? Judith?" he called, making his way to the other set of stairs.

Bill Whitley came around a corner, all but tackling him. "We have to get out. The entire place is going to collapse."

As if to prove his point, there was rumbling from the east wing, and debris rained down onto the flames.

Caleb was dragged back out the front door before he could stop Bill. "Wait. What about Judith?"

Bill shook his head. "She's dead. My father too, and most of the servants."

The wind left Caleb's lungs. Dead? She was dead? "But . . . where? How?"

"The quake collapsed the roof on her room. The entire west wing is in shambles. I tried to get to her, but I was too late."

Caleb stumbled back a few steps and looked at the house. "She can't be dead. I have to help her!"

He tried to push past Bill. "You can't. The fire is consuming the house. The gas is leaking, and there isn't time."

Caleb went still, and Bill let go of him. The thought of his beautiful Judith being dead—burned in the fire—was too much. He could scarcely draw breath.

"I'm going to see if the butler made it out," Bill said. "You should come with me." When Caleb didn't answer, Bill shook his arm. "Come on. There's nothing you can do."

Caleb looked up and met Bill's eyes. There was something cold and calculating in his expression. Caleb felt a stirring in his spirit.

Judith needs you.

He shook his head and pushed Bill away. "She's alive. I know she's alive."

Caleb raced back into the house and took the stairs as quickly as he could, jumping over fallen debris and pushing aside anything in his way. The fire had spread and appeared to be engulfing the entire upper floor and roof.

"Judith!" he yelled.

He heard what sounded like another collapse of walls or roof. They needed to hurry.

"Judith!" He roared her name and pushed at her suite door. It would only open part of the way. "Judith, are you in there?"

"Caleb!"

Her voice was like music to his ears. "I'm coming." He forced open the door to her suite, pushing against whatever wreckage was holding it in place. "Where are you?"

"I'm here, on the floor."

Light filtered down from the hole in the roof. Caleb frantically scanned the room, finally spotting Judith on the floor, a piece of the roof pinning her in place.

He maneuvered through the mess, tossing rubble aside to make a path. With strength born of desperation, he lifted the debris and tossed it to one side. He helped Judith to her feet. "Try to stand."

"It hurts, but I think I can manage."

"Come on, then, the entire house is about to go up in flames."

She grabbed his arm. "Bill is out there somewhere. He's the

one who's been trying to kill me. He told me so when he left me here to die."

Caleb seethed. He had known something wasn't right about the smarmy young man. There had been something in his tone, in his expression, that bordered on cruel. "We'll deal with him later. Right now, we have to leave."

He pulled her along with him, helping her maneuver out the door. He could tell by the way she moved that she was in pain.

"I know this is difficult." He coughed as the smoke thickened around them. "But we have to keep moving."

They were out of the room and heading for the stairs when Bill appeared in the smoky haze with a gun in his hand. He looked at them both and shook his head.

"It seems killing you is a difficult task." He aimed the gun directly at Judith.

Caleb pushed her behind him. "I won't let you kill her."

Bill only laughed. "I'll kill you both."

He squeezed the trigger, but nothing happened. He looked down at the gun.

Caleb was going to charge him, but an explosion rocked the entire house, sending Caleb and Judith to the floor. Knowing Bill wouldn't be stopped by the growing conflagration and destruction of his home, Caleb jumped to his feet and drew Judith up with him. He looked to see what Bill was doing and found him pinned facedown by a large portion of wall. Only his head and upper shoulders were clear.

"Get out of the house," Caleb told Judith. He pushed her toward the stairs. "Hurry, the fire is out of control."

"I don't want to leave you, Caleb."

He was already trying to pull the wall frame from Bill's back. The wreckage wouldn't move. "Bill?" Caleb tried to feel for a pulse in his neck, but could find none.

"We can't help him," Caleb said, rushing back to Judith. Without waiting for her to say a word, he pulled her down the stairs. Flames danced all around them, and the hot air burned every breath as they pressed through the foyer and out the front door.

In front of the house, a handful of people had gathered. Caleb recognized Ramsay, the butler. Mrs. Whitley's cat was in his arms. Caleb and Judith joined him as he looked on in dumbfounded silence.

"Bill is dead. He was crushed by debris," Caleb told the older man.

"He said that Uncle William was dead, too," Judith announced. She shivered. "I don't know where Sarah is. I don't know if she made it out."

Caleb glanced around. "I don't see her here. Bill told me most of the servants were dead."

Ramsay shook his head. "I don't know where anyone is besides those who are here, and the stable boys and groom. They managed to get the horses to safety on the lawn."

Judith shivered and hugged her arms to her body. It was only then that Caleb realized she was wearing nothing more than a nightgown. He pulled his coat off and put it around her shoulders. He would get her back to the house, where Kenzie and Camri could care for her needs. There was certainly nothing he could do here.

"I'm taking Judith back to my house," he told Ramsay. "I doubt you'll have any help from the fire department. It looks like there are at least a dozen fires in the city."

Ramsay said nothing. His gaze was fixed on the destruction of the grand Whitley mansion as he mindlessly stroked the cat. Caleb put his arm around Judith and led her down the drive.

They had walked nearly two blocks before Judith finally

spoke. "What about my grandmother? Do you suppose the hospital was destroyed?"

"I don't know. The earthquake did a lot of damage, as you can see." He motioned to one of the houses across the broken street. It had shifted sidewise down the hill. The morning light through the smoky skies revealed more and more damage. People were everywhere, milling about, the same shocked expression on each face.

Judith stopped. "I must go to her. I must know."

Caleb nodded. "We will. I promise, but you need to get clothes first. Camri and Kenzie will be able to help you at home."

"Then everyone is all right?"

"Yes. Everyone, including the Wongs. We got the gas turned off before it could cause problems."

She looked at him with a dazed expression. "So your house . . . it's all right?"

He smiled and shook his head. "I have no idea of what damage was done, but it was still standing when I came to find you."

To his surprise, she wrapped her arms around him. "Oh, Caleb. Thank you for saving my life. Thank you for coming for me."

He encircled her with his arms, and for a moment relished the feel of her against him. Safe. Breathing. Alive. If he'd listened to Bill, she would be dead, and he would have never had the chance to tell her that he loved her—that he wanted to spend the rest of his life with her.

She pulled back just enough to look up into his eyes. "I . . . I need to tell you something."

He didn't give her a chance. Instead, he lowered his mouth to hers and kissed her.

CHAPTER

26

*Y*ou two there!" a man's voice called out.

Judith was so stunned by Caleb's kiss that she could only look at the approaching man in dazed wonder. He wore a soldier's uniform, and a dozen more men were with him. Judith was glad Caleb was able to take charge. She felt dazed.

"Can we help you?" Caleb asked.

"Where have you come from?"

"The Whitley estate." Caleb pointed back in the direction of the house. "It's engulfed in flames. Many people are dead. We're heading to my house four blocks to the south."

The soldier nodded. "You should get your family to safety. The fires are burning out of control. The fire department and army are doing what we can, but the damage from the quake is substantial, and many are dead."

"I understand. Are you recommending a particular place to go?" Caleb asked.

"There's less damage to the west on the coastline. I believe tents are going to be erected there to house those who've lost their homes. We'll know more by afternoon. There's to be a meeting of the Board of Supervisors and mayor later this morning."

Caleb nodded and waited until the soldiers moved on to say anything more. He put his arm around Judith once again. "We need to get you home so you can dress."

Judith had forgotten all about the fact that she was wearing little more than her nightgown.

A woman with three children walked toward them. The littlest of the children was crying and clinging to her mother's skirts. The woman looked at Caleb and Judith for a moment, then crossed the mangled street, herding her brood without a word.

There were others along the way. Judith could see by their expressions that everyone was still in a state of shock. She wondered if she looked just as stunned. Her uncle and cousin came to mind and only perplexed her more. How could Bill have done what he did? How could he poison an old woman who was already nearing the end of her days? How could he have poisoned Judith without so much as a single thought of remorse? And now he lay dead. She supposed it was God's justice, and yet she felt bad for the cousin she barely knew.

"Judith!" She looked up to see Camri and Kenzie running toward her. They swept her into a group hug. "Oh, we were so worried," Camri continued. "Are you all right? Is your family all right?"

"No. I mean, I'm fine, thanks to Caleb." Judith looked at Caleb and smiled. He was watching her with affection.

"What happened?" Kenzie asked.

"Maybe we could get some clothes for Judith," Caleb said. "And then we can tell you everything." He looked at Patrick. "What about the house? Is it safe enough for us to go back inside?"

"For sure I'm not seein' any reason that we can't go back. There's damage, but it looks solid enough."

Caleb nodded. "Do you have anything Judith might borrow?" he asked his sister.

"She still has clothes here," Camri said. "Her grandmother didn't want her to bring anything. Come on, Judith. We'll help get you cleaned up and dressed, and you can tell us everything."

Camri took her from Caleb's side, and Judith immediately wanted to return. She said nothing, however, as Camri and Kenzie each took hold of her and led her up the many steps to Caleb's front door.

Once inside, they made their way to Judith's old bedroom. She could see cracks in the wall, and the contents of the room had been scattered about.

"Where's the rest of your family?" Camri asked.

Judith looked at her for a moment, trying to convince herself that it hadn't just been a bad dream. "They're dead. Well, Bill and Uncle William are. Victoria left on Sunday for Switzerland, so I suppose she's safe."

"Were they killed by the quake?" Kenzie questioned as she closed the bedroom door.

"Yes. Bill said Uncle William was killed by a collapsing chimney, but I didn't see him. The house was falling down around us. I got trapped, and Bill showed up. I thought he'd come to help me, but he wanted me to die. He was the one who poisoned me and Grandmother."

"Oh, my word!" Kenzie said, shaking her head. "He actually admitted to it?"

"Yes. He was also the one who put a rattlesnake in my bed."

"A snake?" Kenzie looked at Camri. "Did you know about that?"

"Caleb told me. He also said Judith killed it all by herself."

Kenzie looked at Judith with a raised brow. "Did you, now? Well, I have a newfound admiration for you, and I already thought quite highly of you."

Judith frowned. "You shouldn't. You and Camri told me not to move there. I should never have gone."

"Spilt milk. Have you heard anything from your grandmother?" Camri asked as she helped Judith sit on the side of the bed.

"No. Caleb promised we would do what we could once we made sure everyone else was safe. I know Micah planned to see her this morning. He was going to help another doctor with an early morning surgery, so he planned to be at the hospital."

Kenzie frowned. "Has anyone heard whether the hospitals were damaged?"

Camri shook her head. "I can't imagine that any of the city's buildings have escaped damage. The concern is whether or not they've collapsed altogether. Patrick said there's been such poor workmanship over the years—all because of Ruef and the mayor allowing corners to be cut. This will only serve to help our cause."

She and Kenzie gathered all of Judith's clothes and helped her dress. Judith felt her spirits and energy renewed as she finished securing her stockings. Her leg was scraped and cut, but mostly just sore. She was determined to ignore the pain, just as she was determined to forget the horrors of that morning.

She stood, slipped back into the shoes she'd worn, and then looked at her image in the mirror. Her blond hair hung limp. She hadn't thought about what a mess she must have looked like to Caleb until that moment.

"Goodness, but I'm a fright." She looked for a brush amongst the objects on the floor. Not seeing one, she began to comb through the tangles with her fingers. She had barely started that, however, when the earth started to tremble again. She looked at Camri and Kenzie. Both women had grown wide-eyed and grabbed for the nearest thing to steady themselves.

The quaking grew stronger. It was nearly as bad, but not as long, as the original quake. Judith fought back the urge to break into tears. The windows shattered as Kenzie and Camri fell to the floor. What was happening? Were they all doomed to die?

She heard Caleb calling for them even before the quaking stopped. He and Patrick bounded into the room just as things seemed to settle once again.

Without thought, she jumped up and threw herself into Caleb's arms, sobbing. It was all too much. She couldn't bear anything more.

He held her tight, stroking her hair. "It's all right, Judith. It's all right. It was just an aftershock."

"Aye, but that one did us more harm than good," Patrick said.

Judith pulled back to see Patrick helping Camri and Kenzie from the floor. "What are we to do?" She knew her voice betrayed her fears.

"Well, it's obvious we can't stay here," Caleb said. "But I'm not exactly sure where we can go. Everyone around us is suffering the same."

"How far out would the quake cause damage?" Camri asked.

Caleb shook his head. "It's hard to say. We met with some soldiers on our way home. They said there are fires burning all over the city, but it sounds like the brunt of the damage is in this five-mile radius."

"Couldn't we go to the warehouse?" Kenzie asked. "Camri, you were just telling me about all the goods delivered Monday and how much Patrick has accomplished there. Maybe the damage is minimal. After all, it's just one story."

"She's right. That might well be the place to go," Camri said.

Caleb nodded. "I agree."

"I have to find out about Grandmother." Judith looked at the others. "I won't be able to rest until I know if she's dead or alive. If she's alive, then I want her to be with me."

"I'll try to call the hospital," Caleb said. "Come on. Let's get back downstairs before another aftershock hits."

Judith wasn't sure she could bear another aftershock, but knowing she had no choice, she let Caleb take her downstairs to his office. She waited with the others while he did what he could to find out about her grandmother.

"I think we should gather what we can," Camri said, looking to the Wongs. "Pack up all the food that's easily transported. Load it up in Caleb's car. Liling, you get all the medical supplies we have—oh, and any liquor we have. You'd better pack your clothes as well."

"The streets are a mess, love," Patrick said. "We won't get far in the car."

"It doesn't matter. We can carry things if need be, but it's several miles to the warehouse, and we'll need to get as far as possible with the car first."

"Aye, you're right. And it might be that we can be drivin' up on the sidewalks and such. Some of the streets are just fine, I'm sure."

Camri turned back to Kenzie. "Come with me, and we'll get all the blankets and sheets and some of our clothes. Patrick, maybe you could scout us out a route—at least for the first few blocks."

He nodded. "I'll be back as soon as I can."

He took off, as did Camri and Kenzie, leaving Judith sitting and staring while Caleb tried to make calls.

He finally gave up. "The lines are down, and there's no hope of getting through. I'll get you all to the warehouse and then see about going to the hospital myself."

"But the fires and the damage." Judith shook her head. "I don't want you endangered."

He grinned. "I won't take chances, but obviously we're all in a bit of danger. Don't fret." He came back to where she sat and knelt beside her. "You're beautiful . . . you know that?"

She shook her head. "I don't even have my hair pinned."

"I know. I like it down." His grin widened. "In fact, I find I like most everything about you."

She looked at him for a moment, then gave a slow nod. "I like everything about you too."

Camri called out from the hall. "We're going to pack stuff in the car."

Caleb stood and frowned. "What's that all about?"

"Camri felt we needed to take what we could with us and figured we should try to take the car as far as we were able. Patrick has gone to scout us out a route."

"Good thinking. I can always trust Camri to get things organized." He helped Judith to her feet as another aftershock caused the floors to rattle and shake.

Judith clung to him, looking into his eyes for reassurance. Caleb ran his hand down her cheek and cupped her chin. He said nothing and did nothing more, but Judith felt a calm wash over her like never before. She smiled.

"Come on, let's go help the others," he said.

———

Caleb had never thought they could load so much stuff in his car, but Camri had every inch of it packed to the hilt, including a suitcase with his clothes. The stacked cases and crates were so high that by the time she finished, it was necessary for the rest of them to walk beside the car and steady the load while Caleb slowly drove.

It took the better part of two hours just to get the few miles down to the warehouse. While many of the roads were undamaged, others were in various states of disrepair, but added to this was the flood of people. Hysterical people. They swarmed the roads en masse, frightened, even angry. They made it difficult for Caleb to maneuver the car, and more than once Patrick had to clear the way.

Word came that the dome of City Hall had crumbled and much of the building itself had collapsed. That was one building Caleb couldn't blame on Ruef. Political boss Chris Buckley had built it for more than seven million dollars back in the 1890s. Everyone admired its classical beauty and marble columns, but from the sound of it, Caleb figured it had been just as poorly constructed as most of Ruef's projects were. Worse still, the basement of City Hall housed the jail, as well as a hospital and an insane asylum. Who knew if those people were even still alive?

When Camri inquired of some soldiers as to the direction of the fires, the man in charge told her they were in all directions and completely out of control. He believed that as many as two hundred structures were now aflame.

The warehouse, well south of the city, yet conveniently located on the bay, looked to be relatively sound. Caleb and Patrick searched through the entire building, finding only minor damage here and there. Patrick's construction work had added additional support to the frame, and except for some of the crates being tossed about and broken open, things seemed to be in fairly good order.

They went to work immediately, setting up what they could. Caleb knew there would be many people in need of shelter before nightfall.

"We've got this under control," Camri told him. "I think you should do what you can to locate Micah and Judith's grand-mother."

"And maybe you could see if Cousin George is all right," Kenzie said. "In fact, I could come with you, and you could leave me near the candy factory."

Caleb shook his head. "I would feel much better if you stayed here. I'll do what I can to check on him. Do you think he would have been at the factory so early?"

Kenzie nodded. "He is always there by five."

"All right. You stay here and help Camri get things set up."

"I'll be comin' with ye," Patrick said, glancing between Caleb and Camri. "I don't like the idea of leavin' the lasses alone, but . . ."

"Patrick should go with you," Camri said, nodding. "We can manage here alone, but you may need him to help."

Caleb wasn't sure it was the best idea. He feared that once things settled down, looters and good-for-nothings would be roaming the streets, looking for what they could steal.

As if reading his mind, Camri put her hand on his arm. "There's nothing here that anyone would want to steal, and the place has been abandoned for so long that no one would even think to come here. The looting and other problems will be downtown at the stores."

He let out a heavy breath. "All right, but I'll leave this with you." He pulled a pistol from his coat pocket.

"I don't know anything about how to use a gun," Camri said, shaking her head.

"I do," Judith spoke up. "I can handle a revolver, a shotgun, or even a rifle. I'm actually a good marksman."

Caleb let out a laugh. "I've no doubt you are." He handed her the pistol, then drew out a small box. "Here's more am-munition."

"Hopefully we won't need any of it." Judith put the revolver in one pocket of her work skirt and the ammunition in the other.

Then, without thought as to what anyone might think, Caleb pulled her into his arms and kissed her. It was briefer than the kiss he'd given her earlier, but just as satisfying. When he let her go, he glanced around at the shocked looks of his sister and friends and gave a casual shrug.

When they remained in their stunned silence, he laughed and slapped Patrick on the back. "I'd suggest you do the same for Camri and join me in the car."

_____

Getting to the hospital took no small effort. At almost every turn, Caleb found the way either blocked by debris and torn-up streets, or by the army.

When they were less than a block from the hospital, Caleb found it impossible to get any closer. "We'll park here and go the rest of the way on foot."

Patrick nodded and jumped out of the car. "Hopefully no one will want to be stealin' the car, what with it just sittin' out here in the middle of everythin'."

"I hope not, but I don't see as we have much choice."

They hiked the remaining distance, weaving in and out of the masses of people who had gathered. Some were being treated at makeshift stations outside, where nurses and orderlies were doing what they could.

Caleb and Patrick made their way inside the hospital. Caleb knew from the directions Judith had given him where her grandmother's room was located. The hospital had taken some structural damage, but for the most part looked to be in decent order. As one of the finer of several hospitals in the Bay area, Caleb figured its construction and maintenance were better managed than most. To be certain, it was better than the hospital in the basement of City Hall.

The entire building was packed with people. Many were injured, and all were terrified. Caleb thought about stopping to pray with some of them, but felt his promise to Judith had to be kept first. With Patrick's help, they finally made their way to the small room at the end of the hall. He pushed open the closed door and stepped inside to find Mrs. Whitley awake but alone.

"Thank God you've come!" she gasped. "How is Judith . . . my family?"

Caleb shook his head. "Judith is fine. She's sent me to see how you are."

"I'm still . . . alive, but I'm . . . certain that won't be the case . . . much longer. With each passing . . . moment, I feel a little of my strength . . . slip away."

Patrick stood watch at the door. He glanced over his shoulder. "There's somethin' goin' on down at the nurses' station with some soldiers. I'll go see about it."

Caleb nodded, then turned back to Mrs. Whitley. "That's my sister's fiancé."

"An Irishman." Mrs. Whitley nodded. "I've always . . . thought rather highly of the Irish."

"They've had it better in San Francisco than other places, but it's still remarkable to hear someone of your social standing say as much." Caleb pulled the bedside chair closer and sat. "Judith wants you to know that she's all right. She's safe with us."

"What of William and Bill?" She put her hand to her heart and drew a ragged breath. "What of my staff? Poor Ramsay."

"I saw Ramsay. I don't know how many of the others made it. The house . . . is gone. The quake caused a lot of destruction, and then a fire started. All over town there are fires, and the gas mains have broken in many places."

"And my son?

Caleb shook his head. "I didn't see him. I . . . " He didn't know what to say or do regarding her family.

Mrs. Whitley grasped his hand. "Are they gone?"

Caleb nodded. "I . . . we can talk about it later."

She closed her eyes and shook her head. "It's just as well. William . . . could never have survived without me. And Bill. . . ." She faded off, then opened her eyes and looked at Caleb with such intensity that he wanted to turn away. "The doctor told me . . . that Judith and I . . . had been poisoned."

Caleb nodded again. "Yes, that's what they believe. When Dr. Fisher insisted on feeding Judith only the food he brought to her, she got better immediately."

"It was Bill."

Her comment surprised Caleb. "How do you know?"

"He . . . was a hateful . . . spiteful child. He . . . wanted everything. I tried to change him . . . I tried." She shook her head slowly.

"He left Judith to burn in the house. She was trapped. I got her out, and then Bill showed up with a gun. Judith said he wanted her dead because he wanted the full inheritance. I never saw your son, but Bill said he was dead. I figure if the earthquake didn't kill him, Bill did."

The stoic old woman nodded. "And now he's dead, as well. I . . . never . . . wanted that . . . but it's just as well. Now we're all dead . . . all but Judith."

Patrick chose that moment to return. "The army is evacuating the hospital. The fires are taking over the city, and everybody is being evacuated."

Caleb nodded. "I'll go speak with the officer in charge. We can take some of the patients, if they need. I'm sure we'll have that warehouse full of people before it's all said and done. Patrick, would you carry Mrs. Whitley to the car?"

"I'd be happy to." The broad-shouldered Irishman came to the side of the bed.

Mrs. Whitley looked up at him and smiled. "I once had an Irish groom. He . . . fancied me. He was . . . quite the sweet talker."

Patrick laughed. "I could be seein' his logic. You were no doubt a fine figure of a woman."

This actually made the old woman chuckle, but that sent her into a series of coughs.

Caleb got to his feet. "I'll meet you at the car as quickly as possible. Be sure to keep her wrapped up in the blankets."

He left the room and hurried down the hall. It took several attempts to locate the officer in charge, but when he finally did, the soldier wasn't at all interested in Caleb's offer.

"We have our orders. The people are being moved to the Mechanics Pavilion."

The Mechanics Pavilion was the city's largest auditorium. Caleb knew it would be big enough to hold the patients from several hospitals. He nodded.

His next order of business was to report Mrs. Whitley's removal to the nurse in charge of the floor.

"You can't just take her," the nurse protested.

Caleb smiled. "Her doctor has assured us there is nothing more we can do for her. She's dying, as you probably already know."

The uniformed woman nodded. "I do."

"Well, then?" He shrugged. "Better she should die in the presence of family and those who care about her. Here's the address where I'm taking her. If the doctor thinks I'm out of line, send someone to tell me, and I'll take her straightaway to the Pavilion."

He jotted down the address and handed it to the nurse. She looked at it for a moment, then nodded.

Caleb turned to leave, then snapped back around. "Is Dr. Fisher here in the hospital? I understood he was performing surgery this morning with another doctor."

"I wouldn't know. You'll have to go to the surgery and ask there." She gave him directions, and Caleb hurried as best he could through the crowded corridors to the stairway that led him to the second floor.

He found that floor to be even more chaotic, as the staff worked diligently to arrange their patients for transportation. Caleb spotted one doctor clad in a surgical gown, blood smeared across the front of him in no small amount.

"Sir, I wonder if you know the whereabouts of Dr. Fisher? Dr. Micah Fisher?"

The surgeon shook his head. "Not since he was asked to assist in an amputation. A man was trapped in rubble down on Market Street, and they thought they could free him if they separated him from his leg."

"If you see him, would you tell him Caleb Coulter said that everyone was safe at the warehouse? He'll know what it means."

The doctor nodded. "I doubt I'll remember, given this." He looked out across the vast sea of people.

Caleb knew he was asking for the impossible. Hopefully in time, Micah would try to get in touch with them, but for now Caleb knew his mind would be elsewhere.

Caleb made a mad dash for the car. He knew if he paused for even a moment, someone would stop him for some reason. Some people were just begging for answers, and others were in need of things he had no way to provide. He'd never felt quite so helpless in all his life, but he could pray for them. Maybe he could even return once he got Mrs. Whitley safely to the warehouse.

Lord, You know what's happened here. You know what these

people need, and I'm begging You to work out the details and provide for each one.

He continued to pray as he ran back to the car, and it soothed his soul like nothing else could. When he reached the Winton, he found Patrick had just finished tucking Mrs. Whitley into the back seat.

"Let's see if we can get to George Lake."

They drove away from the hospital and headed farther into the most dangerous part of the city. Caleb only got a few blocks, however, before the army roadblock refused him passage.

"We've got buildings still falling to pieces," an army sergeant explained. "There's too much danger from that and the spreading fires. Fact is, we're ordering everyone to leave this section of town for their own safety."

Caleb knew it wouldn't make Kenzie very happy, but it seemed he had no choice but to forget about finding her cousin.

"Let's swing by the house," he said, maneuvering the car in a U-turn. "We'll leave a note on the door explaining where we've gone and encouraging others to join us there."

CHAPTER

27

*I*t quickly became apparent that San Francisco was not going to recover from the earthquake anytime soon. The worst of it, however, were the fires. Many had been started by the ruptured gas mains, while people's carelessness or ignorance started others. Caleb tried to keep abreast of the news. It seemed the army had taken charge of things and evacuated the entire city, including the Mechanic's Pavilion where the hospital patients had been sent. When he learned what was happening, Caleb went to the Pavilion and offered use of the warehouse for as many as they could take. He learned however, that most of the patients were being taken to the Ferry Building for transport to Oakland, so instead of transporting sick and injured to the warehouse, he spent several hours driving them to the Ferry Building.

Meanwhile, plenty of other people took up Caleb's offer to come to the warehouse. He was relieved that caring for the refugees seemed to come naturally to his sister and the others. Camri made records of everyone who came to stay with them, then she turned the new arrivals over to Kenzie with instructions as to where they should be placed. Once Judith had seen to her grandmother's comfort, she and Patrick went to work setting up spaces outside where they could boil water in large kettles. Drinking water was going to be critical for everyone, Judith told him. Caleb was proud of her for putting aside her own desires to be with her grandmother. She never complained about her own injuries either. She had assured Caleb that she was just fine, but he noticed her limping from time to time.

A meeting of what was to be called the Committee of Fifty gathered at the hall of justice at three in the afternoon. Caleb hadn't been called to the meeting, but he figured it would do them all good if he found a way to be present. To his pleasant surprise, Abraham Ruef had not been invited.

"We aren't having the meeting after all," Rudolph Spreckels told Caleb as he arrived at the hall of justice. "The fire's moving this way. We'll have it later tonight at the Fairmont Hotel, provided it hasn't caught fire. Right now, they're trying to evacuate this building's records and the dead in the basement. They'd set up a morgue down there, but it's clear it will have to be moved."

"Is your family safe?" Caleb asked, knowing that Spreckels' wife was soon to have a baby.

"They are. I've sent them to our friends in Oakland." Spreckels shook his head. "It's all madness."

"It's definitely a difficult time, but even so, we can be assured God is still in control."

"Better Him than Ruef and his cronies. The mayor has put the army in control, which has only served to panic people all the more."

"Yes, but they'd be panicked anyway. Their homes have been destroyed and family members killed. Someone has to keep law and order."

"Well, we'll see what's to be done after our meeting." A loud explosion rocked the room. "Fools! They're trying to dynamite against the fire. They'll kill us all," Speckels shouted, leaving Caleb without another word.

The wind picked up by nightfall, causing the fires to spread like water through a ruptured dam. Caleb wondered if the warehouse would be safe much longer. He stood outside, looking toward the heart of the city some miles away. The smoke was thick in the skies overhead, and the fires so numerous and consuming that the skies glowed red.

"I've been looking for you," Judith said, carrying a pail of water in each hand.

Caleb quickly took the buckets from her. "How are you doing? How's your leg?"

She looked at him oddly. "My leg?"

"I know it's hurt. I've seen you limping."

She smiled. "It's nothing, really."

He knew she wouldn't allow him to baby her. "Why were you looking for me?"

"My grandmother wanted to see you." Judith bit her lip, then drew in a long breath. "She's slipping away from me. Each time I see her, she's weaker."

"I know." If only he could save her from further pain. "Why don't you show me where you want this water, and then we'll go see her."

Judith nodded and led the way. Inside at the makeshift kitchen, she instructed him to give the water to the women who were busy making soup.

"I see Camri has put everyone to work." A large woman grabbed the buckets from him before he could say anything more.

Judith took his arm. "Everyone seems happy enough to help. I think it keeps their minds occupied."

"I'm sure it does."

They wove their way through the lines of cots that had been set up. In one of the back rooms, Judith's grandmother was settled with her own cot and a modicum of quiet.

"Grandmother, I found Caleb." Judith dropped her hold on Caleb and pulled up an empty crate to sit on. She took the old woman's hand and placed it against her cheek.

"Glad . . . you came," Mrs. Whitley murmured.

Caleb crouched beside Judith and the bed. "What can I do for you, Mrs. Whitley?"

"Find . . . Mr. Pettyjohn . . . he has my instructions for . . . when I die. Burial and such."

"I will, I promise you."

A small aftershock rocked the room, but there had been so many since the early morning hours that no one paid them much attention any more.

"I'm so grateful," Mrs. Whitley continued, "that you brought . . . Judith . . . back to us."

"I am too." Caleb patted the woman's icy hand. "I'm glad she could get to know you and that you could see for yourself what a fine woman she's grown up to be."

"We were . . . robbed of time." Her eyes grew watery. "Robbed."

Caleb only nodded.

Judith leaned over and kissed the old woman's cheek. "But what time we had together was enough to last a lifetime. I learned the truth, and I won't forget all the stories you told me about my parents and sister."

"Forget about the bad things . . . about Bill."

"I will, Grandmother."

Mrs. Whitley looked at Caleb. "And you . . . you will take care of Judith?"

Caleb glanced at Judith, then nodded. "I will, I promise you."

324

Ann Whitley closed her eyes. "I'm going to rest now. Don't worry . . . about me."

Judith nodded. "I'll come sleep in here when I get my work done. That way I can keep an eye on you." She leaned over. "I love you, Grandmother."

The old woman smiled. "I've . . . never . . . heard you say that before now."

Judith returned the smile. "I don't suppose I knew it for sure . . . until now."

Ann Whitley nodded. "It's all I've longed for. I love you . . . my sweet Judith."

Caleb stood and helped Judith rise.

"Oh, there you are," Camri said, poking her head around the door. "I've been looking for you, Caleb. Someone is here to speak to you."

Caleb let Judith go, but he gave her a wink. "Seems we're always being interrupted. Find me later." She nodded, and he smiled. "Don't forget, because there's something I want to ask you."

Reports continued to trickle in, along with horrible stories about things that people had endured. Judith found it all appalling but knew there was nothing to be done about it. One thing was certain—the fires were doing far more damage than the earthquake. Three especially large fires were raging out of control. The South Market fire extended from Sixth Street to the waterfront, and the North of Market fire traveled from the Ferry Building to Sansome Street, consuming the financial district, Chinatown, and spreading to Nob Hill. Last of all was the Hayes Valley fire, which someone had jokingly called the Ham and Eggs fire because a woman cooking breakfast with a faulty flue had apparently caused the blaze. They were all far too close for comfort.

Judith tried not to worry about it, but she couldn't help but wonder what the future held for any of them. Such a short time ago, she had lived in the lap of luxury with everything she could have ever wanted. Even now she thought of how all those beautiful new gowns her grandmother had purchased for her were nothing more than ashes. It was a good reminder that earthly treasures weren't meant for eternity.

Shortly before midnight, Judith finished washing the last of the dishes. She had been unsure how Camri had managed it all. A wagon filled with food had arrived earlier in the day, and they had fed more than two hundred people who had crowded into the warehouse for shelter. There was no telling what they'd do tomorrow . . . or even if there would be a tomorrow.

Making her way to the room where her grandmother rested, Judith encountered Camri. She handed Judith a short candle, then lit it from her own.

"Are you just now going to bed?" Camri asked.

"Yes. I finished with the dishes and wanted to check on Grandmother. I think I'll sleep on the floor beside her in case she needs anything tonight."

"Nonsense. I'll get your cot and blankets. You go ahead."

Judith nodded and made her way into the small office room. She glanced around and decided to put the candle on the empty plate sitting atop a crate at the foot of the bed. She dripped wax onto the plate, then secured the candle stub. For a moment, she just watched the flame flicker. How strange that a little flame should be so helpful, while so much fire was devastating everything around them.

She went to her grandmother's cot and knelt down. Placing her hand on the old woman's cheek, Judith was startled by its chill. It was then that she realized her grandmother was no longer straining to breathe. She was gone.

Judith broke into sobs and buried her face in her hands. How unfair it all seemed. She had wanted a family so much, and God had given them to her. Now, however, they had all been taken away again. Life was so cruel.

"Judith?" Caleb whispered.

She looked up. "Oh, Caleb, she's dead."

Caleb lifted her up. His arms went around her and pulled her close. "It's all right. We knew this would happen."

She cried, wetting his shirt with her tears. "But she's gone, and now I'm all alone."

"No, Judith. You aren't alone. You'll never be alone again. You have all of us."

She shook her head. "But I have no family."

He lifted her face to his. In the glow of the candlelight, Judith could see the love in his expression. "You do. You have me, and together we'll make a new family."

Her heartbeat quickened. "What are you saying?"

"I'm saying that I love you. That I've loved you longer than I even realized." He wiped away her tears. "I'm hoping—praying—that you might return my feelings. I think you do, but I long to hear you say so."

"I do. I love you so very much. I've loved you from the first moment I laid eyes on you." She shook her head in wonder. "I never dared to hope you might feel the same about me, a poor girl from Colorado. A nobody."

"Judith, you could never be a nobody." He grinned. "You've become the most important somebody in my life." He glanced down at her grandmother. "I know the timing is terrible, but. . . ." He looked back into her eyes.

Judith swallowed the lump in her throat. "But?"

"Will you marry me? Marry me and play beautiful music for me. Marry me and let me love you for the rest of your life."

The tears came anew, and for a moment Judith wasn't sure she could even speak. How she had dreamed of this moment. "Yes," she managed to whisper. "Oh, yes."

He pressed his lips to hers and pulled her closer. His strong arms tightened around her, making Judith feel safer than she ever had. She thought of all they had gone through together, and of the life she'd known before ever meeting Caleb Coulter. The past and the present melded together in dreams forgotten, creating the promise of a new future.

Judith felt Caleb's hold loosen as he raised his face from hers. For a moment he did nothing but gaze into her eyes, then he stepped back.

"Come on. Let's find you somewhere else to sleep, and then I'll come back and take care of your grandmother."

"No. Let's do it together." She looked at her grandmother and for a moment thought the light was playing tricks on her. It looked as if the old woman's lips had curled ever so slightly into a smile.

———

"And you proposed, just like that?" Camri asked the following morning as they shared breakfast with hundreds of strangers.

"I did," Caleb said, giving Judith a nudge. "And she said yes."

"That's wonderful." Camri grinned at Patrick. "We can have a double wedding."

"Well, that should be something we discuss," Caleb interjected. "After all, I want my bride to have whatever she wants."

Judith shrugged. "I think it sounds like fun."

"What sounds like fun?" Kenzie asked, joining them on one of the benches Patrick had thrown together.

"A double wedding," Camri replied before Judith could speak. "Caleb proposed to Judith, and she said yes."

Judith caught the look of pain that momentarily flashed in Kenzie's eyes. It was there and then gone, replaced by Kenzie's stoic acceptance.

"Congratulations to you both." She looked at Caleb, her eyes narrowing slightly. "You'd better be good to her. She's loved you since we walked in that day from church and learned you'd returned."

Caleb laughed. "I know, she told me. If I'd had any sense, I would have known that I lost my heart to her that day as well."

"Seems mighty strange to have folks laughin' and makin' merry when our town and all we had is burning to the ground," a woman on the other side of Patrick said. She got up in a huff and motioned to her children. "Come now, we'll find another place to eat our breakfast and mourn."

Patrick shook his head. "Maybe 'tis better that we spend our day bein' thankful rather than mournful. After all, didn't the Good Lord save us from the fate of so many others? Didn't He give us a shelter for rest and food for our bellies?"

The woman stopped and opened her mouth, then closed it as she seemed to consider his words. Her children stood, bowls in hand, looking to their mother for instruction.

Finally, she gave a nod. "Sit back down and eat your oatmeal."

The children did as she instructed, and the woman didn't say another word.

The matter was forgotten, and soon they were sharing ideas about the future and the weddings that would take place. Even Kenzie seemed to have put aside her past in order to offer thoughts on Camri's suggestions. Never had Judith experienced such a sense of belonging. Not even when she'd lived at the Whitley mansion.

She looked around the large open room, seeing the people there—strangers who had come together in need. Just as she and Camri and Kenzie had come together the year before. Maybe family didn't need to be blood related. Maybe you could be a family just because you shared a common need and a mutual love for one another.

"You haven't said a word about their ideas," Caleb whispered in her ear. "Are you really going to let everyone else plan our wedding?"

She laughed and shrugged. "So long as you are included in the plans, I will be quite content."

Caleb chuckled and slipped his hand around her waist. "I fully intend to be in those plans, because I'm certain they're God's plans for me."

"So you are finally feeling more certain of where He wants you?"

He motioned to the people around them. "He wants me here, with them. I'll share the Gospel and see to their legal needs. I'll provide shelter and whatever else I can. It will never make me a lot of money, but if I wisely invest what I already have, I know God will never let us go hungry."

"I feel the same way." She looked into his eyes and smiled. "My inheritance is yours to use as you will. In fact, everything I have is yours. Especially my heart."

"And that's truly the only thing I need."

Tracie Peterson is the award-winning author of over one hundred novels, both historical and contemporary. Her avid research resonates in her stories, as seen in her bestselling HEIRS OF MONTANA and ALASKAN QUEST series. Tracie and her family make their home in Montana. Visit Tracie's website at www.tracie peterson.com.

Sign Up for Tracie's Newsletter!

Keep up to date with Tracie's news on book releases and events by signing up for her email list at traciepeterson.com.

Also from Tracie Peterson

In the early 1900s, Camri Coulter's search for her missing brother, Caleb, leads her deep into the political corruption of San Francisco—and into the acquaintance of Irishman Patrick Murdock, who her brother helped clear of murder charges. As the two try to find Caleb, the stakes rise and threats loom. Will Patrick be able to protect Camri from danger?

In Places Hidden
GOLDEN GATE SECRETS #1

You May Also Like . . .

Katherine and Jean-Michel once shared a deep love that was torn apart by forces beyond their control. Reunited in the 1920s at the Curry Hotel in Alaska, have the years changed them too deeply to rediscover what they had? And when Jean-Michel's nightmares of war return with terrifying consequences, will faith be enough to heal what's been broken for so long?

Out of the Ashes by Tracie Peterson and Kimberley Woodhouse
THE HEART OF ALASKA #2
traciepeterson.com; kimberleywoodhouse.com

Zanna Krykos eagerly takes on her friend's sponging business as a way to use her legal skills and avoid her family's matchmaking. But the newly arrived Greek divers, led by Nico Kalos, mistrust a boss who knows nothing about the trade. Yet they must work together to rise above adversity after the mysterious death of a diver and the rumor of sunken treasure.

The Lady of Tarpon Springs by Judith Miller
judithmccoymiller.com

Though Aunt Gerd has softened towards them, Uncle Einar remains a harsh landlord as two more Carlsons, Nilda and Ivar, join Signe and Rune at the farm in Minnesota. When tragedy lays a dark secret bare, the Carlsons and Strands will have to come together and become a true family.

A Breath of Hope by Lauraine Snelling
UNDER NORTHERN SKIES #2
laurainesnelling.com

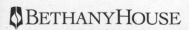
BETHANY HOUSE